her backup boyfriend

a Sorensen Family book

ASHLEE
MALLORY

Entangled Publishing, LLC
2614 South Timberline Road
Suite 109
Fort Collins, CO 80525
Visit our website at www.entangledpublishing.com.

Bliss is an imprint of Entangled Publishing, LLC. For more information on our titles, visit http://www.entangledpublishing.com/category/bliss.

Edited by Alycia Tornetta
Cover design by Jessica Cantor
Cover art by iStock

Manufactured in the United States of America

First Edition January 2015

Bliss

To Shawn, Lily, and Harrison, my most devoted fan club.

Chapter One

Sheesh. It was hot as Hades in here.

Despite the brisk early October chill and the fresh white snow that powdered the ridge of the Wasatch Mountains that she could see from the window, Kate Matthews could feel beads of moisture forming on her upper lip. She tugged at the cuff of her wool blazer and tried not to squirm while her boss finished his phone call. Her curiosity at the reason for this impromptu meeting had become overshadowed in the last couple of minutes by her longing to throw off the stupid jacket.

But unless it burst into flames, that wasn't an option.

She cursed her haste in running out the door this morning without taking her usual perusal in front of the full-length mirror. If she had, she would have noticed the white tag billowing like a flag at her waist and realized her new silk blouse was on inside out. Unfortunately, it wasn't until she'd arrived and was sprinting toward Tim's office that she'd noticed the slight wardrobe malfunction.

At the time, the best solution had been to take the ten seconds to slide on the spare jacket she kept behind her office door.

She hadn't expected it to be, like, a hundred and ten in here.

Kate took a quick peek from the corner of her eyes at the other participant in today's last- minute conference. Nicole Bancroft, the latest addition to Strauss and Fletcher's litigation division, didn't seem to be having any problems with the temperature of the room if the smooth, shine-free polish of her clear, porcelain skin was any indication. Her shiny raven-black hair was secured in an elegant chignon Kate couldn't help but envy. She resisted the impulse to pat her own bristly red hair already escaping from the confines of her hair clip.

No wonder Michael was in love with this paragon of perfection.

At least, according to the rumors that linked the pretty new associate with the firm's most eligible bachelor—and Kate's ex-boyfriend. Kate had been trying to convince herself that the rumors didn't bother her. Sure, they had dated for three years, and she might have been expecting a proposal—not a plea for space—when he'd broken up with her. But that had been fourteen months ago. Give or take eight days. All the same, it still stung to be sitting next to such flawlessness.

Why were they both here, anyhow?

"Sorry to keep you waiting, Tim," Kate offered the moment he hung up. "I had a meeting this morning." She decided not to mention the meeting was personal. She doubted Tim would care she had waited over an hour for a contractor to give her a bid for her home renovation, or that he'd failed to show up. Firm business always first.

Tim nodded brusquely. "You're probably wondering why I called you both here today. I had a call this morning from the CFO of McKenna and Associates. Our client is anxious to present an aggressive defense at the upcoming depositions."

Kate almost sighed out loud. The McKenna case was her slam dunk into making partner at Strauss, one of Salt Lake City's most preeminent law firms. Even if the client was more demanding than all of her clients combined. And a jerk. But a jerk who had ties with several of the senior partners.

"Although they think you've done a great job of things so far, Kate," Tim continued, his blue eyes cool and discerning, "they want to make sure we hit the other side hard and have asked for more manpower. I decided Nicole would be an excellent second chair."

Kate's stomach tightened. Sure, she understood. She was a team player; she could work with another attorney.

But did it have to be *her*?

Kate glanced over and met Nicole's gaze. They smiled briefly, and Kate noticed the clean, straight line of the woman's teeth. Instinctively, she pulled back her own smile, conscious of her two slightly crooked front teeth that she had always wanted to get fixed.

"I know you've spent a lot of time preparing for the upcoming depositions, but perhaps you can give Nicole a chance to look over your notes. She might give you a new perspective on things you haven't seen." With a glance at his Rolex, Tim stood. "I've got to run. I'm sure you two will be able to handle this without any problem."

"Absolutely," Kate assured him, a response echoed by Nicole that he acknowledged with a wave.

And then they were alone, the room quiet and growing hotter by the minute.

Nicole spoke first, brisk and businesslike. "If you can have your assistant drop off the file this afternoon, I should be able to get a feeling for the issues. We can meet tomorrow to discuss our plan."

"Of course. I look forward to hearing your thoughts."

There. They almost sounded like friends. Almost.

Up to this point, Nicole's hands had remained clasped together on her lap. Now, as she came to her feet, she stretched her fingers out in front of her. A gleaming explosion of light beamed from her left hand. Kate's carefully held composure deflated into shock.

Oh, dear God of all that is good and holy, please say that isn't what I think it is.

As if aware of Kate's gaze, Nicole held her hand out to catch the light.

Kate had to say something. Anything.

"Wow. Is that an engagement ring?"

Original.

Nicole held her hand up higher and the light flashed off the enormous chip of ice. "It's beautiful, isn't it? I'm still getting used to it."

A boa constrictor seemed to be wrapped around Kate's neck, squeezing ruthlessly as she managed, "Congratulations." With the back of her hand, she tried to covertly swipe the dampness from her upper lip.

Nicole's cool green eyes gazed back at Kate at that inopportune time and her upper lip curled in vague disgust. But her tone remained polite, if not chilly, as she said, "Thanks. I'll see you tomorrow."

Kate barely heard Nicole's footsteps retreat from the office as sharp pain stabbed her in the chest, and she worked to suck in oxygen.

Michael was getting married.

But not to her.

. . .

Why hasn't this idiot gone already? The light changed five seconds ago.

Kate gritted her teeth. The driver's left arm rested on the truck's open windowsill, his hands tapping to some unknown beat. Kate counted another five seconds, then released her foot off the brake. Her car rolled forward until it was inches from the offending fender. She hit the brakes.

Message received, the guy lifted his hand in a brief greeting and puttered through the intersection. But his speed didn't pick up measurably. The truck crept down the street.

Kate stifled a screech of frustration and, for the sixth time since leaving her office, pressed redial on her Bluetooth headset. *Don't go to voicemail. Don't go to voicemail*, she prayed.

"Hi, Kate," Payton answered, out of breath. "Sorry I missed your calls. I've been meeting with a wedding videographer for the past hour and had my phone off."

Two months before, Payton became engaged to someone whose trust fund miraculously exceeded her own. Massive planning had since ensued, not only for the wedding but for the upcoming engagement party. Payton was a Vaughn, after all, as her mother would say.

It also left Kate with not just one but two parties for which she needed to find a date.

In short order, Kate relayed the events of the afternoon — particularly the massive diamond perched on Nicole's slim finger, still conscious of the fact the truck in front of her was cruising at an easy speed of *twenty-one* miles an hour.

In a twenty-five-miles-per-hour speed zone.

"You're kidding me. Nicole and Michael are engaged," Payton mused. "How are you holding up?"

Kate sighed. "Been better. I'm on my way home."

"Before eight? That's a record. Wait a minute, you're not listening to that depressing Bonnie Raitt song again, are you?"

Kate paused just as the familiar refrain about making someone love you when they didn't streamed loudly from her speakers. Too late to turn it off now. "Maybe."

"I thought I tossed that CD a year ago."

She had. But that was the beauty of everything being digital. Kate only had to repurchase it and add it to the breakup playlist she'd created months ago. For moments like this.

"You should go home and have a bottle of wine. I'd come over but I'm running a few minutes late for my appointment with the caterer for the engagement party. Supposed to finalize the menu. But I'll call you later?"

"No, don't worry about it. I plan on drowning my sorrows in a large bubble bath and a pint of coffee ice cream. If I can get my bathwater above a balmy sixty-four degrees, anyway."

"I warned you about buying a fixer-upper. You've got to

find someone who can help."

"I'm working on it." Ahead of her, the truck eased to a halt at the four-way stop. Kate said a hasty good-bye and disconnected. Reaching forward, she flipped the volume of the radio back up and glanced at the road.

Shit! She slammed on the brakes, almost careening into the truck, now stopped in front of her at the stop sign. Her cell phone flew out of the center console and clunked to the floor somewhere around her feet. Great.

The truck idled for a moment and she said a quick prayer he would hang a right or go straight. As long as he got the hell out of her way.

He took a left. *Frick.*

Kate turned left in reluctant pursuit. Up ahead she could finally see the roof of her newly purchased two-story house. The down payment alone had rivaled her total student loan debt, but the century-old home, built in the esteemed Avenues neighborhood just east of downtown Salt Lake, had all been worth it.

Nirvana was a moment away. A wave of calm drifted over her.

Until she realized the guy had slowed down. A lot.

Oh. Lord. What if this guy was one of her new neighbors? Although she'd moved in almost a month ago, with her late nights at work, she hadn't met anyone save for her next-door neighbor, Glenda, a friendly widow who'd brought over a batch of cookies the day after Kate moved in.

He crept past her house, and Glenda's, and the next house…

Phew. Relieved, she turned left into her driveway. Out of the corner of her eye, she saw the white truck make a

U-turn. He stopped at the curb in front of Glenda's.

Kate parked her Audi and slumped down in the soft beige leather seats. How much worse could this day get? She considered waiting him out in the haven of her car, maybe pretending to be rooting for something in her purse until he went away. But that would have been the coward's way out, and she was anything but cowardly.

A glance in her rearview mirror showed the guy had eased open his own door. A crown of coal-black hair appeared over the top of the cab and the guy stepped around to the front of the truck. An unbuttoned light blue chambray shirt acted like a jacket over a white T-shirt that hugged his taut upper body. Loose, ripped jeans hung from narrow hips.

She swallowed with some difficulty. He certainly was something to look at.

Even from here, his light eyes stood out against warm, sun-kissed skin. Watching her.

. . .

Dominic Sorensen stood outside of his truck, well aware he was under the she-devil's scrutiny. Other men might have lost their temper at the crazy woman's display of road rage, but he found it…amusing.

So this was his aunt's new neighbor. The lawyer Glenda had been trying to get him to meet since she'd moved in. His aunt was delusional if she thought for a moment the two of them were remotely compatible. Her Audi cost more than his entire income last year. He'd made the mistake once of thinking that he would be enough for a woman like that. And it had only earned him heartache when she left, claiming he lacked sufficient ambition for her taste.

Still, he'd better go introduce himself or his aunt would never let him hear the end of it.

Her door swung open as he drew near but she was hunched forward, not aware of his arrival. From what he could tell, she was searching for something near her feet. Probably the cell phone three inches from her right foot. So focused in her search, he didn't want to interrupt.

Particularly since the top of her shirt gaped open to reveal an interesting amount of cleavage. He was human, after all.

Phone in hand, she sat up and her eyes widened when she saw him waiting outside her door. Gray eyes, maybe blue. Whatever their color, they were bright and blazing in contrast to the hot, fiery red of her hair that, even tied up, seemed to glow under the fading autumn sun.

Glenda had said she was pretty, but that was only half the story.

He delivered his most charming smile. "Never known anyone to drive so…determined."

She stepped out of the car and stood to an impressive height. But even with her heels, he still towered over her. "I'm afraid I was only concerned with your well-being." Her tone was friendly enough but the sarcasm was clear. "Seeing as how you were traveling ten miles *under* the speed limit, I thought you might be elderly and had lost your way or perhaps were suffering the sudden onset of a stroke…"

"Gee, and I thought you were trying to get close enough to check me out."

Her eyes narrowed. "Hardly."

"Hey, it's been known to happen."

The screen door of his aunt's house creaked open and

her backup boyfriend

a familiar blond head poked out. "Dominic? Is that you?"

Without taking his gaze from Kate, he smiled even wider. "In the flesh."

For a woman just shy of seventy, Glenda Sorensen moved remarkably fast as she sprang down the steps and the steep driveway that ran parallel to her new neighbor's.

"You're earlier than I expected, but I sure am glad to see you," she said and wrapped her arms around him in a hug, then stepped back. "Kate, I'd like you to meet my nephew Dominic Sorensen. Kate's the lawyer lady I was telling you about, Dom. She works for one of those fancy law firms downtown. They usually have her working long into the night. Although, come to think of it, you're home awfully early." She glanced down at her wristwatch. "It's not even close to eight o'clock."

"Yes, well, I had some stuff I thought I could work on from home." Kate dropped her gaze and lifted her bag up. He caught sight of a laptop and several file folders peeking from the top. "Speaking of which, I should get going."

"Why don't you join us for dinner tonight, Kate? I made lasagna and there's more than enough. I even made apple strudel for dessert." He had to give his aunt an *A* for effort in her obvious attempt at matchmaking. It was a like a conspiracy between her and the rest of the women in his family to see him dating again.

"That does sound delicious," Kate said. "But I ate a late lunch and don't think I could eat another bite. Thank you for offering."

She'd been careful to keep her gaze from his but he couldn't help but notice the slight pink around her lids that, at least with his two sisters, had usually been caused by tears.

Maybe she had a heart, after all.

"Another time then, dear. Oh, by the way. About ten minutes after you left this morning, a guy in a truck advertising a carpentry service showed up. Were you looking for someone to do some work around your house?"

Glenda didn't wait for a response but placed her hand on Dominic's arm, and he repressed a groan, knowing what was coming.

"If you are, you should look no farther than this man before you. His family runs a construction company, mostly large commercial projects, but Dominic has always had an eye for restoration. He does wonderful work. I bet he could probably give you a reasonable quote."

"I will definitely keep him in mind," the redhead said in a tone Dominic knew meant *no way in hell*, even if his aunt wasn't as perceptive. "I really have to go. It was nice meeting you, Dominic."

He inclined his own head slightly in return. "Pleasure was all mine."

Before Glenda could make any further interruptions, Kate turned and strode up the driveway. Her long legs made quick work of the distance and he couldn't help but appreciate the generous curves that even her boring black skirt couldn't hide.

Glenda was saying something about the length of time until dinner was ready, and he nodded while he continued to watch Kate's exit. She pocketed a business card squeezed in the doorjamb and turned her key in the door. From out of nowhere an orange tabby cat shot up the porch steps and wrapped itself around her feet. She took a moment to disentangle her heels from the feline and they both disappeared inside.

He nodded toward the place. "Does it still look like it did when the bank had the house up for sale this past summer?"

Back in June, he'd stopped by out of curiosity when he saw the FOR SALE sign planted in the law. The house was beautiful, with the low-pitched tile roof and overhanging boxed eaves, all of which he placed as turn of the century. It certainly had lots of potential, but it had been too small for his taste. He wanted something with a lot more space. Something for a family.

"I only caught a peek last week, mind you, but it looked close to the same. Poor dear still doesn't even have her window coverings up."

He nodded. She had her work cut out for her, then. Ordinarily, he'd be more than happy to get inside the place, see what he could do. But it was probably better this way. No sense working around someone—someone as pretty as her—knowing that nothing could ever come of it. It'd be like dangling a carrot in front of a horse. Torture.

Mentally he wished her luck and followed his aunt inside.

Chapter Two

"Hey, Kate."

Hearing the familiar voice, Kate's chest tightened. She glanced at the time and paused to write it down on the yellow legal pad in front of her, earning herself a few extra seconds to try and collect herself. She pulled a few slow breaths into her lungs.

And looked up into his face.

Michael was smiling fondly down at her. Kate knew what he was thinking. She'd always been a bit of a hard-liner when it came to tracking billable hours, not comfortable with rounding up to two-tenths of an hour when a call might be closer to a tenth. But she was well aware that to the average person working forty-plus hours just to put food on the table, one hour of her billable time could cost as much as their weekly income. Not that money was an issue for any of Strauss and Fletcher's clients, but for Kate, old habits died hard and she insisted on being meticulous.

Whereas Michael, whose family's money traced back to the earliest settlers, had no idea what it was like to live hand to mouth. He'd always thought she was a bit of a lark when it came to her diligence at keeping track of her time. Or so he used to say when he tucked a strand of hair from her eyes and kissed her soundly. The memory caused another twinge in Kate's fragile heart.

Stop it, damn it. Pull it together.

"What case are you working on? Finnegars?" Michael asked and glanced down at the files strewn across her desk. Judging from the way his brown hair arched evenly above his ears, she guessed he'd had a haircut recently.

Without waiting for an invitation, he took a seat across from her, throwing his right leg over his knee, and sat back comfortably, almost like things had never changed. So much like…before. Except he wore a blue-striped tie Kate wasn't familiar with. He must have come from a client meeting, because he hadn't taken the time to shed his tie and jacket or unbutton the top two buttons of his shirt as he usually did.

He was, in her estimation, perfect. The picture of confidence, sophistication, and power. A picture that had always made Kate's heart skip before. It just ached now.

Michael's brows furrowed, and he pressed his hands together in front of him. He spoke slowly and deliberately. "I understand from Nicole the cat may be out of the bag about our recent…development."

He could say that. She pinched the inside of her hand, willing herself not to tear up.

Michael, fortunately, didn't seem to notice her distress. "I wanted to come and see you myself. Make sure you're okay with everything."

"Me?" She forced herself to laugh and gave him a perplexed expression. "Why wouldn't I be all right? I'm happy for you. Really."

Her assistant, Trish, arrived in the doorway with a notebook in hand, ready for their meeting. She froze when she saw Michael, and her face drew into a grimace. Shooting Kate a brief, sympathetic smile, she scurried out.

Momentarily distracted from the conversation, Kate tried to remember what she had been about to say, aware Michael was looking at her expectantly. *Yes. That's right. About being completely happy for him.* "Besides, you and I have been over for ages. It's not like I didn't expect you were seeing someone. We've *both* moved on, after all."

He raised his right brow. "Oh? So you're seeing someone, then? I hadn't realized."

Crap. It had sounded like that. How had that happened? But she sure as Hades wasn't going to take it back and look like a liar, or worse—like she was single and still pining for him.

Because she wasn't. Much.

Certain her face was as flaming red as her hair, she smiled wide to cover her mortification. She might as well go with it, make it appear like embarrassment in talking about her guy. She glanced down at her hands twisted together in her lap, unable to meet his gaze. She'd never been any good at lying to him. "Oh. For a little while. Nothing too serious, yet."

She was so burning in hell for this.

"Good for you. Good for you," he said, perhaps a tad overexuberantly. "I've been worried how this would affect you. Especially since we all work at the same firm. Nicole told me I was being ridiculous. *We're all professionals*, she said. Looks like she was right."

her backup boyfriend

"Absolutely. No need to concern yourself on my account. I'm happy for the two of you. Nicole is so, so..." Bitchy? Snotty? Somehow, she didn't think either of those descriptions would be appropriate here.

"She is, isn't she?" Michael answered and a smile tugged at his mouth as his brown eyes lost focus for a moment before continuing. "With the two of you working together on the McKenna case, it's probably best to get it out in the open. And with the firm's fall retreat coming up and then Payton's engagement party, it was only a matter of time before you'd see us together."

Frick. That's right.

Kate had resigned herself to seeing Michael at Payton's engagement party, since Kate knew the Vaughns were close friends with Michael and his family. But that didn't mean Kate was ready to see him moving on with her new second chair. Not at Payton's engagement party and certainly not for a whole weekend retreat under the fishbowl gaze of the entire law firm.

Especially since she still hadn't found anyone to bring as her own date.

She only hoped the horror she felt didn't register on her face as she smiled so wide her cheeks were hurting.

Michael came to his feet, pausing a moment. "I'm glad things are going so well for you, Kate. You deserve it."

She looked into those familiar brown eyes, remembering how she'd once thought the future was theirs. Together.

"Thanks, Michael. You, too," she lied.

• • •

Kate managed not to look too horrified as she stared at the bottom figure on the bid that the contractor handed her. Corroded pipes that needed to be replaced? Electrical rewiring? It just didn't mesh with the information she'd learned from house's inspection report done only two months before.

"Thanks for your time. I have a couple more people I'm talking to and then I'll be in touch." Kate followed the guy out to the front porch. She watched his slow gait as he plodded his way toward the truck parked in the driveway. With a marked grimace, he managed to pull himself into the cab and shut the door.

Good riddance.

The air a little nippy, she rubbed her hands along her arms and looked around the neighborhood. Quiet, peaceful, and painted in bright, vibrant fall colors thanks to the leaves from the large, century-old sycamore trees that lined the streets.

She noticed the mail truck at the end of the block, and a sense of dread overcame her. Payton had mentioned she'd sent the engagement party invitations out on Thursday. It was bound to be there. She supposed she'd better go look.

The contractor's rusty brown contraption sputtered to life as she passed it, but he remained in park while he read something from his cell phone. She tried not to crinkle her nose in distaste at the gray plume of smoke that spewed from the tailpipe.

Things were not looking good on the contractor front. She'd already contacted five different guys since Tuesday. The only one with an opening on a Saturday at such late notice had been this guy. Two had told her the earliest they could stop by was next week, although the soonest they could start any work would be mid-December, after some of their bigger projects slowed down. She was keeping her fingers crossed until then.

Kate grabbed the pile of mail and snapped the mailbox shut. There it was. The dreaded cream-colored envelope addressed to Ms. Kate Matthews and guest.

She opened it, despite already knowing what it said, having seen a copy a couple of weeks ago. But this was official. Only a few more weeks until Payton's party, where she would be surrounded by several wealthy and prestigious families—including Michael's—at the city's most exclusive country club. Payton's mother wouldn't hear of anything less.

Maybe she should take Payton up on her offer to set Kate up with one of the groomsmen. At least then she wouldn't have to go solo or to explain to Michael why her fabulous new boyfriend was absent.

For a moment, the image of the sexy contractor with the devious grin came to mind. With someone like him as her escort, Kate would be sure to score some jealousy points from Michael.

Preoccupied with her thoughts, Kate almost didn't look up in time to see that her near contractor had thrown his truck into reverse and was hurling down the driveway.

Headed directly toward her.

She leaped to the left and fell to the ground just as the truck screeched out onto the road—almost colliding into another oncoming truck. Fortunately the other driver responded quickly and managed to swerve in time. With barely a wave of his hand, the contractor put his truck in drive and continued down the street, unconcerned with the near wreckage he'd caused.

The other truck moved forward again, made a wide turn, and pulled into Glenda's driveway.

Of course, it would be him.

. . .

Dominic parked his truck and stared outside his window at the redhead sitting in the middle of her lawn. She was surrounded by mail and wet leaves, a few of which almost matched the color of her hair, save for a couple stuck in the thick riot of waves and curls. Gone was the cool lawyer, replaced with someone more touchable—and human. Not to mention cute when she was flustered like that.

He opened his truck and climbed out. "You two related? I may have to take out extra hazard insurance to park here."

She sprang to her feet and started gathering the letters, not bothering to look up before she answered. "It seems as if the whole contracting profession believes common courtesy, speed limits, and other rules of the road are optional."

He leaned back against his truck, enjoying the view. He'd bet she had no idea how the damp fabric of her jeans practically molded to her backside as she bent down. He should probably help her, but by the way she was huffing and throwing disgruntled looks his way, she'd sooner eat the mail than accept his help.

"Don't take this the wrong way," Dominic said and scratched his chin like he was pondering something, "but I think there's a city ordinance that requires you to keep the walkways clear of all debris. It's a safety issue. That mound of leaves you're accumulating could earn you some hefty fines if you're not careful. Even a fancy lawyer should be able to handle a rake if she puts her mind to it."

"I was already planning on getting to it today, but thank you for your concern." She brushed a wad of hair from her eyes, and the last leaf in her hair loosened and fell to the ground. Too bad. He'd liked the effect.

Dominic straightened from his perch and lumbered toward Glenda's side door. "I only mention it because we might see some snow in the next few days. You don't want those leaves sitting on your lawn all winter long. It'll rot the grass."

He tapped on Glenda's door then let himself in.

• • •

Kate peeked around the corner of her front room window for the fourth time in the past hour, holding her breath.

The white pickup was still parked in Glenda's driveway.

Dominic Sorensen didn't appear to be in a hurry to leave, making her efforts to avoid him and any further embarrassment impossible.

What, was he moving in?

For the last hour or so, Kate had confirmed that there was, in fact, a city ordinance that mandated home owners keep the walkways unobstructed. But having grown up living in a series of trailer homes, then a small condo apartment with her grams, and, later, one rented half of a duplex after she graduated from law school, she'd never had any experience with the obligations of home ownership.

Kate tried to figure out her options. If she could put this off until tomorrow, she would. But Sunday was not a possibility, and the rest of the week was no good, either, not with her work schedule.

Sure. The stupid leaves might look amazing, as she was just appreciating earlier, but they were quickly losing their appeal now that they'd hit the ground.

How diligently did the city enforce this rule? Did she dare risk a citation? From the way the sun was waning, she guessed she only had about another hour of good light to get the task done. She was going to have to risk it.

With resolve, she strode through the front room toward her half-gutted kitchen—with the hideous blue floral wallpaper—where she kept a light jacket and rubber boots by the door. When she'd bought the house, she'd found a few gardening tools in the shed out back, including a rather decrepit rake. But since she didn't have time to go to Home Depot, it would have to do.

Glenda's small terrier barked from her backyard. Kate stuck her head out the back door for a minute to hear the low murmur of voices, confirming they—meaning, Dominic— would be preoccupied for the time being. She didn't need an audience. Especially since she had no clue how someone raked a lawn.

It can't be that difficult. Right?

She took another deep breath of the smoky-scented October air and marched around the back of her yard. At the top of the driveway she collected the garbage can and rolled it behind her to the sidewalk. Pensive, she stared at all the work now spread across her lawn. A little awkwardly, she took a large swath of the leaves with the rake. The crush of the dry leaves bristled loudly in the air. She took another sweep, revealing damp grass underneath.

Actually, this might not be so bad. It is kind of peaceful out here.

By the time she had three large piles of leaves and the lawn green and naked again, the sun had hit the Oquirrh Mountains, leaving the evening sky a purplish hue. Satisfied, she wiped a sleeve across her nose, which was cold and slightly damp from the chill in the air. Now all she had to do was get these leaves off the ground and up into the can. She wished she had a pair of gloves and would bet Glenda had some she could borrow, but there was no way she was going to ask for them now.

She could do this. How difficult could it be? She bent down and scooped up an armful of leaves and with the other hand clapped the teeth of the rake over the leaves and started the slow process of getting them into the canister. Kate was at the bottom of the first pile when a strange tickling sensation on her right wrist caught her attention.

She glanced down in time to see a brown-legged spider crawl up her sleeve.

A high-pierced screech of terror ripped from her throat. She tore the jacket from her body and threw it to the ground, trying to find the spindly-legged arachnid. She didn't hear the approaching footsteps until Glenda's voice reached her.

"Kate, dear, what on earth is the matter?"

A choked-off laugh told Kate that her neighbor hadn't arrived alone. She ran her fingers through her hair, frantically searching for the beast, but tried to keep her voice level and even despite the frantic beating of her heart. "Oh. Just a large spider. It—it kind of surprised me."

No use. Where the hell was it? Wait. Was that another tickling at her neck? *Shiiiit!*

Her composure abandoned, Kate danced in a circle, her fingers scraping against the skin of her neck to try and get rid of any creepy crawly things. She still couldn't feel anything, though.

Okay. Take deep breaths.

The fog of fear began to lift and Kate looked more carefully down her body—and became aware of the silence from her two visitors. At another attempt for calm, she smoothed her hair and paused when her gaze met Glenda's wide, questioning eyes. Kate tried to give the woman a reassuring smile. She darted a quick glance at the taller figure standing beside her neighbor. Although his mouth was set in a straight line, his blue eyes looked suspiciously bright.

Humiliation flooded through her and she was at a loss of how to explain her behavior. "A—a spider. I saw a spider crawling up my arm and I—" A shudder racked her body. Oh, God. She really, really hated spiders. Worse than anything. And the size of that one? Uneasy, she glanced back at the piles of leaves waiting to be loaded into the garbage.

"I don't see anything, dear. There now. You don't even have any gloves for your poor hands. Dom, why don't you grab your work gloves and take care of these for Kate."

"No, really, I wouldn't want—" she attempted.

"Not a problem," Dominic said smoothly, and without waiting for any further objections, headed over to his truck and grabbed some gloves from the seat.

Kate really wanted to object. She wanted to be able to refuse his help, only—another glance at the leaves assured her there was no way on God's green earth she was going near those piles again. Instead, she watched Dominic bend down and grab an armload of leaves, his back to them.

"Why don't you come inside for a few minutes while Dom finishes up? I have some water on for tea and a plate of fresh butter cookies I made this afternoon."

Kate's gaze, however, was on the figure before her, whose jeans had crept dangerously low to reveal a small expanse of tanned skin under his plaid flannel shirt. Hunched over, with his weight supported by his quads, Kate couldn't help but notice the tautness of his jeans as they stretched over his upper thighs and backside. He stood easily and dumped half the pile of leaves into the canister and turned to meet her eyes.

That's right. Glenda had asked her a question. Something about tea…

"Thanks for the offer, but I'm fine. Nothing a long, hot bath couldn't cure."

At that statement, Dominic broke into a wide, easy smile, and an impish gleam entered his eyes as he watched her. Oh, great. Now he was probably picturing her naked.

Glenda waved her hand. "You can take a bath later. You're coming with me right now and we're having some tea. I won't take any arguments. We've had so few opportunities to visit, now seems as good a time as any."

She grabbed Kate firmly by the shoulders and led her up the driveway, and Kate, realizing the decision was already made for her, quietly followed. Maybe if she hurried she could get in and out before Dominic finished.

Chapter Three

When Dominic opened the door, the scent of cookies assailed him, and the warm air bit at his cheeks. It was colder outside than he'd thought. The two women seated at the kitchen table paused in their conversation when he stepped in.

"There's a mug of tea on the counter for you. Earl Grey," Glenda offered. "I was just giving Kate the name of a couple neighborhood kids who could help her with the yard work in exchange for a few bucks."

He nodded and headed to the kitchen sink to wash up. "I pulled the garbage can up the driveway and left it next to the recycling bin. Your rake is in the shed out back. It's definitely seen better days." He reached for a paper towel and glanced over at Kate.

"Came with the house. I've been meaning to get to Home Depot—"

"Well, look no farther in the meantime, honey," Glenda said and scooped two teaspoons of sugar into her tea. "Feel free to use whatever I might have in the garage. My Danny always loved tinkering around in our garden, which for Danny meant we had to have state-of-the-art everything. Half the stuff I don't even know what to do with," she said and laughed merrily at the memory of her husband.

A loud buzzing sound from the basement brought Glenda to her feet. "That's my whites. I'll be a minute. If I don't hang up a few of those shirts they'll be a mess when I try to iron them later."

Dominic tossed the paper towel in the garbage and picked up the mug Glenda had left for him. He preferred coffee but this would do. He brought it to his lips, using the opportunity to watch Kate, who squirmed in the quiet of the kitchen. He would bet she was wishing she'd finished her tea before he'd arrived.

Which was why he'd made sure to work fast.

Almost absentmindedly, she tried to run her fingers through her windblown hair but grimaced and gave up halfway through when it looked like a certain knot wouldn't budge.

She looked up at him, her expression serious and intense. "Thanks for the help outside," she said with absolute sincerity, distracting him enough so he took a large swig of scalding tea. "I was—what you might say—acting like a freak out there. I hate spiders. And when I saw one crawl up my sleeve…" She stopped, her cheeks getting rosier by the second. But she didn't look away, still meeting his gaze. "Well…thanks."

"Like I said, no worries. We all have something we're afraid of. If there had been a snake out there, you probably would have heard a few girlish shrieks followed by some choice words from me."

Her mouth cracked into a very slight smile. Progress.

"You and Glenda must be close. Two visits in the same week." She raised her mug to her lips and sipped.

"She's a sweet lady. Since my uncle died, my brother and I try to get over here as often as we can. Lend a hand. These old houses always seem to have something or another going on, as I imagine you'll figure out soon enough." From the way she flinched, he had a feeling she probably already was. "Did you find someone yet?"

She looked at him, perplexed initially, and then he saw understanding dawn. "I've talked to a few people," she said vaguely. He translated that into a no.

"I told you," wheezed Glenda as she reached the top of the stairs, a laundry basket with clothes in her arms. He hustled over and relieved her of her burden, and she took another breath and continued, "Dominic is the only person you want. At the least, let him in to have a look. Glance through the estimates the other clowns gave you. He'll tell you what's what."

"I couldn't impose—" Kate started.

Did she ever let anyone help her out? "I could take a look," he said easily and cut off the rest of her objection. "At least give you an idea of what needs to be done, and you can compare it to the bids you've received. Besides, I'm curious to see the inside the old place. Turn of the century, right? What have you got to lose?"

She raised those gray-blue eyes to his, and he could see her trying to assess the situation as her brow furrowed.

"Okay," she said slowly. "I guess it wouldn't hurt to get another bid."

He smiled. "I can swing by Monday evening."

"Wednesday will work better for me."

Was she trying to be difficult? "Wednesday it is."

Glenda smacked her hands on the table. "Darn. I completely forgot to take the cookies out."

"Actually"—Kate glanced down at her cell phone resting on the table—"I really should be going."

"It's only seven thirty, dear. Oh. Are you going out?" His aunt's surprise couldn't have been more evident and he worked to keep a straight face.

"Not tonight." If she had been pink before, her face turned a deep purple now as she looked everywhere but at him. "It's been a long week. All I want is to relax in a nice hot bath."

"I understand, dear. But don't think I haven't noticed, other than working upward of fifteen hours a day, you never get out and do anything fun. You're only young once. Lord knows the trouble Danny and I used to get into when we were your age. We never could have kids of our own, you see, so we were determined to be kids ourselves, living every moment to the fullest." Glenda looked off with a fond smile on her lips and a bit of mist in her eyes.

"Save for those weekends when my parents lassoed you into watching the four of us, if you remember," Dominic teased. "By Sunday night, I think you were both counting your blessings you *didn't* have kids."

Glenda chuckled. "As exhausting as you four were, I loved every minute of our time with you all. We both did."

Kate stood abruptly. "Thanks again, for your help. But I really do need to be going."

"Let me grab you some cookies at least." Ignoring Kate's objections, Glenda stuffed a sandwich bag with as many cookies she could cram in. Kate accepted them reluctantly and sailed out the side door before Glenda could delay her further.

"You enjoy your bath, dear!" Glenda called out from behind her.

Kate blanched and gave them a halfhearted wave.

He joined Glenda at the table and nodded while she continued to make conversation long after Kate left. About what he didn't know. His mind was still on the redhead.

And that damned bath.

• • •

Dominic stepped out of his truck the next evening, pretending not to notice the faces that peered at him from the windows. The front door swung open, and before he could reach for the handle a small figure threw himself at his legs.

"Uncle Dominic!"

"Oomph! Take it easy, Paul. You almost took me out."

Even though his presence in his six-year-old nephew's life has been sporadic at best thanks to Paul's nomadic father, the kid was eager to give his affection without restraint. Paul's two older sisters, Jenna and Natalie, wise already at nine and seven years of age, watched him warily from around the corner. Their affection wasn't as quickly given. He'd win them over with time.

"Hello, girls. What's your grandma been brewing over her pot for dinner?"

"I heard that," was the quick response from the kitchen. With Paul holding on to his legs, Dominic strode down the hallway to the large room at the back of the house.

"You'll eat what I make and won't complain," scolded the dark-haired, petite woman washing her hands at the kitchen sink. But the wide smile belied the true affection she had for him. She briefly wiped her hands on a towel and opened her arms for a hug.

"Hey, Mama," he said and folded her in tightly and lifted her off the floor.

"*Dios mío.* You'll drop me," she squealed and he set her down. "It's not like you didn't just see me last Sunday."

Her accent was faint, something more than forty years in the United States had softened over the years but couldn't quite erase. Elena Marguerite Eschaban Sorensen was as beautiful and youthful at fifty-seven years as she appeared in her wedding photos. Dominic could see how someone like stoic, fair-skinned Petter Sorensen had fallen for such a warm, lively woman with mischievous dark eyes. Four kids later, they were still very much in love, something all their children looked on with pride and possibly a little envy.

It was exactly the kind of love he was looking for.

He wanted Sunday dinners with his own large brood. Dinners where he and his wife shared warm looks of love that made everyone around them roll their eyes or grimace in disgust knowing what they'd be doing later.

He sneaked a carrot from the saucepan and took a bite. "How's Dad doing?"

She shook her head. "Stubborn. He's in bed and refuses to come out for dinner. He's been hiding out there all afternoon. I think he's afraid the slightest stress will set him back for his surgery. Why don't you go see him? Maybe you can get him to at least come to the sofa. I'll fix him a tray."

"A lot of good I'll do, but I'll try my best."

Although his dad had recovered from the heart attack that nearly took him from his family three years earlier, the heart condition that caused the attack—dilated cardiomyopathy—

still plagued him. His doctors hoped the pacemaker he was scheduled to receive in a few more weeks would improve his health.

Ten minutes later, Dominic appeared for dinner—without his dad. He shook his head at his mother's expectant face. She tried to smile, but he could tell she was concerned.

Dominic and his family had done their best over the years to ease the stress on the old man. He'd even pulled out of the U, where he had been working toward his architecture degree, to help cover for his dad at the family construction business. It had been the right things to do at the time—even if his then girlfriend, Melinda, hadn't agreed—and he had no regrets. If it helped his dad's stress level and the toll on his heart, it was worth it. Family came first.

He only hoped that his dad would understand that now that things were taking a positive turn, Dominic was ready to get back to his own life. Realize his own dreams. And he hoped his dad wouldn't be too hurt.

"Hey, I want to sit with everyone else," Paul whined when he saw the adults take their places around the table and realized he and his sisters were to sit up at the bar.

"There's only one spot left, little man, at the head of the table," Cruz said, referring to their father's empty spot. Cruz took his usual seat at the foot of the table. The eldest, he liked to remind his siblings of his place as leader. They let him think so. "Are you ready to assume the responsibility of sitting as the head of the family?"

Paul nodded. "Mama already tells me I have to be brave because I'm now the man of the house. Right, Mama?"

"That's right, buddy." Daisy attempted a smile, but her heart was clearly not in it. Her wide, dark brown eyes looked drawn and tired. Not at all like the bossy older sister he knew. When he got a hold of Leo, her two-timing shit of a husband, he was going to give him something to remember. "I suppose you can sit here. Let your aunt Benny help you cut your food."

Paul picked up his plate and strutted to the table, almost preening. Dominic's mom smoothed his dark hair when he took the seat next to her, pride shining in her eyes.

"Make sure you eat every bite, kiddo," Benny said and leaned over to cut his pork chop for him. "You don't want to end up weak and frail like your uncles."

"Listen to your auntie. She'll show you how to grow hair on your chest," Dominic quipped, earning an elbow in the belly even as Benny's blue eyes sparkled.

"Can I see? Really?" Paul chirped, his gaze already steady on his aunt's chest, which in her overlarge tee looked as shapeless as a potato sack.

"You won't find anything there," Cruz chimed in and Dominic chuckled while Paul looked up at the adults, truly perplexed.

"I could take you both anytime," Benny bit back. Beautiful in a more understated way than Daisy, Benny was the youngest, and had never been apologetic for her tomboyish ways. "You've both gotten soft in your old age. What are you guys pushing, like forty? I'd bet Paul could put you down in under a minute."

"Thirty-five, brat," Cruz said. "And I can whoop pretty boy's ass here"—he pointed to Dominic—"as well as yours. Anytime."

"*Language,*" their mother reminded them, and Cruz grinned.

"Should we have a little game after dinner?" Benny just didn't give up. "Two on two. Let's put your false bravado to the test. Dominic and I could totally take you and Daisy, as always. I'll even let you have Paul."

Paul whooped and immediately started begging to be included. Daisy, however, didn't bite and barely realized what was going on around her.

Dom exchanged looks with his siblings. He knew that aside from his sister's heartache, she was trying her damnedest to keep her family afloat, struggling with all the debt her ex had taken on but was now nowhere to help pay it off. She needed help—legal help—and that was going to cost her. For a minute, he considered the possibility of talking to his aunt's feisty new neighbor, even if to get a referral for a reliable divorce attorney, but dismissed the thought right away. Because as proud as Daisy was, she wouldn't take any financial assistance from them. She wanted to figure it out herself.

Even if it killed her.

He shook his head. There was more than one heart that needed fixing in this family.

Chapter Four

Kate opened the door Wednesday evening, surprised at her nervousness. Almost like she was going out on a date or something, which was completely ridiculous. This was strictly business. She needed someone to help figure out what work had to be done on the house, and Dominic was offering some guidance.

But…he looked good. His too-long hair was wavy and, from the sheen on it, looked wet, like he'd just stepped out of the shower. As if planned, the wind chose that moment to kick up and blow a lock of his hair across his forehead.

Lord, help her.

His dark, tanned skin looked warm and toasty underneath the dark hunter-green T-shirt that clung to his chest. For an agonizing moment, she fought the urge to kiss the small crevice below his neck and inhale the delicious clean scent wafting toward her.

"I don't know where you want to start," she said after

they offered the preliminary greeting, and she shut the door behind him. "This, of course, is the great room. You can see there's not really much that needs to be done in here. Before they abandoned ship, the previous owners finished this and the dining room. Oh, and the staircase." She looked in admiration at the beautiful work someone had done in restoring the old curving staircase and the maple-toned hardwood floors to their original beauty. It had been love at first sight when she'd walked in.

Even after she'd seen the rest of the place.

"The dining room is through there." She pointed to the closed French doors on the opposite end of the room.

"It's gorgeous." His eyes swept the room in obvious appreciation, stopping to touch on her in a way that made her pulse increase.

She quickly turned away, dismissing the possibility his compliment was intended for anything other than the room. She looked around again, as if for the first time, appreciating the contrast of the white wainscoting and white French doors with the rich wood floors. The warm, off-white linen shade of the walls that kept the room feeling large—but still warm and cozy. The surprising amount of sunlight that streamed in from the two large windows that looked out over her front yard, even with the large sycamore tree front and center on her lawn.

The only things missing were the teal silk draperies that sat in a box on the floor.

Dominic ran his hand along the dark walnut wood that framed the century-old fireplace. "Nice work," he said softly.

For an insane moment Kate wondered what it would feel like to have that same hand on *her* in appreciation.

Then quickly blocked it from her mind. She was acting like a lovesick teenager. With his easy smile and swagger, Dominic doubtless had a string of women he dated. Women flashier and more fun than she could be—or wanted to be. Women whose only ambition was making him the center of their universe. *Definitely* not something she wanted to be. "On that note, let me show you the rest of the house."

• • •

Dominic followed Kate into the kitchen, quietly admiring her soft scent, the few red tendrils of hair that escaped the band holding most of that hair up off her neck. Her conservative navy suit with a formfitting knee-length skirt was an interesting contrast with the furry red slippers on her feet. He'd noticed the abandoned high heels near the door when he came in. Even without the added height, she was only half a head shorter than him. It wouldn't be very difficult to lean down and press a soft kiss at the nape of her ne—

He stopped when he finally got a look at her kitchen. Well, if you could call it that. He let out a low whistle. "You've definitely got your work cut out for you."

It wasn't that the room was a disaster or a flashback to the seventies, with appliances in shades of avocado green or anything. In fact, the previous owners had gotten a fair start on the breakfast nook that overlooked her backyard. But they'd begun dismantling the cupboards, leaving half on the floor and the other half hanging without their fronts when they left. They'd also stripped about a third of the hideous blue-flowered wallpaper from the walls, leaving the rest for the new owner to get around to tackling. At least the kitchen was still usable, even if the oven was circa 1977 and the old fridge not much newer.

"How does the electrical look?" he asked taking a step into the room. "Or the plumbing? Those can be the bigger costs when you buy an old home like this."

"I had an inspection done when I first looked at the property, and the guy was optimistic in his estimate. I have a copy here." She headed over to the counter where she picked up a quote from the last contractor and then handed it to Dominic.

Dominic saw the guy had clearly been trying to bilk Kate for everything she was worth as he took in the unreasonably high estimates. Being a single woman with little knowledge of anything home improvement–related probably made her a target for predators like this. He shook his head. "Why don't you show me the rest of the place?"

Forty-five minutes later, they were back in the kitchen where he was drawing up what he believed was a more than fair bid. Actually, generous might be a better word for it. But he told himself it was because he felt sorry for her. If he didn't do the work, who knew what some joker might try to con her for? It had nothing to do with the fact he was drawn to the woman. He'd already concluded they would not be the right fit. She was too much like…Melinda.

He slid his bid across the counter to her. "This is what I'd estimate the costs to be, including labor," he said, pointing to the first number. "And this is what I'd charge you. Keep in mind that I'd be doing this as a freelance job. Working mostly weekends and in the evenings, so it may take a little longer than you'd anticipated. But I could start Saturday."

She studied it and looked up at him warily. "Why would you do this for me?"

"Glenda would have my hide if I didn't give you a deal. Plus, there's the bonus that maybe now you'll stop trying to run me over whenever I visit my aunt." She couldn't repress her smile in time for him to catch it.

"May I ask what your qualifications are? Do you have any references? Other than your aunt."

He smiled, not at all offended by her question. He'd have been worried if she hadn't asked. "Been helping my dad with his construction business since I was twelve. Like Glenda said, Sorensen Construction focuses mainly on commercial projects, but there are the odd jobs we've taken on in the off-season that, over the years, have given me experience in residential. You could say I've developed a special interest in home renovation and restoration. This isn't my first freelance job, I promise. I can get you the numbers of some of my past clients."

She nodded and stared down at the sheet. His bid was half the cost of the other one. He could almost hear her thoughts as she weighed in that fact along with the fact he was offering to get started this weekend. Not in another month or in the new year, as would likely be the case with most other contractors as they wrapped up existing projects.

She gave a quick nod, as if coming to a decision. "All right. Deal."

"Deal it is." He smiled, the right side of his lip curled a little higher than the other, something he'd been told had a certain charm to it. "Why don't we start first thing Saturday morning? I'll pick you up at eight?"

She scrunched up her brows. "Pick me up for what?"

"Thought I could take you to Home Depot. Look at some paint swatches and cabinets to get a feel for what you're looking for. Maybe even buy a rake or two."

"I usually spend Saturdays putting in a few hours of work, but…" She sighed. "You make a good point. Okay. It's a date." She stopped, a fusion of blood rushing to her face. "I don't mean *date* date. I just meant—" She paused again when she caught him trying to contain his own smile. He was enjoying her discomfort. More formally, she said, "See you Saturday."

"See you Saturday, Kate."

This was going to be an interesting job, to say the least.

• • •

"Hey, Kate. Have a minute?" her boss asked from her doorway, a smile on his face and a few sheets of paper in his hand.

"Of course. Come in." She noted the time on the brief she was reading and set her pen down, crossing her hands in front of her.

Tim shut the door and took a seat. Kate tried to fight a rising panic. Usually Tim stood by the door when he had a question or wanted to make a few comments on a brief. Entering into her office for an unscheduled visit *and* closing the door? It was unprecedented.

"Have any plans for the weekend?" he asked easily.

Tim wasn't here to discuss weekend plans, even if it was Friday. But she'd play along. "I'm going shopping for some things for the house, and then I'll probably put in a few hours on the McKenna case."

"Kate, how long have you been with Strauss? Five

years?"

Clearly the small talk was over. She nodded. "Five years last June."

"I've been watching your progress with the firm for some time, and I've always been impressed. Your work on the Landers settlement last month was exceptional. You're a great asset to us, and I said as much at the last board meeting." He paused and studied her carefully. "When I recommended you for junior partner."

The knot of anxiety tying up her stomach started to loosen, and she felt almost buoyant. This was exactly what she'd been working for since she first walked through those doors. Partner. "Thank you. I sincerely appreciate it—" She stopped when he held his hand up.

"I recommended you. But the decision is still theirs. I'll be honest with you. Most associates who attain this distinction have a different profile than you, Kate. They're married. Have a family. A life outside of the firm."

The knot began tightening again.

"I know what you're thinking. It's ridiculous. But keep in mind, an attorney with a vast background of friends and family also tends to have strong roots in the community. They or their spouses are members of the PTA, they're church or Scout leaders. And with these community connections, these same attorneys can bring in business. A lot of business." He paused to level those piercing blue eyes on her.

Contacts. Social connections. Family. Did it always come down to that? Instead of plain old hard work and dedication? But she only nodded.

"You're single, no children, and from what I've seen, no visible ties to any outside organization, which in the past when the topic of making you partner was broached has been a point of discussion. Until now."

She blinked. Until now? What had changed?

Tim actually cracked a smile. "Word is that you've recently become involved with someone. Something pretty serious."

How on earth did this kind of information spread? She said one little word to Michael and suddenly she's the latest gossip. Typical.

Before she could comment on the truth or fiction of this latest tidbit, Tim continued, "I think that's great news. You're not getting any younger and, truthfully, your lack of male companionship has been noted and commented on." He actually chuckled and Kate had an image of the eight stuffy male attorneys who made up the senior partners, sitting around the conference board trying to determine her sexuality.

"And now with this McKenna case, you'll have that extra boost to send you over the top. You know, Mark McKenna and his family have been clients since this firm originated. You'd do well to bring your best game. Anyway, I just wanted to share the good news with you." Tim stood. "Well, I look forward to meeting the guy. He'll be coming to the fall retreat with you, right?"

She coughed, trying to find her voice. "We're still working the details out, but I'll do my best."

He stared at her. Hard, with a penetrating, laser-like focus. "You do that. Just remember everything I said."

Kate stared at the open door long after Tim left.

To think. Four years as an undergraduate in the top 10 percent while working full-time to pay the bills. Three years of painstaking, competitive work in law school and two grueling summer clerkships. Five years of burning the midnight oil at the firm to be number one in billable hours among the other associates. But all of that, apparently, wasn't what might be the clincher to her getting that promotion.

This was the twenty-first century. How could one's marital status still be so pivotal?

And what would the senior partners say if they discovered she was actually single? Without the impending social connections a marriage and kids and family might bring with it...

She risked losing it all.

Which meant, for the time being, she'd play along. Keep up the pretense that she had some guy devoted to her who might even now be checking out engagement rings. As to the retreat...she'd come up with something. Heck, half of the spouses usually stayed home for some reason or another. She'd be no different. Yes. She could make this work and, in the meantime, win the McKenna case, making it easier for everyone to overlook the tragic news when her "boyfriend" dumped her. Or she dumped him—whichever.

She just needed to buy time.

. . .

It was like a warehouse. One large, endless warehouse that— she inhaled deeply—smelled funny.

It was also packed. Who knew so many people would have the urgent need to purchase rakes and paint and God knew what else on a brisk Saturday morning when they could be at home enjoying coffee and a good book—or, in her case, a brief?

"You'll definitely want to have this socket wrench set in your tool box," Dominic said and dropped the item next to the hammer, drill, picture hanging kit, and a bunch of other items of which she'd already forgotten the names. She liked to think it was just the overwhelming amount of stuff she'd never heard of before that had her mind drawing a blank.

But that was only half of it.

As Dominic bent down on his haunches to stare at an array of something or other, her gaze wandered helplessly down. She carefully checked the side of her mouth for drool.

It had been fourteen months. No wonder she was acting like a hormone-driven lunatic.

Kate hoped her own attire looked similarly casual and thrown together—even if she had spent most of the morning agonizing over this "effortless" look of faded curvy-fit Levi's and a simple white T-shirt. She'd topped it off with her new brown leather jacket that accentuated her narrow waist. Probably the only thing about her that was narrow.

Kate might have decided that things had to remain professional between them—but that didn't mean she couldn't enjoy the thrill of having an attractive man look at her with appreciation.

Dominic turned his head to her, and she barely had time to pull her gaze away from his derriere. She pretended to be staring at the cart instead. "Why do I need all this stuff again? I thought you've done this before. Shouldn't you already own it?"

"Do you want to rely on a contractor to come and help you whenever you need to hang up a few measly pictures? Or fix a leaky faucet? You'd be broke within the year." He straightened and tossed another packet onto the pile. "Of course I have the necessary equipment to do the renovations, but with the proper tools and common sense, you could be prepared to handle some basic home maintenance on your own. That's what all this stuff is for. You. You're a home owner now. It's time you started to *own* it."

She shrugged and took the last swallow of her venti latte that they'd picked up from Starbucks first thing. They moved to the next aisle.

Half an hour later they were looking at several paint samples. A fun project initially—until Dominic began explaining the difference between matte, flat, eggshell, satin, gloss, and semigloss finishes as her own eyes glossed over. Until she heard a familiar voice.

"Kate?"

Instinctively, she turned her head before she could process *why* it was familiar.

Oh, Lord.

Michael. And he wasn't alone. Her nemesis was glued to his side, looking chic and slight in dark, skinny jeans that Kate doubted she could get an arm through, let alone a leg. For an early Saturday morning, Nicole's hair still looked exceptionally silky and luxurious. How could Kate not hate her for that reason alone?

"Hi, guys!" Kate asked a little too brightly, "What brings you two here?"

Stupid question now that she was collected enough to see the paint samples in Michael's hand. Michael actually looked a little uncomfortable before he responded, "Nicole and I were thinking of doing some…um, repainting."

This still begged the question of what Michael was doing

here, since as far as she knew from their three years together, he'd never done any house maintenance on his own, leaving it to his very expensive decorator.

Nicole continued, "The master bedroom is this hideous shade of blue that begs me to slash my wrists every time I wake up."

Ah. Now she could see why he was uneasy. Kate and Michael had chosen that particular shade of blue together. Michael had the courtesy of avoiding her eyes.

The silence drew out and Kate finally noticed the couple's attention had turned toward the tall, strangely quiet figure behind her. From the strange look that entered Michael's eyes as he looked back and forth between her and Dominic, she had a pretty good idea where his thoughts were leaning.

That this was the guy. *Her* guy.

Her pulse seemed to double as she tried to figure out how to handle this without everything blowing up in her face. *Let's go for simple first.*

"Michael, Nicole," she said, inclining her head to them, "this is Dominic."

Both men shook hands, each studying the other, Michael with a look of suspicion, Dominic with only mild interest. Nicole already had her cell phone in her hands and was busy scrolling through, dismissing all of them.

Kind of like the first time Kate tried to interact with her. In Nicole's first weeks at Strauss, Kate had reached out to find some common interests. Frankly, there hadn't been too many female attorneys in the ranks at the law firm, and she'd thought they could both use an extra friend. But Nicole had dismissed her requests and barely drawn her gaze from her phone screen to say hello. Not much later Kate heard the rumors linking Nicole and Michael together as a couple, and she'd given up the effort all together.

"Dominic. Good to meet you. I've heard a lot about you," Michael said.

Dominic gave her a sidelong glance. "Really? I'm afraid I'm at a disadvantage, then."

Michael's eyes narrowed.

Crap.

"Michael and Nicole are attorneys at my firm," Kate rushed in. But she gazed nervously over at Dominic, her eyes pleading with him not to blow her cover. "I'm sure I've mentioned them, sweetie."

Other than raising an eyebrow, Dominic didn't give anything away.

So far, so good.

"We were picking up a few things for the house," Kate said and stepped closer to Dominic. She thought about placing her hand on his arm but figured that might be pushing her luck. "Looking at paint samples, getting a few odds and ends. I don't want to keep you two…"

"That's right," Michael said, not taking the hint. "I heard you took the plunge into home ownership. You know, if you're looking for professional help, I have some contacts of my parents I could send you."

Kate couldn't help but notice Nicole's ramrod posture stiffen measurably, even if her gaze didn't leave the phone screen.

"Actually, Dominic is helping me out." She'd have to skate carefully here. "It just so happens his expertise is in restoration. It's how we met." Her face had to be three shades past radish red, and she kept her eyes on the row of paintbrushes behind Michael, wondering if Dominic had figured out her little story yet. Not that what she'd just said wasn't perfectly true.

It was what was said between the lines that was giving her a small anxiety attack.

"And you're a contractor? Have I heard of you?" Michael asked. Lord, he was relentless. "Are you licensed professionally?"

"My family runs Sorensen Construction," Dominic said. "We recently completed the new office building on the Draper Parkway for that pharmaceutical company."

Michael nodded but didn't seem to want to let it go. "And how are you qualified for residential construction?"

Kate laughed uneasily. "Michael, I've already vetted Dominic. I'm satisfied." Her tone took on a warning note.

"Michael, honey, we should be getting on our way," Nicole intervened, not looking particularly happy. "Remember we have brunch with your parents in an hour? They get worried when we're running behind, and we still need to stop and pick up dessert." She delivered a megawatt smile to Kate.

It was as if the woman knew where to hit her where it hurt most.

Despite dating Michael for three years, Kate had never scored an invitation to the Langfords' weekend brunches. After a disastrous first dinner where Mrs. Langford peppered Kate with not-so-subtle questions about her family and social connections—none of which Kate had—Michael's mother had deemed her unworthy. Kate was too blue-collar for them and, more particularly, their son. Something that wasn't exactly new to Kate, having attended a private school on scholarship for six years with people very much like the Langfords. All the same, it had stung.

"You're right," Michael said, still not meeting Kate's

gaze. "We should go."

"Besides, I'm sure you'll be able to catch up with them next weekend," Nicole said and tucked her cell phone back in her pocket. "I'm assuming Dominic will be your guest at the firm's retreat?"

Kate clenched the cart. And there it went. She'd been so close…

"I—well, we haven't—" Lord. She was a terrible liar.

"She's working on me," Dominic cut in smoothly, saving her from further stuttering. He was a godsend.

Michael took a last look at her and smiled. But it didn't seem like the smile quite met his eyes. "We'll look forward to seeing you both."

Kate watched them walk away, hand in hand, with a heavy lump in her throat until they were well out of sight.

"How long did you date him?"

"Three years." She turned to face him. Color returned to her cheeks as she remembered the lie she'd been caught in. "Thanks for covering for me."

Dominic nodded and looked at her carefully. She braced herself for the next round of questions he would inevitably ask.

But instead, he turned back to the paint samples. "I'm thinking for the kitchen, something light and warm. Maybe this one?"

He was holding up a bright canary yellow.

She laughed, forgetting for a moment the pain of the previous moment. "Not a chance."

And at that moment, when Dominic chose to let Kate off the hook, she realized she liked him a little more than she probably should.

Chapter Five

"Okay, you're doing fine, just hold it steady and it will go in easily. I promise."

"I'm not sure, I feel like it's going out of control. Look. I'm shaking."

Dominic could hear the panic in Kate's voice. But he refused to help her and after another twenty seconds, she drove it home. And looked down at him, a surprised but satisfied look in her eyes.

"I think I did it."

"That you did. Now get down and give me a hand with these drapes. Which one goes in front again?"

Kate hopped jubilantly down the two steps of the new stool she'd bought earlier that morning, her cheeks flushed and her eyes shining. She'd only drilled the posts for her new drapery rods into the wall above her front room windows, but from the way she looked, you'd think she had invented a cure for cancer.

"The white panels go between the windows and the teal draperies. This way I can pull the heavy drapes back but still have some privacy," she said holding the gauzy fabric up. "See what I mean?"

"Oh, yeah. I can't see through it at all," he said sarcastically, since he could still see that hourglass shape of hers through any kind of fabric. She'd discarded the jacket from earlier, leaving him to try to keep his eyes off her curvy assets.

"Here, hold this," she said.

She climbed up and slid a panel across the rod, leading him to a few not-so-professional thoughts. Thoughts he was crazy to entertain when this one came with so much baggage, if today's scene was any indication. Something he was more than a little curious about.

Michael was exactly the type of guy Dominic would have pegged for Kate. Wealthy, well educated, and cultured. Likely from a family of some means and social standing. Probably also drove a late-model Mercedes he leased new every year. Throwing away money hand over fist.

Kate probably fit well in that type of world. She had beauty and class, education and obvious wealth. Hell, look at her car. These all served as reminders that despite the fact he had spent the morning in the company of a beautiful and smart woman— who definitely knew how to fill out a pair of jeans—she was way out of his league. Getting mixed up with her would only inevitably cause them both pain. Was a shame, though. Her pining over such a douche bag. She could do better.

And against his better judgment, he decided to ask. "About earlier. With that guy, Michael. Want to help me understand what was going on there?"

Her shoulders tensed, and she didn't answer him at first,

arranging the curtains back and forth. "It's…complicated."

"Try me." Not that he hadn't already filled in most of the puzzle, after seeing the rock that snotty chick had been sporting. But he wanted to torture Kate a little bit.

She climbed down from the stool and sat on the top rung. "Well, long story short, in a moment where I apparently totally lost my mind after hearing the news of his impending nuptials, I may have given Michael and…a few others the impression that I was in a serious relationship myself. And thanks to this morning's fateful meeting, you've kind of become that someone."

"I see. And how long have you been pretending you've had a boyfriend? And is this something you usually do?" he teased.

She actually laughed, and her eyes lit up her face. "No, I don't usually make up phantom boyfriends. I was just taken off guard. And thanks to how quickly the rumor mill works at the firm, it didn't take long for my boss to hear about it and make his own congratulations."

"Aw, the intrigue. And what were you planning on at this little firm retreat? Were you hoping no one would notice your boyfriend was imaginary?"

"To be honest, I hadn't thought about it at all until my boss made a point of telling me how my shot at partnership was tied into convincing the senior partners that wedded bliss was on the horizon." She studied her fingernails. "The next board meeting is in early December, where they make the final vote. If I can keep up the charade through then, I'll be in. And then I can make up a sad breakup story and move on. As to the retreat, I'll just say *you*"—he noted the mischievous gleam in her eyes—"couldn't get away. Some construction emergency, blah, blah, blah. I think now that there's been an actual boyfriend sighting, I'll be okay."

"I'm glad I could be of service. But to tell you the truth, from the looks of this Michael guy, I don't see why you felt the need to have to make up any boyfriend at all. He's kind of a douche."

Her laugh was deep and full, her head falling back to reveal a smooth pale expanse of skin. She should do that more.

"I think that's exactly what my friend Payton called him. She'll be glad to hear someone else is of the same opinion."

His phone buzzed in his back pocket. He pulled it out and glanced down. His brother.

"I've got to take this," he said with some reluctance before heading to the kitchen.

"Mom just called," Cruz said. "Some guys just came and repossessed Daisy's car. She's a mess. When she got Leo on the phone, he admitted he stopped making the payments. Told her he wants a divorce. He's decided Daisy and the kids are no longer his responsibility. I'm going to kill him."

Dominic would join him. He'd never trusted the guy, but Daisy could be damn headstrong when she wanted. Seeing only the good in people, what little there might be. "What she needs is an attorney. Someone to go after the bastard."

"Yeah. But you know Daisy. Proud and stubborn, she's refusing my help. I told her it would only be a loan, until she got back on her feet. She won't hear it. She went down to Legal Aid, but according to Mom, resources are pretty limited and it might be months before she hears back from them. If she does."

And Daisy needed someone now. Someone smart and passionate.

And he could think of one person right now who might

fit that description.

"We can figure it out tomorrow at family dinner," Cruz said finally. "I'm thinking about bringing Becca. She's been hounding me for weeks to meet the family. You know, she has a roommate, a really cute dental assistant that I can line you up with."

Not a chance. "Not necessary. But thanks."

"You've got to move on sometime, Dom."

"I'm doing just fine. But look, I've got to get going. I'm in the middle of something."

"Fine. But just be nice to Becca. And please don't regale her with any stories circa high school or earlier. Payback can be a bitch."

"Hey, I'm always nice. Besides, women love to hear how the serious, always stoic Cruz once wrote a love note to his sixth-grade teacher. They eat that stuff up."

"Ha-ha. Just remember. Payback," Cruz said.

"Yeah, I'm worried. I'll talk to you later," he said and hung up before his brother could say anything more. Not just to avoid another lecture about not letting one woman scar him for life, but because an idea had struck him. Was it as ludicrous if he said it out loud as it was running through his head?

Dominic returned to the other room, where Kate was sitting on the couch glancing through one of the home repair books they'd picked up.

He sat on the edge of the step stool. "This retreat thing with your work," he started. "It's going to be pretty tough keeping up the charade of being in a happy, dedicated relationship if your boyfriend can't bother to show for such a pivotal moment in your career, don't you think?"

Kate grimaced. "I don't really have a lot of alternatives,

do I?"

"Maybe you do."

She shook her head, her brows furrowed in confusion. "I do?"

"What would you say if I agreed to go with you? Continued the charade to your senior partners, as well as your former boyfriend, that you were in a happy, committed relationship."

"Why would you want to do that for me? Wait. This isn't some proposition thing, right? You're not trying to sleep with me or anything. Because I can tell you now, I'm not willing to whore myself out for—"

"Easy there. I wasn't implying we were going to sleep together. Well, not in the biblical sense." *Unless she wanted to.* "I'd just be there to add credence to your lie. That's all."

She narrowed her eyes in suspicion and bit her bottom lip. "Uh-huh. What's the catch? What do you get in return?"

"I need your help. Your legal help," he added. He briefly explained his sister's marital situation and the urgent need for reliable legal service right now, not in a few months. "We've offered to pay for an attorney, but she won't accept any financial assistance. But don't firms like yours do free legal service on occasion?"

"Pro bono. And of course. At Strauss, we're usually expected to do at least fifty hours of billable work a year pro bono."

He nodded, the idea sounding more and more plausible by the minute. "The thing about Daisy is she'll never accept it if she knew I sought you out, asked you for help, or gave you any sort of compensation to help her. Even just pretending to be your boyfriend. But if you're my new, totally devoted girlfriend, who mentions you do this sort of thing on a regular basis and offer to take her case pro bono—something you would do for your firm anyway—she just might buy it if for no other reason than for the sake of the kids. Of course, this goes without saying, we need to hit that bastard hard. You are good, right?" he added, almost as a dare.

She narrowed her eyes. "Damn straight. I've worked several domestic and custody cases, most pro bono, and my clients have been nothing less than satisfied." She paused. "So if I understand you correctly, you're proposing that for the next month, we actually perpetuate this charade that we're together, publicly? That you'll do this for me, provided that I represent your sister in her divorce? What if she declines?"

He shrugged. "She declines. But I'll hold up my part of the deal. See you through until they hold that meeting and that partnership is yours."

"I don't know." She stood. "I've got to think about it. I mean, if we do this, pretend to be a couple, I'm putting myself at a lot of risk. One wrong word and everyone will know I lied. And I could definitely kiss that partnership good-bye."

"You don't have to make any decisions now. When is the retreat?"

"Next weekend."

"Okay. Take a few days. Think about it, and then you can let me know. We can both win here, Kate."

She looked at him, her expression thoughtful. "Okay. I'll think about it."

He smiled. "Good. I'll be here Monday evening to start work on the bathrooms. Let me know then."

There was another bonus here that he hadn't thought out loud. Passing Kate off as his girlfriend could have the added perk of getting his brother and everyone else off his back about finding a new relationship.

Help convince them that he wasn't permanently damaged.

And his family was bound to adore Kate. From the short time he'd spent with her, he could tell that despite her education and obvious wealthy background, she didn't put on airs. She was down-to-earth and friendly—well, when she didn't look like she wanted to kick him. And if he played it right, he might even find an opportunity to see if her lips were as soft and sweet as he'd imagined.

He'd just have to be careful. Remember this wasn't real. Because when the whole thing was over and they each had what they wanted, she was only going to leave him. For someone better. They always did.

• • •

Kate took a sip from her Shiraz and waited for her friend's reaction to her current dilemma. The lights in the bar where Payton had dragged her were dim and the music low enough to allow the occupants to hold a conversation—barely. But dim light or not, with her long, shiny strawberry-blond hair, dimples, and a smile that charmed everyone, Payton shone. Especially as her laughter filled the space around them, drawing a few more gazes their way.

"I'll tell you one thing, I like this Dominic's style already. I wish I could have been there to see the look on Michael's face when he met this mystery man. He sure must be something to look at."

"How on earth could you know that?" Kate paused, middrink. She had specifically refrained from relaying any physical descriptions.

"Because I know you." She took a sip and watched Kate

over the rim. "And then there's the fact Michael sounded almost jealous when he ran into you. Which would imply this guy's got to be hot."

Kate couldn't argue with her logic. "Okay. I suppose he's… moderately attractive. But I don't know about Michael being jealous. Remember, he dumped me. Why would he be jealous?"

"We both know why he broke up with you."

Yes. She did. Michael hadn't been willing to stand up to his family for her. He'd made the decision to let her go rather than bear their disappointment and judgment.

He'd let her go.

The bartender interrupted them. "The two guys at the end of the bar would like to buy you ladies a drink. Should I make it two more glasses of Shiraz?"

"No. I think we're going to try a shot of Patrón Silver and two rum and Cokes." Payton delivered a look that warned her not to argue.

Kate gave Payton a stern look when the bartender left. "Remember who's the designated driver tonight." It was the only way Kate would agree to coming, her car keys secure in her purse.

"I want you to have fun. I'll order us a cab if it comes to it. But for now, try to relax." Payton turned around on the bar stool, her hair swinging behind her, and studied the crowd until their drinks arrived. "Now, as to your question, I say go for it. What the hell have you got to lose?"

"Um, my dignity, my promotion, maybe even my job if anyone finds out I made this whole thing up."

Payton rolled her eyes. "Dramatic much? You're not planning a bank heist here. You're just playing the game. Hey, they're the ones who are making this whole promotion about you having a man. You're giving them the impression they need. But the reason you really are where you are, being considered for partnership, is because of your hard work and determination. Nothing else. You can't let them take that away from you because of some archaic beliefs of what makes a better partner."

Which was similar to what Kate had been telling herself.

"And if you have a little fun while you're doing it..." Payton wiggled her brows, earning a laugh from Kate.

"I'm not having sex with him, Payton."

"Unless you want to. Come on. It's been over a year since you and Michael broke up, and you have yet to show any interest in anyone. Maybe a little diversion is just what you need to move on."

Two shot glasses were set in front of them, followed by their drinks.

Payton took a shot glass and held it up as she smiled over at two guys in suits who were watching them. The angle she held the glass made the diamond on her hand hard to miss. The men smiled and nodded, apparently not discouraged by her impending marital state.

"To moving on," Payton said and waited for Kate. "And taking a risk."

Kate only hesitated another moment. Payton's fearless take on life was always something Kate had admired. And here was the perfect opportunity. Why not?

She lifted a glass, and realizing her mind was made up, she tapped Payton's before throwing the fiery liquid down.

An hour later, bold from another shot of tequila, she picked up her phone and dialed Dominic's number.

"I'm in."

Chapter Six

"So Ms. Herrera is claiming Mark came in to her office, sat on the corner of her desk, and unbuckled his belt while asking her to..." Nicole paused as she read from Kate's chronology. "'Give it a pull and let's see what comes up'?"

"According to her discrimination complaint, yes. But she also provided a written statement to the company that didn't mention anything about this alleged incident," Kate answered. "Seems to be a significant detail to have missed. If it really happened. Which is why I want to thoroughly review the details of that day with her."

It was almost five Monday evening and they'd been at this for a couple of hours. And it was agony. Kate was fine with working a case with another associate and had done so many times in the past. But Nicole had that dismissive way about her. Just like Michael's mother. No wonder they got along so well.

"I think it would be helpful to lay out their individual

schedules for that day before we jump into questions about the details of their meetings rather than develop schedules *after* the fact." Her tone making it clear she thought Kate was making a mistake.

"I'll consider it," Kate said and continued to skim Ms. Herrera's past eight years of performance reviews.

Ava Herrera had worked at McKenna and Associates, a large accounting firm downtown, until she resigned more than a year ago. According to Ms. Herrera, her boss, Mark McKenna, made several overt sexual advances toward her during her employment.

Mark's story, of course, was entirely different. According to Mark, Ms. Herrera had been desperate to keep the accounts she'd been warned about losing if her performance continued to slip. Desperate enough that while they were on a business trip, she'd come to his room in a long trench coat and nothing underneath. He claimed he'd sent her away immediately.

Kate had contacted the hotel, but it was their standard practice for the video surveillance footage to be purged after ninety days. However, she had kept at them and they'd conceded IT might be able to pull something off a network drive. She was still waiting to hear back.

Nicole flipped through a few more pages of Ms. Herrera's complaint, pausing to jot some notes down. Leaving Kate to her thoughts.

Usually the details of a case, particularly at this stage, would take over her every waking thought, and sometimes even her nonwaking thoughts. But today, Kate was distracted. She wanted to get things wrapped up so she could get home.

She and Dominic had a lot to discuss if they were going

to pull their ruse off.

"You know" — Kate sat back in the chair and stretched — "I'm pretty wiped out. Would you mind if we finished this up in the morning? I think we have all the documents in order."

Nicole barely glanced up at her. "No problem. I was planning on leaving soon anyhow. Michael and I have dinner reservations at Caffe Molise for seven."

Ouch. That had been their favorite Italian restaurant, usually going there before hitting the theater. But she refused to let Nicole know her comment had had any effect. "Well, enjoy your dinner. Don't let Michael get carried away with the bread basket. He always feels guilty later, you know."

Kate couldn't help but note Nicole's hand tightening on her pen. But she kept her attention on the file in front of her and barely nodded when Kate said good-bye.

She grabbed her notes and made a beeline for the door. She could be home in thirty minutes. She checked herself as she raced down the hall, telling herself that the excitement and nervousness she was feeling had to be because of the planning she and Dominic had ahead of them if they wanted their charade to be a success. Nothing else.

But it wouldn't hurt to brush a quick layer of polish on her lips. She had to moisturize, after all. And if the color and shine perked up the fatigue that might be evident on her face, it was purely coincidental.

That's right. She could be professional.

Only Kate couldn't deny the small bubble of excitement in her chest when she saw Dominic's truck parked in front of her house and the lights on upstairs when she pulled up. It was almost six and it was already dark outside, but her house looked warm and welcoming. Like home. She loved it.

"Hello?" she called when she walked inside, dropping the keys on the hall table.

"Up here," he called. "Come and take a look."

Kate found him standing at the sink in the guest bathroom with a smile on his lips and her cat curled at his feet. His light blue T-shirt was rolled up at his arms. Who knew forearms could be sexy? Or the display of muscles that were hard to miss in the fitted shirt as he crossed his arms in front of him. She almost licked her lips, which would have displaced the layer of gloss she'd put on. "Give it a try." He nodded toward the sink.

Her fingers skimmed the shiny, cool surface of the new faucets she'd selected last Saturday. Chic. She turned the handle and waited. Usually the water took a good minute to even reach tepid, but within ten seconds, it was running hot. She smiled and looked up. "You did it."

"You'll find the same in your bathroom, but since we'll be tearing out everything for the remodel, you'll only have a few more days to enjoy it."

"It will definitely be worth it," she said as she pictured the bright pink-and-white tiles that ran across the floor and up to the ceiling of her master bath. They had to go. Kate looked around the small guest bath that Dominic had turned his attention to today. Even with just the small tweaks of the new faucets, towel racks, and new lighting and mirror, it looked brand-new.

"Did you get a chance to decide on some paint shades for the master bath and kitchen?" he asked and turned those impossibly brilliant blue eyes in her direction. Had he chosen that shirt because he knew the way it brought them out? Yeah. Probably. Men like him absolutely knew the kind of effect they had on women. Take that grin of his that he had to have practiced in the mirror a few times.

She noticed he was still waiting for a response. Right. "I think so. I have it narrowed down to three shades of yellow for the kitchen and two different blues for the bath."

Dominic gathered all the trash from the floor into a black plastic bag and she purposely turned her attention to the new faucets in the sink instead of his backside. It about killed her.

Unaware of the serious self-control she was exerting, Dominic said, "I was thinking about heading to Home Depot for a few things. Want to come with? We can pick up the paint samples and maybe a pizza for dinner. Give us time to discuss some of the details about our little arrangement."

"Let's do it," she said without hesitation. For a moment she worried she'd answered too quickly. "I mean, I'm pretty hungry, and pizza sounds great. Let me put some jeans on first."

They debated all the way out to the driveway whose car they were taking, and Dominic ended up victorious, but only after pointing out they might find more things than they anticipated and his truck could hold more than her sedan.

She slid into the cab of his truck, already feeling its familiarity from last Saturday. It even had his scent. Clean. Masculine. There was an empty bag of chips on the seat and a Big Gulp cup. It was completely unlike Michael's, which had only had the faint aroma of his Polo cologne and was immaculate to the point of obsession. As weird as it might be, she found Dominic's truck—gas-guzzling monster and all—preferable.

He slipped the keys into the ignition and she laughed

when she heard bluegrass playing over the radio.

Okay, so that was a little unexpected. Kind of like him.

• • •

A couple hours later, Dominic and Kate stood with their mouths full of pizza, staring at several long swaths of paint crisscrossing the wall. He was careful not to get too close to her since he'd been struggling all evening to keep his hands in his pockets instead of wrapped up in her hair or settled on those lush hips.

This was going to be harder than he'd thought.

"So far I think I like the third one best." She took a sip of wine. "The first one, under the lights, appears more lime green than buttery."

He nodded. "Fortunately you have some time to make the final decision. It's probably going to take me a good week to gut the bathroom and get the new walls and tile in place, maybe longer since I'll be taking a weekend off for that retreat of yours. Then comes the paint. I'll do the kitchen last, which should time well with the arrival of those cabinets we ordered. By then you may have changed your mind several times."

"Sounds good." She turned back to the island to top off her wineglass. "And now that the shoptalk is out of the way, I think it's a good time to discuss our other little arrangement."

"Is it safe to say you haven't changed your mind since you called me Saturday?" he asked. Something he probably should have double-checked before he'd mentioned it at Sunday evening dinner with his family. His mother had practically wept at hearing he was seeing someone again, which had given him a twist of guilt. But any joy, no matter how short-lived, would make it worth it. And keep his family off his freaking back.

"I'm 100 percent on board. I can almost see my new letterhead now. Kate Matthews. *Junior partner.*"

"So tell me about this retreat. What do I need to know?"

"It's at one of the lodges in Park City. Friday to Sunday morning. Fortunately, other than a cocktail hour the first night and a dinner on Saturday evening, we'll be left to our own devices. As long as we make brief appearances, we should be okay. Now, the firm booked a block of suites for the event, which I doubt has any available rooms left at this late stage. And I think it would be risky for us to stay in separate rooms and keep this up. So you're going to need to stay with me."

"Okay. As long as you don't try to violate my moral code."

"I think your virtue will be safe. You'll be on the sleeper sofa. In the other room. Believe me, I've been there before — we'll have plenty of space to keep ourselves out from under each other."

That gave him an image he wasn't ready to let go of. Kate. Under him. Him under her. Probably not a good thing to be considering about now. He coughed. "Easy enough. Now, as to introducing you to Daisy, I think we need to ease into that. We have a big family dinner every Sunday at my parents' that would be the best place to introduce you. I already mentioned I was seeing someone yesterday, so it wouldn't be a surprise." She nodded, but she seemed to be looking a little green. "You okay?"

"Yeah. I'm just not really good at the whole meeting-the-family thing."

"You'll be fine. They'll be so overjoyed to see me even bringing someone home they'll overlook anything. Taxidermist, psychic, serial killer…I promise they won't care." She was still too damn quiet.

"It must be nice having someone looking out for you like that. I always wondered what it would be like to have a brother or sister around."

"It's hell." But he was smiling. "With an older brother and two sisters, let me tell you, there is no such thing as privacy. They're up in your business all the time, thinking they know what you want better than you know yourself."

"Kind of sounds like my friend Payton. She's the closest thing I have to a sister." She managed a smile and lifted the wine bottle in a silent inquiry as to whether he wanted a refill.

He shook his head. "What about your parents?"

Whatever small smile had curved her lips was gone and he saw a wariness cross her face. Before she could tell him to mind his own business—which she had every right to—the doorbell rang. It wasn't hard to see her immediate relief at having a reason to end the conversation as she headed over to open the door.

He saw the mop of silvery-blond hair first and then his aunt's twinkling eyes as she stepped into Kate's foyer.

"I just wanted to pop in and see how things were coming along," Glenda said. Only he wasn't fooled. He'd bet anything her arrival had something to do with a phone call from his mother as the two women tried to put together who the mystery woman was.

Glenda crossed the room and went to the windows, where she slid her fingers across the silky fabric of Kate's new drapes. "These are lovely. You're probably relieved to have the extra privacy. I am so glad you decided to take my advice and go with Dominic. He certainly is a wonder. In fact, he's part of why I'm here. My dishwasher is on the fritz again. Do you think you could take a look for me?"

"Sure. I was just wrapping things up, I'll be over in a few minutes."

"Oh, please. Don't let me interrupt you two. Take your time." His aunt's tone told them both she was insinuating more than just his contractor services. "I just knew you two would be a great team. In fact, your mother mentioned you were seeing a special someone these days. I was wondering if I might know who the lucky woman was…"

He rolled his eyes at her subtlety. Dominic had known it wouldn't take long for her to figure it out, but he had to give her credit, because he hadn't expected her to be so bold.

"You're killing me here. But if Kate's okay with it"—he looked over at her, seeing the bemused look on her face as she watched the old lady in action—"then I don't see the harm. Kate and I are dating. There. You happy?"

"Why wouldn't I be happy? I knew I saw the sparks between you two from that first moment you met. I'm just glad you recognized the undeniable attraction and didn't let her slip between your fingers."

He and Kate both opened their mouths but stopped as they met the other's gaze. Any objections they made to her far-fetched observation would not help their cause. This was what they both wanted, right? To convince people this was real.

"Well, you really nailed it on the head this time, Glenda," Dominic said. "But it's getting late. If you want me to take a look at your dishwasher, I probably better get over there."

"Oh, before I forget," Glenda said and stopped before the front door. "That's the other reason I wanted to stop by. Wednesday is my seventieth birthday—something I'm sure you already know, Dominic—and I'm having a small party. Nothing fussy or anything. Only family and a few friends. I'd really like it if you could come, Kate. Meet everyone."

Dominic hadn't remembered his aunt's birthday but realized how fortuitous this party was to their plan. Kate, however, looked like Glenda had asked her to run around naked on the front lawn.

"Oh, I'm not really sure if I could make it. I usually have to work late, and I'm sure you want to keep things small and intimate."

He came to stand next to her, easing his arm over her shoulder. If her shoulders tensed up any more, her head might just pop off. "What time should we be there?"

"Party's at six." Glenda smiled impishly and started for the front door. "Well, enjoy your new drapes, dear. They're gorgeous. You coming, Dominic?"

Kate started forward to get to the door, and his arm slid back to his side. He stopped in front of Kate, who still looked a little dazed by this new turn of events as she turned her gaze up to his.

Her eyes were a dark bluish gray in the dimming light. He stood so close to her, he could see the trail of freckles across the bridge of her nose. Could breathe her scent, a mix of sweet and floral, like vanilla and bright sun-kissed petals rolled into one. Kate looked as startled as he felt at their close proximity, her eyes widening a fraction of an inch, and her lips parted.

"See you, Kate." He realized that his aunt had paused at the bottom step and was watching them now. Well, since they had a part to play…and with Kate still watching him, he leaned down to place a simple, chaste kiss on those soft lips. She blinked but didn't pull away, but he noticed her eyes narrowed at his boldness.

He winked, unable to stop the slow smile that spread across his face as he took a step back. "'Night Kate. See you tomorrow."

He could feel her gaze still on him as he crossed the drive-way and up Glenda's steps. But by the time he'd turned around, her door was shut.

This boyfriend act certainly had its advantages.

Chapter Seven

Dominic managed to stifle a yawn the next morning as he and Cruz inspected the plans for their latest project. Cruz looked him over. "So what's all this about you and some mystery woman? How come you've never mentioned her before?"

"Probably because she's a client. Not someone I would usually get involved with."

"Who is she?" Cruz challenged, evidently not yet convinced.

"She's an attorney at some overpriced law firm downtown. And more importantly, Glenda's new neighbor. She moved into the house next door. You'll have the pleasure of meeting her tomorrow night at Glenda's birthday party."

"A lawyer, huh? So are things serious?"

Dominic shrugged. "Serious enough if I'm bringing her to meet the family. How serious are things between you and Becca?"

"Point made." Cruz turned his attention to the contracts

in front of him, accepting this line of questioning wouldn't end well for either of them. While Dominic might be considered, from his family's perspective, wounded and still recovering from his breakup with Melinda and thus in need of someone to get him feeling again, to their knowledge, Cruz had never suffered true heartache from any relationship for which he'd needed to recover. His practice had always been to end relationships before they could grow too serious. And Cruz had gotten away with it because the family felt—or more like hoped—that he just hadn't met *the one*. Cruz took another moment before continuing. "I'm glad you're bringing someone. Maybe it can distract Mom. Between worrying about Daisy and Dad and his heart, she's been pretty stressed."

"His surgery can't come soon enough. For both of them."

Cruz looked up. "And for you, too." Dominic felt his brother's gaze on him. Cruz took his time mulling over his next words. "Once Dad's surgery is behind us, how much longer do you think you'll stick it out here?"

"Guess as long as Dad's health takes to recover."

"Sorensen Construction could survive without you. We did before Dad got sick and we'd manage now. Have you contacted the university to see about getting back into the program?"

Dominic sighed and straightened. Cruz was not going to let up today. "I don't know about the whole architectural license thing anymore. You know that."

"Don't get your license then. But don't hide away here, either. It's time you start focusing on getting things in order. Get on with your life. You don't have to sacrifice your dreams any longer—we'd be all right. You know your heart isn't in this."

"I'll keep it under advisement."

Cruz shook his head and sighed heavily before looking back down at his desk. The sound of the pencil scratching across the smooth surface of the paper assured Dominic he wouldn't have to worry about Cruz revisiting the topic today.

It was quiet in the room and Dominic thought over what his brother had said. He knew his dad and the business would probably be okay if he left. So what was holding him back from getting out there and doing what he wanted?

For a long time, it had been Melinda. She'd crushed him when she left him. She hadn't been interested in being the wife of a general contractor. Or a carpenter, as she'd called him. She'd wanted more. He hadn't realized how much she had bet on him getting his architectural license to finish the picture. When he'd told her he was going to have to bail to help out with the family business after his dad had his heart attack, she'd warned him it wouldn't be enough for her. And she'd meant it. He'd heard she'd married some banker a couple of years ago.

He'd been hiding out here ever since, going on three years. It had been okay for a while, reeling from Melinda's decampment and worried about his dad and the business. It was the right thing to do. At the time. But now…

Cruz had the business end of things well under control. In fact, he'd made quite a name for Sorensen Construction in the past couple of years. And Dominic was itching to get out on his own again. Immerse himself in his own designs, his own plans for renovating and designing homes, new and old. Making each one special.

Suddenly Dominic realized, with a jolt, that the thought

of Melinda had barely caused him any pain. In fact, this past week only one woman had been filling his waking thoughts and his dreams.

Kate. She intrigued him. She wasn't what he expected, and he itched to find out more of what made her tick.

He also had to admit to wondering if their ruse was for the sole purpose of earning partnership, or if there was another agenda. Like making her ex jealous. Maybe even getting him back.

Something he'd have to remind himself of many times over the next month. He'd already fallen for the wrong woman before. He wasn't going to repeat that mistake again.

• • •

From her position spying behind the folds of her new drapes, Kate stared at the cars parked in front of Glenda's house and her driveway. Laughter echoed in the night air. In Kate's estimation, there were about two dozen people inside. None of whom she knew.

Frick, she hated these things.

She'd been watching the house for the past ten minutes, not sure if she was relieved that Dominic was running behind and she'd earned a reprieve or frustrated that she was just prolonging the inevitable. But truth be told, they didn't look that bad. Actually, they looked pretty nice. Friendly. Down-to-earth. Unlike the guests at the parties she and Michael used to attend. And the people at the events the Vaughns hosted that Payton had dragged her to. They had seen through her. Known she wasn't one of them.

Which was why she hated these kinds of things.

She looked down at her watch as the time edged closer to quarter after. Had she misunderstood the plan? Last night she'd worked past ten, arriving home to find Dominic had finished an hour earlier. He'd left a note on the fridge saying he'd see her at six.

Had he meant she should meet him there at six?

Crap. She really didn't want to go over there alone, but if her grandmother had taught her anything, being punctual was the most important rule of etiquette. Actually, her grandmother had been fond of sharing a lot of her own personal rules. Her favorite being that opportunity knocked only once, while temptation leaned on the doorbell. A weird little saying that hadn't meant much to Kate before.

Then she'd met Dominic.

He was nothing but temptation. And she'd be sure to remember that this was nothing more than a business arrangement. She didn't want to get caught up again in something that could have no future, only inevitable heartache, since Dominic didn't seem like the type of guy who let himself get wrapped up in any one woman. He was a love-'em-and-leave-'em type of guy.

And if he wasn't? Well, even if he could commit, it wasn't likely he'd appreciate a woman who worked upward of sixty hours a week and chose billable hours at the office over a late movie with him. That's why being with Michael had been so…perfect.

A purr from near her ankles reminded her she still needed to feed Oscar. Kate stepped away from the curtains and went to the kitchen to crack open a can of cat food. She wasn't procrastinating. Not at all.

Although she *should* wash her hands for a good sixty

seconds after handling the cat food. There could be a pregnant woman there or something. Or was that the kitty litter?

Quick tapping at her back door broke the quiet of her kitchen and nearly sent her jumping out of the skin. She leaned back until she could make out a face peering through the glass panes of the door.

Dominic. Temptation itself.

She sucked in a deep breath and crossed the kitchen to flip the dead bolt and open the door. As if on cue, he smiled in that dangerous way of his that made her body hum with a discomforting need. The kind of hum that was going to get her in trouble if she wasn't careful.

"Sorry I'm late. I had an emergency at a job site to take care of. You ready? I have about a dozen texts from the family already telling me I'm late and that if I didn't get you over there I would suffer bodily harm. You're not thinking of bailing or anything, are you?"

"Of course not," she said, trying to sound indignant, but she couldn't quite bring herself to meet his gaze. "I have every intention of coming, which is why I'm here and not at the office."

He didn't look like he believed her.

"Hello?" called out a female voice. "Is everyone decent?"

A dark-haired, ponytailed woman who was somewhere about Kate's age appeared behind Dominic. Her figure was obscured by hospital scrubs that had to be three sizes too big. But what really stood out to Kate were the woman's large, bright blue eyes fringed with long dark lashes that Kate would have killed for. Eyes the same shade as Dominic's.

"I thought I'd come over and see what the holdup was. You must be Kate. I'm Benny." She pushed past Dominic and stepped into the kitchen. "Dominic's sister."

"Benny is the youngest and also the family brat. Be fore-warned."

Benny smiled sweetly at her brother and slugged him in the arm.

Kate couldn't help but chuckle. "Nice to meet you."

"Wow," Benny said, taking a look around Kate's kitchen. "I can see why you hired Dominic. The previous owners didn't leave you with much to work with, did they?"

"I'm just grateful the sink works and I can use the microwave."

"Excellent point. I'm a Lean Cuisine gal myself. I'd sooner give up my stove than my microwave. Do you mind if I take a look? I always wondered what it looked like in here."

Kate gave her the tour, letting Dominic take over when they reached the decimated master bathroom. "Believe me," Kate said while Benny gaped at the bathroom walls and the exposed pipes, "this is an improvement."

"I'll take your word for it. Although I'm sure Dominic will make it beautiful in no time. It's kind of his talent. You should see what he's done with the place he bought over the summer. His house is going to be amazing."

That surprised Kate. With his playboy good looks and easy charm, she'd pegged him for the eternal bachelor. She'd been sure an apartment with a hot tub on the premises was more his style than something with…roots. Something so respectable. Curious, she looked over at him. "Really?"

He shrugged. "We probably should be going," he said, obviously trying to steer the conversation off of him.

"He's an artist, is what he is," Benny continued. "Did he tell you he majored in architecture? Would have his license by now if he hadn't pulled out of the program to help with the family business after Dad's heart attack."

Of course Kate didn't need to know Dominic's whole biography or anything. But she wondered why he hadn't mentioned any of this before.

"Unless you guys want Glenda calling nine-one-one, we should get going," Dominic said.

They shut off the lights and headed downstairs. Kate's thoughts whirled as she considered what Benny had said about Dominic. Of him giving up his career goals to help out his family. Giving up on his passion, his dreams. How many people would do that?

Definitely not her own mother.

An uncomfortable emotion swept over her, something akin to shame. For someone who'd grown up having people judge her because of her lack of money and social status—never once basing their decision on who she was and what she'd accomplished—she had make the same snap judgments about Dominic. Assumed the worst of him without really knowing him.

Dominic held the back door for them, his eyes on her as she passed. He wasn't smiling now. He clearly didn't like his sister blabbing his history.

They stepped outside into the brisk fall air, Benny in the lead, Kate behind her, and Dominic following. Kate was conscious of the crackling of the leaves under their heels, the visible steam from her breath—and Dominic's presence behind her. She wouldn't turn to confirm it, but she was certain he was watching her. She knew the goose bumps that trailed up her arms were as much from Dominic's nearness as from the chill in the air.

The havoc his presence was creating had temporarily displaced Kate's nervousness over the party, but when they reached the steps leading to Glenda's side door, the nerves returned in full force. Until Dominic's hand grazed hers, and she flinched at the unexpected heat such a slight touch could create. When his arm went back around her shoulders, she almost shot out of her skin.

"Here they are," Benny announced and swept into the kitchen.

A dozen faces turned in her direction at once. She tried to smile and raised her hand in greeting.

Act natural. Breathe.

Glenda jumped up from her seat and bustled over. "Everyone, this is Kate. I'd tell you all to watch yourself or you'll answer to me, but since she's also a highly paid lawyer, I have a feeling she can take care of herself. You're all forewarned," she finished to laughter. She turned to Kate and gave her a wink. "Can I get you anything to drink?"

Kate nodded.

"I'll take care of it. You go take a seat," Dominic said to his aunt. "You're the guest of honor."

"Such a gentleman," Glenda said. "Come sit down, Kate. You'll find everyone scattered in here and the next room. But you're welcome to sit wherever you'd like." She patted Kate on the arm and returned to her seat.

Kate stood awkwardly for a second until Benny grabbed her arm and dragged her over to a table laid out with food. "Tip number one. In my family, grab any food that may tempt your palate now and decide later if you want it, because things go fast."

There was an array of dishes to tempt her, but Kate

wasn't feeling hungry. Still, at Benny's urging, she took some samplings of a few items and, without much choice, found herself settled in a seat between Benny and a tall, dark, brooding guy who, if he smiled, would look like a dead ringer for Dominic. Save for the guy's dark, velvety-brown eyes. Dominic brought her a glass of white wine as Benny introduced her. "If the gray hair and wrinkles don't tip you off, this is Cruz. The eldest of us four."

Kate worked to bite back her own laughter at the annoyed look Cruz—who didn't have a sign of a gray in his dark, shiny hair—leveled at his sister. "Nice to meet you, Kate. I see you've met the brat?"

"Behave yourself, you two. Is this how you act in front of strangers?" A small, petite woman with dark, wavy hair cut in a chin-length bob scolded them as she sidled next to Kate. Her dark eyes were friendly and bright as she surveyed Kate. "I see you've met most of my brood."

This was Dominic's mother? She didn't know what she'd expected, but after meeting a number of terrifying mothers—Michael's and Payton's, cases in point—she was unused to such unabashed friendliness. Kate could see the obvious similarities between mother and son—particularly in the eyes. Mischievous. That's all they could be described as.

"I'm Elena. Over there"—she waved her arm to a stern blond giant at the other end with clear blue eyes who didn't seem likely to miss anything, even if his face didn't register any emotion—"is my husband, Petter. Don't mind the grumpy look on his face. Underneath the scowl he's a big teddy bear, aren't you, *mi corazón*?"

Kate watched as the stern-looking man's face flushed

and his mouth crept up a hair in what she guessed was a smile.

"My other daughter, Daisy, is over at the children's table." Ah. That was the heartbroken Daisy. Another beauty, with long, jet-black hair and dark brown eyes. This family had definitely hit the gene-pool jackpot.

Elena continued her introductions, pointing at the children surrounding her daughter. "That's Daisy's youngest, Paul. Across from them is Jenna, who just turned nine"—the little girl with serious, wide eyes smiled sheepishly—"and Natalie, who will be eight next month."

This earned a big grin from Natalie. It was hard to miss the two front teeth missing. The kids were adorable, making Kate's determination to convince Daisy to let her represent her in the divorce even stronger.

Dominic, she noticed, was lingering close by, leaning against the wall and holding a plate in front of him. But he wasn't eating anything. Only watching. She quickly diverted her gaze back to Elena.

"I understand you and Dominic met because he's helping you fix up your place, is that right?" Elena asked.

"Fixing? That might be putting it mildly." Benny interjected. "It's definitely a beautiful house, Kate, don't get me wrong, but for myself? I'll buy new every time. I've had enough leftovers my whole life that when I bite the bullet and get a house, 'new' and 'upgrade' will be the only words in my vocabulary. I've never understood the allure for old and antiquey, like Dominic."

"Is that why your last boyfriend looked like he'd just graduated high school, Benny?" Dominic joked. "I worried a few times that he might need his mom's permission slip to stay out past curfew."

"Well, you know the saying, it's easier to teach a new dog old tricks than an old dog…like you."

Elena spoke over the laughter and teasing, obviously used to the banter. "Cruz, you'll have to lend Kate and Dominic a hand. That doesn't sound like something Kate can or should be tackling on her own. What about your family, Kate? Are they around to help?"

Kate looked up at the faces of Dominic's family, and her heart ached for a moment. Other than her grandmother, she'd never really known what having a family meant. Until now. Fortunately, before she could respond, Dominic cut in. "Mama, let Kate eat. Let's not overwhelm her with your inquisition. Give her at least until dessert."

Dominic's little nephew looked over as if just realizing his uncle had arrived. He raced over to Dominic, who swung his nephew up into his arms and tickled him while the boy giggled helplessly.

Kate felt a tug in the area of her womb.

Clearly seeing Dominic in such a nurturing role was playing crazy with her mind. It was making her think of impossible things. Impossible dreams. Because she and Dominic weren't even right for each other. Had no common interests other than convincing people their charade was true.

Finally catching his breath, the little boy looked up at his uncle. "When are you going to let me come to work with you? I want to build things, too."

Dominic set his nephew down and tousled the little boy's thick hair. "If your mom says it's okay, maybe I can bring you to the site next Monday."

"Yes!" Paul cried and jumped up.

"Not so fast. You have kindergarten until noon." Paul let out a cry of protest. "But I suppose afterward you could tag along," Daisy added, apparently not up for a fight.

Paul raced around the room, pumping his arm and calling, "Yes, yes, yes."

Benny shook her head. "Let's not give this kid any more sugar."

Kate laughed along with everyone else. But silently, she reminded herself that her place here today, with these people, wasn't real.

So stop wondering what it would be like if this was your family. Or if Dominic was anything more than a business partner.

It would only make it harder when this was all over and she was alone again.

• • •

The next two hours passed by easily for Dominic, especially with the sound of Kate's infectious laugh filling the room. It was—irrationally—something he liked to hear. Even if it was at his expense.

"He loved that thing so much, he spent a whole summer in it," Cruz was saying. "We'll have to show you the pictures sometime. There must be half a dozen."

Kate looked over at Dominic, humor brightening her eyes. "Who knew you had a fondness for wearing girls' swimsuits. Pink? With cherries?"

"I was four," he said defensively and shot a scowl at Cruz, who from the look on his face, was letting him know this was the payback he'd mentioned before.

Best to leave now before they remembered the pics of him and Daisy hamming it up—in her princess dresses. Dominic glanced down at his watch. "It's just after ten. I have to get to the site early. Weren't you saying you had an early morning, too, Kate?"

Kate looked down at her own watch, surprise on her face. "I hadn't realized it was so late. But you're right, I should be going."

"I'll walk you home," he said, coming to his feet, a movement that was premature when his mom, sisters, and aunt rushed forward to give Kate hugs and personal good-byes. Each time someone threw their arms around her, Kate froze, almost unsure how to reciprocate the attention.

"They definitely seem to like you," he said ten minutes later as his aunt's front door swung shut behind them.

"Good. I really liked them, too." She was quiet another moment. "They're pretty special."

"They're all right. You did great in there. Although you didn't have to pretend to laugh at Cruz's jokes. He'll be insufferable from now on. Well, more insufferable."

"Oh my gosh, I love your brother," she gushed, and for a moment he felt a twinge of jealousy. "He's hilarious."

"Sure. When it's at my expense."

She laughed and the sound went right to his gut. "I'll have to get a peek at one of those pictures of you in the swimsuit. I don't think I quite believe it."

He shook his head, vowing to himself to make Cruz pay. Best to change the subject. "Daisy even seemed to warm up to you by the end of the night. This was a good icebreaker for Sunday dinner."

"Oh. Right." The easy smile was gone suddenly, and her

brows drew together.

"Come on. You just said you enjoyed yourself."

"I did. But maybe that was a fluke. In a smaller, more intimate setting, things are bound to be different."

She'd been great tonight and she'd be great Sunday, but what she needed was confidence. Assurance. "Maybe a little different. But also better. Just make sure you compliment Mom's cooking and continue to laugh at Cruz and Benny's jokes and you'll be gold."

Their breath was cool in front of them as they climbed her front porch. The smell of burned leaves still hung on the air. He watched as she fumbled for her keys, trying to decide if this was the right moment. Hell, when was there ever a right moment? "I should warn you, my sisters and mom can be relentless sometimes. And they're bound to ask a few more personal questions. Like about your family?"

Her hand paused as she took a second to process that.

"The night is so quiet. Peaceful. Do you want to sit out here for a minute with me?" he asked, afraid that once she went inside she'd shut the door to him and their night would be over.

She looked up, and he waited to hear her decline, but surprisingly, she agreed. They sat on the top step, looking out across the yard and to the street ahead. Her cat arrived and pressed against his leg, purring softly. He reached out to massage its head.

"Want to tell me about them? Your family?"

She shrugged and kicked her legs out in front of her. "Not much to say. My dad took off before I was even born. And my mom has always been better at finding boyfriends than raising her daughter. When I was eight she dumped me on my grams and took off. She sends postcards every now and then. Last year she was up in Montana somewhere with her latest squeeze. Now my grandmother"—she paused and he heard the warmth that entered her voice—"she's my real family. Her love was the one and only true thing I could depend on." She shivered and gripped her arms to keep warm.

"Here." He shrugged his jacket off and placed it around her shoulders, despite her objection. "Sorry. When did she die?"

"Oh. No. You misunderstand. She's still alive, it's just that…well, she's not really herself anymore." Kate took a deep breath of the air and slowly exhaled. "A couple years ago she was diagnosed with dementia. It happened so quickly, which I guess is a relief, compared to some other stories I hear where people—their minds—slowly and painfully degrade. In the space of a year, my grandmother was lost to me. She's been in a home, of course. I go see her every Sunday. Spend the day with her, sometimes playing cards or watching an old Fred Astaire movie."

She smiled and looked up at him, but he could see the extra glistening to her eyes, the trickle of a tear at the corner.

His heart hurt for her, and he couldn't stop from reaching out, wiping the tear away with his thumb. She didn't pull back, just looked at him. "I'm sorry, Kate." Simple words that didn't seem enough to express the depth of his feelings just then.

"We all have a sob story in us somewhere, right? I'm really just glad that I still have her. She's an amazing woman."

"Just like someone else I know."

He wanted to kiss her. No. He ached to kiss her. Not a

kiss for show, or to tease. A real kiss. But he could still feel the wetness of her tears between his thumb and finger. This wasn't the right moment.

Wait. He shook his head. What was he thinking? There wasn't *any* moment for real kisses. That's not what this was about.

She wasn't looking at him now, but back at Glenda's. "Having met your sister, I'm glad that we're doing this. I want to help her." She came to her feet. "Thanks for tonight. And for listening to me."

He stood and walked her back to the door, the cat winding around their legs again. This time she didn't hesitate as she pushed the key in the lock and opened the door.

He almost wished someone was watching them so he could plant one on her. But the view from Glenda's would be obstructed now, so that wouldn't quite wash.

With reluctance he watched as she waved good night and went inside.

Chapter Eight

"I can't remember if I left the basement door open." Kate chewed on her bottom lip, her eyes still on the road as they headed up the canyon. "Maybe I should call Glenda and have her make sure, since if it's closed and Oscar is inside, he won't be able to get to his litter box."

Kate had of course insisted on driving and since it was her car, he didn't argue. Much. But before this weekend was over, he was going to take it for a spin. With Kate barely cracking the speed limit, he was itching to see the speed he could get on these turns.

"I'm sure Oscar will manage until Glenda stops by later." Dominic gave her a sideways glance. "He's a cat. He'll be fine. Haven't you ever left him alone overnight before?"

"No. I only got him a couple of months ago. I always wanted a pet but when you're renting, the rules are such a pain that I didn't find it worth the hassle—or expense. But the minute I closed on my house I went down to the humane society and adopted him. He was so skinny then."

"Well, I'm sure Glenda will be spoiling him plenty, so you have nothing to worry about." He glanced up at the sky. "Looks like that storm they've been promising is finally coming in. Good thing I packed for snow."

"Snow? It's the first week of November. No way."

He glanced at her black heeled boots. "Hope you brought something more weather worthy than those."

"Even if by some miracle it does snow, I'm not planning on leaving the lodge. I'll be fine."

"What? There's tons to do up there. Even without the snow we can take the ski lift up the mountain to enjoy the view, ride the luge down at the Alpine slide, go barhopping in downtown Park City." But she kept shaking her head. "You're kidding. What do you usually do when you go on these things?"

"Work. When Michael and I were together, we'd get the fire blazing and pull out our laptops and work in peace and quiet."

"Seriously?" From the look on her face, he could tell she was being serious, which was pretty sad. "Wow, Michael sure was…adventurous."

"We always enjoyed ourselves," she said primly.

"I'll have to take your word for it. As for me, there's no way I'm sitting holed up in that suite—not matter how nice it is—for three days. Okay, scratch that. I wouldn't be holed up in some suite *on a computer* for three days. Maybe doing some other *activities*." Her cheeks were definitely growing pink, but she didn't turn to look at him. Man, Michael was such an idiot. "Anyhow, if we're going to pull this little charade off, I think it will do you well if we actually leave the room on occasion. Have fun."

"Maybe. We'll see." From her tone she might as well have said, *Sure, when hell freezes over.* "So what's the plan again?" he asked.

"Cocktails from seven to nine and then we're free until tomorrow. There's a thing in the morning, supposed to be some psychologist or something who's going to give people tips on managing stress and maintaining a balanced life or some crap like that. I was thinking of a way to skip it." He smiled. Of course she was. "Then nothing until dinner and a guest speaker at seven."

He nodded and looked out in time to see the first snowflake settle on her windshield.

"Frick." She glanced at him. "Don't even think of saying, 'I told you so,' or I'm putting on my Broadway music. I have a Gershwin CD just waiting for me to hit play."

He just laughed and held his hands up as more snow started falling. He hoped Kate had something warmer than that light jacket with her this weekend, because he knew something she didn't. He could be really persistent when he wanted to be, and it was going to be his mission to get Kate out of her comfort zone—and her room—and trying something new. Something that he would have to admit had been in short supply in his own life these past few years.

Having fun.

• • •

"Can you believe all this snow?" Jody from the bankruptcy department was saying to Kate and two other associates. Since they'd arrived over an hour ago, the snow hadn't let up, and from the looks of the storm still raging outside, it wasn't going to stop anytime soon.

Kate just nodded and agreed along with everyone else. She wasn't very good at this small talk stuff and she couldn't help but wonder what everyone would have to talk about if it wasn't snowing.

She looked over at the bar where Dominic was placing their order, something in hindsight they should have done straight off. She could really use that drink.

From the corner of her eyes she kept an eye on the steady flow of attorneys streaming into the lounge. No sign of Tim. Which meant she had to stick around a little longer, until she could say hello and introduce him to her living, breathing, genuine boyfriend. Hopefully before they ran into Michael and Nicole.

Drinks in hand, Dominic turned from the bar and headed in her direction. Making her excuses to the group, she met him halfway. She took the glass of wine he offered and sipped. "Let's grab a seat over by the windows."

It was hard not to notice all the interested glances that kept coming their way as they crossed the room. Well, Dominic's way. Not that she could really blame them. He certainly knew how to clean up when he wanted to. In dark jeans and a long-sleeved black polo that clung to his well-defined chest and nicely muscled arms, he looked casual but still sexy as sin. Throwing in his sculpted jawline and trademark crooked smile, he had the women from her firm bumping into walls to get another look.

Almost to their destination, she spotted Tim and two other partners seated in an alcove across from the seat where she and Dominic were heading. They must have been there the entire time.

Seeing their arrival, Tim came to his feet. "Kate. Good to see you made it before the storm hit. Jon and Martin here also just made it, but it looks like a couple of other senior partners might not get in until morning." He shook his head in disgust. "Californians. They see a snowflake and they're ready to call in the National Guard. You must be Kate's boyfriend," he said.

"Tim, this is Dominic Sorensen. Dominic, Tim's the head of the labor and employment division at Strauss," Kate continued as the two men shook hands and nodded. "And my boss."

"Nice to meet you, Dominic. I'm afraid Kate's been a little mum when it comes to her personal life. What line of work are you in?"

"Design and drafting. My family owns Sorensen Constru-ction. We're a small commercial construction company that works primarily in the Salt Lake Valley. Although we've recently been expanding statewide."

"Sorensen Construction, huh? What are some of your current projects? Maybe I've seen them."

"We recently completed some office space down at the Draper Parkway, and we're negotiating for a contract with Eastman Motors."

"Impressive. But knowing Kate, I wouldn't have expected anyone less than impressive. She certainly has a solid head on her shoulders. Which reminds me," he said and turned his laser-sharp focus on her, "Mark McKenna called earlier today, sounding a little…anxious, about the upcoming depositions. I told him he was in good hands, but when you get a chance, you may want to just give him a call. He needs a bit of hand-holding."

She managed not to roll her eyes and instead assured Tim she'd take care of it.

"So what do you two have planned for the weekend? Hope you're going to get out and have a little fun," Tim added.

"I'm thinking that with all this powder, I might convince Kate to hit the slopes after lunch," Dominic said.

She was about to tell him he was seriously deluded if he thought he was getting her out in that snow, let alone on *skis*, when he wrapped his arm around her waist. Making it almost impossible for Kate to breathe. Or think about anything other than the warmth of his arm. Of the pressure of his hand on her hip. His long expanse of muscled body pressed against her side. She managed to hide the shiver that shook through her, not of cold but of liquid heat.

"The snow will be spectacular," Tim continued, seemingly unaware of Kate's precarious state. "I'm afraid with my back, skiing is something I do at my own risk, but you two are young and healthy. You should get out there. Well, I don't want to keep you guys. It was good to finally meet you, Dominic."

"You, too, sir."

Dominic pulled her along beside him, not yet relinquishing his hold on her, and she managed to keep her feet underneath her. "Nicely done," she managed to say. "But I think you can let go of me now. You made your point."

"Are you sure about that? Because while Tim was grilling me on my family's business, you missed Michael's entrance. He certainly didn't miss you, however. I'd lay bets he's watching you even now."

She nearly stopped in her tracks but other than the slightest stumble, she managed to keep stride with him. "Really?"

"Really. So I thought we'd take this opportunity to show him and that fiancée of his that you have no interest in him anymore. How could you, when you have such a sexy, virile Latino glued to your side?"

She crooked a brow up. "Virile? Did you actually just say that?"

"What do you want to do? Go over and say hello to the happy little couple?" He came to a stop in front of the hors d'oeuvres table. Setting his glass down, he finally dropped his hand from her waist and grabbed a plate. "Or do we pile our plates with food and go upstairs and see if there's anything good on HBO?"

She hazarded a glance around the room, spotting Michael and Nicole standing in front of the windows at the far end of the room. Dominic was right. Michael was watching them, not so subtly, as he took large sips from his drink. Nicole didn't look like she'd seen them, too engrossed in whatever she was talking about.

Kate looked back to Dominic, who had piled his plate with cocktail wieners, coconut shrimp, and mini chicken salad sandwiches. "I think we've accomplished what we came here for tonight," she said. "But instead of HBO, I have another activity in mind."

The plate Dominic was holding slipped sideways, and he would have lost its entire contents had she not reached out to save it. She laughed, feeling a little powerful at the reaction she'd gained. "I was talking about Scrabble. I saw it in the entertainment center back at the room."

"But you were going out on such a high note this evening. Why would you want to go back and play a game that I'm sure I'll whip your ass at?"

She smiled. "Is that some sort of challenge?"

"Just a promise, babe," he said and gave her that lazy sideways smile.

Usually hearing someone use such ridiculous endearments would send her eyes rolling. Only coming from Dominic, she found the words had a sweeter meaning.

"Let's just put your money where your mouth is."

His brows crooked. "Oh? Are you saying you want a wager?"

"Absolutely." Little did Dominic know she had never been defeated in a game of Scrabble. Michael had given up playing her, calling her too competitive.

"Good. Because I know just what I'm going to want when I win."

Poor deluded guy. This was going to almost be too easy. She almost felt bad for him.

• • •

Dominic leaned back against the couch, his legs sprawled in front of him on the floor. He waited as Kate continued to study the board and then looked back at her tiles.

"I'm setting the timer. You've gone way past three minutes," Dominic warned.

"Fine," she said, heaving a deep sigh. "I'll go."

Only he could see the corners of her mouth twitch as she tried to suppress a smile while placing the letters across the board. "Q-u-i-c-k. With the triple letter, should give me... forty points."

He focused his attention on recording the score, aware of her barely suppressed glee. He glanced at his own letters, only taking a minute to see what he needed before placing two letters down. "Q-u-i-c-k-e-n. And with the triple *word* score," he emphasized, "gives me…sixty-six points."

Kate stared in shock at the board, her mouth slightly open. She didn't say anything for another long moment. Then, as if she had envisioned this from the beginning, she nodded. "Lucky move."

"Of course. And that leaves our scores at…217 and 163. I believe I'm in the lead. Your turn."

She took another sip of her second mug of hot chocolate laced generously with Irish cream liqueur and leaned back, her feet tucked underneath her. She looked up and stared into the fire he'd lit earlier, her mind clearly running in overdrive as she tried to think of a way to best him. He should have warned her before that his family were championship Scrabble players, having spent most every weekend sharpening their skill as he grew up. Daisy was the best by far, but he'd given her a run for her money a time or two.

Outside, the snow continued to fall big, heavy flakes that accumulated on the banister outside on their balcony. By morning he'd bet they'd have over a foot of snow, easy.

Kate jumped to her feet. "Are there any more of those cocktail wieners left?"

"You're stalling," Dominic said. "And no. You finished them all. I think there were a few pieces of shrimp left, though."

She headed to the fridge and peered in. It was hard for him to ignore her luscious backside when she leaned down like that. "Nope. Looks like that's gone, too. Only a sandwich is left." She shut the door, her nose curled up in distaste. "Why'd they have to put walnuts in a perfectly good chicken salad?"

When she returned, she plopped down on the floor, on her stomach this time. Damn.

From this angle, it was impossible not to look at the tantalizing gap in her sweater that was displayed. Her face propped on her hands, she was studying her letters again and couldn't know where his lecherous gaze was wandering.

He swore she was wearing a deep grayish-blue bra. Almost the exact shade of her eyes. Why the hell would she go out of her way to match her undergarments to her eyes if she didn't want people to appreciate the comparison, right?

"You know, I'm kind of tired. Why don't we just call it a draw."

"Not on your life." He grinned. The bag of letters had less than a handful remaining. The game was almost over, in his favor, and he knew what he wanted in return for their bet. Letting her gracefully bow out was not going to happen. "You know, you can always draw new letters and skip your turn."

She didn't respond, just shot him a scornful look before returning her attention to her letters. He sat back and crossed his arms, ready to enjoy the show.

But that satisfaction only lasted another twenty seconds. About the moment she took a long slurp of her cocoa, leaving a creamy chocolate mustache on her upper lip. She then used her pert little tongue to slowly lick the foam from across her lip. He closed his eyes.

Maybe keeping his eyes on the board would be a better idea.

An eternity later, she dropped her next word. Seventeen points. And then scooped up the last letters. It was cruel, really, to keep her in such suspense. He should just put her out of her misery and call it good.

But this was more fun.

He laid out the last of his letters and tallied up his score. "Only fourteen that time, but with a bonus for using all my letters—"

"I can add. Fine. You won this round."

"Round?" He looked up at her.

"Didn't I tell you?" She smiled sweetly at him, but he could see the determination in her eyes. "Best out of three."

She really didn't like to lose. Well, neither did he.

• • •

"I cannot believe you're making me do this," Kate said the next afternoon, trying to keep the rising panic from her voice.

Was this thing even safe? She clutched the side of the chair as the ski lift hurled them up into the sky. The once picturesque mountainside she'd been appreciating only this morning had gone from beautiful to treacherous in the space of a minute.

She was going to die.

The unrelenting snowfall that continued through the night had slowed to nothing more than a light dusting of snow that settled on her face and pooled into droplets of water. She was certain her nose was already akin to Rudolph's, so a little water dripping from her chin seemed irrelevant.

"You'll be fine. I promise," the spawn of Satan was saying next to her. As if he'd anticipated snow, he was decked out in his own parka and ski pants—which she'd already noted seemed to emphasize the firmness of his tush and slimness of his hips and abs, despite their padding. Even the ridiculous ski cap on his head couldn't take away from the sexy allure of his smile and those bright, hypnotic eyes. So hypnotic she'd been too busy staring into them to realize she was heading toward her death. He'd have been a great executioner. "I won't let anything happen to you."

Yeah, easy for him to say. He knew what he was doing. She, on the other hand, despite living the majority of her life in the Salt Lake area and attending a preeminent private school where 99.9 percent of the student population—her being the obvious holdout—went skiing every weekend, had never been. Ever.

She cursed her luck. She'd been so certain she was going to win last night with those tiles in her hand and that double word score that she'd stupidly agreed to go skiing if she lost. Something she'd had no intention of doing, because she was going to kick his butt.

Until she didn't.

"I can't believe you've never skied before. You live in a state where half the license plates brag about having the greatest snow on earth."

"Right. And who would have taken me? My grand-mother?" Not to mention the fact that lessons, slope passes, and ski equipment rentals cost money. Something that had been in short supply in her house.

"I think you're old enough now to go by yourself," he teased.

"So I can be humiliated when four-year-olds whiz by and heckle me as I plow my way down the slope? No, thank you. Not to mention that I could break a leg or an arm—or my neck." God. She was really going to die.

He laughed. "I'll make sure you don't go flying off any cliffs. I promise."

Cliffs? He was kidding. Right?

One hour. She just had to survive for one hour. Then they could go back to their room, where he'd promised to leave her uninterrupted while she soaked in that massive tub in her bathroom.

But what good would a bath be if she was crumpled at the base of a tree with a concussion?

"Okay. We're coming up to the crest," Dominic said in a soothing voice like he was talking to a toddler. "Hold on to your poles, slide forward to the edge of the seat, and when I say go, slide off and veer to the right. Got it?"

Oh my God. Oh my God. What?

"Go."

Dominic slid off and easily skied to the right, like he'd directed her. Kate, however, was still frozen to the seat, clutching the arm for dear life. The lift started to curve and within a few seconds she was facing back down the mountain. The lift came to a bone-jarring halt, almost throwing her from the seat.

"Kate. *Kate.*" It was Dominic, she realized. And he looked like he was trying not to laugh. Another guy showed up at his side and from the emblem on his jacket, he must be an employee of the resort. "You're going to need to let go. Come on. I'll catch you."

Kate looked around and noticed the dozens of eyes on her. The whole freaking lift was stopped as everyone waited for her to get her ass off the seat. Mortified, Kate made the decision that nothing could be worse than this and let herself slip off the seat and down to the powdery snow below.

She was wrong. She fell hard on her butt.

"Okay. We'll work on that," Dominic said and offered his hand to help her up.

Coming to her feet, Kate found the skis slipping, and she started falling back again, but this time Dominic's strong arms wrapped around her and steadied her. Even through the layers of their clothes, she could feel the furnace of his body. It was hard not to nestle up to his natural heat and she leaned in to him a little longer. "Remember what I taught you. Snowplow."

She nodded and reluctantly pulled away. She turned her heels out so the fronts of her skis almost crisscrossed in front of her.

"That's it. But first we need to move out of the way." With his arm firmly around her, he helped her slide off to the side and to the top of the slope.

Kate looked down just as the wind picked up, blowing the powdery snow around like a small blizzard, almost making it impossible to see anything. Except for what looked like a sheer drop to the valley below ahead of them. From the way Dominic was pointing, she was supposed to head that way.

Oh. My. Dear. God. Save me.

"I can't do this, Dominic. I don't know what I was thinking. Is there another way off the mountain?"

His lips quirked up. "Only one way. You're going to have to ski it. Come on. I'll help you."

With surprising patience, Dominic began talking to her, explaining how to twist and glide her skis in motion and then, if she lost control again, to bring them in front of her and snowplow to decrease her speed and gain control. She followed his instruction and after a few minutes, found she had moved a few feet down the hill—granted, very slowly—and had managed to turn her skis and was now sliding in the opposite direction.

And then she did it all over again. She was doing it, she was actually skiing.

Wait…

Shit. She was going too fast. Her arms flapped and her skis slipped dangerously fast across the surface of the snow.

What the hell was that tree doing in the middle of the slope?

There was only one way to save herself and she felt her ankle twist underneath her as she turned to the side and fell not so gracefully into the snow. She coughed out chunks of snow and tried to wipe the crystals from her mouth.

Dominic sashayed over to her, not looking even mildly alarmed that she had almost died. He was actually smiling. "You're getting it. No worries. Come on. Let's try again."

Again? Was he insane?

Dominic held his hands out to her and in a moment had her on her feet. Only he didn't release her hands immediately, holding her steady so she didn't fall back down. She had to admit, in his hands, she felt safe. Her worries almost washed away.

"Kate? Is that you?"

The vision from her goggles was slightly obstructed from the snow that her graceful fall had kicked up and she wiped away the moisture, even though it was unnecessary. She knew who was bearing down on her.

That's right. What was hell without more abject humiliation?

"Hi, guys," she said and tried to smile. She wiped away a few chunks of snow clinging to her hair.

Michael was shaking his head in disbelief. "I would never

have believed it if I hadn't heard that bloodcurdling scream from clear over on the other run"—he pointed to another slope adjacent to the one they were on, where people were whipping by at alarming speeds—"and had to come see for myself. You. On the slopes."

Kate looked over at Nicole, who still managed to look cute and chic in slim-fitting white snow pants and an ice-blue parka. Kate was wearing an oversized pair of black snow pants and a frumpy parka they'd found for sale in the resort's gift shop that made her feel more like the abominable snowman than a ski bunny.

"You always insisted you couldn't ski. No matter much cajoling I did," he continued, actually managing to sound affronted.

"Just had to find the right incentive, I guess," Dominic said, the innuendo clear. He smiled, and Kate thawed a tiny bit from its warmth.

Michael nodded a little curtly. "Well, be careful, Kate. This isn't the best resort for beginners. I could have taken you to a couple of other places more appropriate if you really wanted to learn."

"Kate's doing fine," Nicole interjected. "Although I learned to ski when I was around three, so I don't really remember the learning process. But it looks like she's in good hands." Nicole brought her snow goggles down and over her eyes. "I'll see you guys at the bottom. Michael, are you ready to eat my dust?" she challenged him.

Michael glanced uneasily back at Kate. He actually looked like he wanted to stay and make sure she got safely down, and she couldn't ignore the rush of excitement she had at the prospect that he still cared. And might actually be *jealous*.

"She's right," she finally said and gave him a big smile. "Dominic and I can manage. In fact, before you know it, I'll be ready to ski the diamonds or black hills—or whatever you call them," she added with false bravado.

"I think you mean black diamond," Dominic said and smiled at her fondly. He turned to Michael, his voice warm but authoritative. "We'll be fine."

Despite the fact she could not longer feel her face, Kate smiled at how easily Dominic dismissed Michael. And how much she actually believed his assurance that they'd be fine. She was almost convinced she'd make it to the bottom in one piece.

Not looking entirely convinced, Michael nodded. "Okay. I'll see you later, then." He brought his own goggles down and, without waiting another moment, followed Nicole.

Dominic said something under his breath that sounded a lot like "schmuck" before turning back to her. Which kind of surprised her. Usually people—men and women—were drawn to Michael. He could be funny and personable. But it she wasn't mistaken, Dominic had taken a definite dislike to him. It was ridiculous how giddy that made her.

"Ready?" he asked.

A group of three skiers flew by, spraying snow up around them.

"Not really." She sighed. "But it doesn't look like I have much choice."

And with steely determination, she tilted her body forward and slid into the turn. She went about five more feet before she fell on her butt. Again.

It was certainly going to take some time, but she'd get there.

Even if it was in a body cast.

Chapter Nine

From his seat on the couch in the living room of the hotel suite, Dominic tried to block out the sounds coming from the room behind him. And the images.

He heard Kate turn the water off and a minute later heard her loud groan.

Good God. What was she *doing* in there?

"Kate? You all right?"

A long pause. "No. I'm hurting in places I didn't know was even possible."

Damn. That put an interesting picture in his mind. He flipped the television on and started switching stations, aware of the swishing of water coming from behind the door.

"This is completely your fault, you know," she continued. "Making me ski today. Risking my life."

"Hey, my deal was that you tried skiing for an hour. You were the one who insisted on skiing another two. Come on. Admit it. You had fun."

She muttered something he couldn't hear, but it didn't sound very favorable.

"What time do you want to leave tomorrow?" he asked again, needing something to distract him from the image of her naked body, immersed in the water. Feet away from him.

"Whenever we want. But I was thinking no later than ten. I want to make sure I'm at the nursing home in time to have lunch with my grams. When should I be at your parents' for dinner?"

"We eat about six, but usually everyone arrives the hour before. Helps with the preparation."

Another moan slipped from her lips. She was killing him. "Is there anything I can get you? A glass of wine, some ibuprofen? You know, I actually give a killer back massage. I might be able to make you more comfortable."

"It's not my back that's hurting."

From the number of times she'd fallen on her ass, he could imagine where the real aches were. "I'm flexible. I'm sure I can knead those sore muscles of yours…wherever they are."

This time he heard her laugh. "Nice try. I took some ibuprofen already. I just hope they kick in before dinner. Or you might be wheeling me in there in a wheelchair."

He gave up on the distraction and flipped the television off. He crossed his legs in front of him, resting them on the coffee table.

"Tim seemed nice enough. Is he the one making the deci-sion about your promotion?"

"No, but he is the one who made the recommendation to the senior partners. There has to be a consensus for me to be voted in, which is what they'll do at the quarterly meeting. And with your presence this weekend as my significant other, my nailing the upcoming depositions, and hopefully getting the McKenna case dismissed on summary judgment, Tim thinks I'll be a shoo-in. I'm betting on it."

He remembered Tim's advice the night before that Kate check in on her client. "Is this the case you were supposed to do the hand-holding on?"

"Yes, and it just so happen to be the bane of my existence these past few months. It's a sexual harassment complaint brought by a former employee. She claims her boss came on to her for months and when she complained, worked to get her fired. I've seen these types of cases before. It's a shakedown for money. I mean, as much I think the guy is a jerk, the evidence—or lack thereof—is solid."

"And you're defending him?"

"Well, defending him and the company."

"Sounds…interesting. But what if you don't win? Would that jeopardize your promotion?"

"I'll try not to take offense from that. Since it's unlikely I won't win, I am not worried about the promotion. This woman's attorney is horrible. A small-time family practitioner, he's out of his element in a full trial like this one. It's almost criminal that he's so incompetent."

More swishing came from the other room and then the distinct sound of the plug being pulled and water draining. He had an image of her standing, water dripping down her hips, and lower…

He jumped up. "I'm going to make some coffee. Want any?"

"Sure."

He stood and went to the kitchen and grabbed a couple of mugs from the cupboard. A few minutes later, Kate came in, bundled in a thick white terry robe. Her hair was combed but still wet and down around her shoulders, her face pink and clean.

Damn, his fingers itched to pull her into him and taste those full rosy lips. Really taste them. No quick chaste kiss. Bad idea, though. In this room? With her alone? It wouldn't end with just a kiss. And that was just too damn dangerous for them both.

He handed her a mug of coffee instead and followed her back to the couch. She pulled her feet up and tucked them under her as she sipped her drink. "Tell me about your work. Benny mentioned that you used to study architecture, right?"

"I did. Earned an associate's degree in engineering and drafting before getting into the program up at the U. Then my dad had his heart attack, and I had to leave. But I don't regret it. I've learned a lot helping out at Sorensen, and I'm glad I was able to be there for my family. Now, though..." He trailed off, thinking about the thrill, the satisfaction of working on Kate's house, improving what was already there, making it beautiful again. Not to mention the home he'd built with his own two hands these many months. With Dad's surgery coming up, he was champing at the bit to return to work. "To be honest, Cruz has that place running like a well-oiled machine. I'm not really as needed as I was before."

"Do you think you'll go back into the architectural program?"

"Cruz wants me to, but I don't know. I suppose I could, but then I'd be putting off what I want to do even longer. Benny's been trying to get me to meet with this web designer, get my own business off the ground. With Cruz's business sense, he could help me get it launched, too. I'm just focusing on Dad's surgery first, and then we'll see. How about you? Did you always want to be an attorney?"

She smiled and looked down at her cup. "Actually, when I was a kid I used to watch *Judge Judy* every afternoon. She was tough as nails and ballsy and I never missed a show. Don't tell anyone else, but I always wanted to be her. Sitting up at that podium in a long flowing black robe, slamming the gavel down while bossing people around. Not taking crap from anyone. I only found out later that to be a judge you had to be an attorney first. So I set my sights on law school."

Not taking crap from anyone? Like who? But he didn't press it. "A judge? Color me impressed." He grinned. "But now that you mention it, I could see it. You'd be great."

"How would you know?" she asked and looked up at him. Her eyes were soft and shining, her skin flushed bright with color. She was lit from within as she talked about realizing her dream. Had he ever looked so optimistic?

"Because you have a soft touch. Even if you don't know it yourself. But if your goal is to become a judge, why are you stressing about this promotion?"

"It's a stepping-stone. Junior partner at a reputable firm like Strauss, the connections I make — they're all invaluable when I look to make that final leap. And the money doesn't hurt, either."

"I suppose it doesn't." He took a big slug of his coffee, barely tasting the nutty brew. Her comment about money hit too close to home when he remembered how important it had been to his ex as well. Damn more important than him.

Kate took the last gulp of her own and shot to her feet, then immediately flinched. "I had better go start drying my hair or you'll be escorting Medusa to tonight's dinner instead of the future Honorable Kate Matthews."

Judge Kate. Hair tied up behind her, that long flowing black robe. With nothing underneath. Kind of like now.

Damn. He'd better go take a shower before he embarrassed himself.

A long, cold shower.

. . .

Hours later, Dominic was tossing and turning on the torturous pullout couch in the living room, trying once again not to think about the soft, sweet-smelling woman in the bedroom.

Kate had looked beautiful tonight and the hour she'd spent putting on the finishing touches had been worth it. Walking into the ballroom with every man turning to stare at her had filled him with contrasting feelings. Pride that this creature was there with him, and the urge to punch every guy throwing salacious grins her way.

Especially Michael. What a freaking weasel. He'd cornered Dominic when he went to get Kate a drink, practically demanding to know how serious things were between them while his fiancée waited across the room.

"I'm not quite sure what business it is of yours, bud," Dominic had said. "Isn't that your fiancée watching us at the next table?"

"Kate is a good friend. The fact that we had…complications in our own relationship doesn't change that we still care about how the other's doing."

Complications, his ass. Michael had been an idiot to ever let Kate go.

The squeaking of the mattress in the other room told him Kate was still awake. He could almost picture her now. Probably in some silky nightgown, maybe a number with a long slit up the thigh. Her full breasts heavy and pressed against the fabric. That red hair cascading on the pillows under her, her body soft and waiting for his touch.

He muffled a groan and nestled farther in his pillows, willing himself to shut the crazy thoughts away and get some sleep.

"Are you awake?" Kate asked softly from the other room.

Hell, if only he was. Instead, he rasped, "Nope."

"Me, either." He heard her toss around again. This was torture. "But I think the pain meds are working. I don't feel like I'm as stiff as I was before."

That made one of them. "Good."

"I think I should take some more ibuprofen, though. Want to be able to walk tomorrow."

This time he could hear her rise from the bed, and then it was quiet.

"I'm just going to get some water," she said from the doorway. The carpet must have muffled her footsteps.

He pressed his eyes even tighter. Not trusting himself to look over to see what, if anything, she was wearing. "Be my guest."

• • •

Kate stood in the doorway for a few seconds, adjusting her eyes to the dark, until she could recognize the pullout bed and Dominic's figure thanks to the light streaming in from the window above the kitchen sink.

Gaining her bearings, she walked into the small studio kitchen and grabbed a water from the fridge and set it next to the medicine bottle.

She should be tired, and Lord knew she had been exhausted when they'd arrived back at their room after skiing earlier. But between then and now, she felt energized. She laughed out loud as an image from earlier came to her. "I'm still remembering that look on Michael's face when you took me out to the dance floor before the dancing had even started and swirled me around. He never was much for dancing."

Not to mention the giddy emotions that she'd experienced when Dominic had held her so expertly, her hand in his as he whirled her around. It had been like a dream. For a minute she'd forgotten everyone else in that room save her and Dominic.

Until she had spied Michael sitting there, his mouth hanging open.

"You certainly left an impression on him," Dominic said after a moment.

"I think you're the one who left the impression. Who knew how powerful the pull of jealousy could be," she mused.

Dominic was quiet and didn't move. Finally, he tossed the pillow that he'd had over his head and rolled over to prop his arm up underneath him. Kate's stomach dropped as she realized that his shoulders were bare. Maybe coming out here hadn't been such a good idea. What did he have on underneath that sheet?

"Is that part of your angle here?" he asked. "To make Michael jealous?"

Concentrate, Kate.

She forced herself to drag her gaze from where he was lying and grabbed the ibuprofen bottle and twisted. "Honestly? It wasn't part of the agenda when you first proposed the idea of posing as my boyfriend, but I'd be lying if I said it hadn't crossed my mind recently."

"And what are you hoping for? If Michael suddenly came to his senses and said he wanted you back. Would you take him?"

She was glad that she had the excuse of tossing the capsules in her mouth and chasing them down with a healthy serving of water to give her a moment to think about the question. Would she want Michael back, now, after all this time? After everything he'd put her through?

She set the bottle back to the counter and sighed. "I wish I could tell you unequivocally no. That I would laugh my head off and send him away with his tail between his legs. But the feelings I had for him? They're still there. We had just seemed so…ideal for each other. Both attorneys at the same firm, both dedicated to moving up the ladder. We understood when the other had to break off a long-awaited evening out for a last-minute motion that needed to be filed. I would have a lot to think about, let's put it that way."

"That's fair." He took another moment and she looked over to see he was still studying her, and she wished his face wasn't so obscured by the shadows. She wanted to know what he was thinking. "What happened between you two, anyhow? If you don't mind my asking."

Ah. She had wondered if he was ever going to get around to asking her that. Grabbing the water bottle, she walked over and took a chair in the recliner adjacent to the couch. She tucked her feet underneath her, making sure she wasn't flashing him.

"I had been working as an associate at Strauss for just over a year when Michael joined the firm. That first year had been…tough. Trying to prove to everyone that I belonged and that I could handle everything they gave me and then some. It was lonely sometimes." To say the least, since she hadn't felt the same camaraderie with the other associates, who all seemed to have been in the same sororities and fraternities. She'd always felt awkward when conversations turned to what fabulous location they'd been to for vacation. "Anyhow, with my student loan payments coming due and rent to pay along with my grams's declining health, I hadn't wanted to take on any new debt at first and was still driving Grams's old clunker. A green Oldsmobile Cutlass, circa 1988."

"Practical. Classic." She could hear the smile in his voice.

"It was, but it didn't make it any less embarrassing that day in the parking garage when it decided to die on me. I had a line of cars behind me, waiting to exit the garage." The horror and humiliation still twisted her gut. "I threw open the car door and for the briefest moment considered the possibility of making a run for the exit. Then I looked up to see Michael. Coming to my aid."

She paused as she remembered how even in the stifling heat of the parking garage that July evening, which had made her own perspiration-dampened blouse cling to her skin, Michael had appeared fresh and cool with the most dazzling smile she'd ever seen. He'd later admitted that it had been the clinginess of her blouse that prompted him to ask her out for dinner that night. "And instead of looking contemptuous at my car or me, he'd smiled and offered to push the car out provided I steer."

Dominic adjusted the pillows behind him and sat up, his arms crossed in front of him. This time she couldn't miss the fact he was definitely shirtless. Holy Hades. *Easy there, Kate. It's just a little chest hair.* On a massively hard and taut chest that she was clenching her fingers tight to stop from going over to outline. *Those pecs.*

She cleared her throat and swallowed some more water. "Half an hour later, my car was safely towed and we were headed to an impromptu dinner. And that's when we started dating. I had never dated anyone like Michael before. I'd had boyfriends, of course, most with ambitions as high as my own, but none of them with the suave confidence Michael emanated. He never seemed to have any doubts about himself." And it had been this sure confidence that immediately attracted her to him. That, and the charm of his smile. As to his attraction to Kate, that had always mystified her. She wasn't perky and exuberant, radiating confidence like him or Payton. Yet he always told her she was beautiful and made her feel like a million bucks.

"So other than this alleged charm I'm still waiting to see, what else made you fall in love with the saintly Michael?"

Did Dominic sound annoyed? Maybe all this sharing wasn't a good idea. How much did it reveal about her as well as her relationship with Michael? She thought about how to put her next words. "Michael took care of me, straightaway. Helped me unload my old car and get a steal of a lease on my first brand-new car. He even helped me fit in at Strauss, seeking me out for lunch and coffee, introducing me to several attorneys at the firm I hadn't yet dared to approach. Things were just…easier with Michael." Easier than they'd ever been in her life. He'd paid for their fancy evenings out, bought her exquisite gifts, planned luxurious vacations, and made her feel better about herself.

After all, *he'd* chosen *her*.

The room was silent, Dominic too quiet. And she was suddenly mortified at how much she'd revealed to him. She slid her legs out and came to her feet. "I'm sorry. I can't believe I just unloaded all this on you. It's pretty pathetic and I should let you get to sleep—"

This time Dominic slid to the edge of the bed, his legs on the floor, and took her hand to stop her. She looked down, noticing the way the sheet wrapped around his waist and what she was almost sure was the top band of his bottoms. She hadn't realized how cold her hands were until his own warm, dry hand encompassed one.

"Kate." He waited until she brought her gaze up to meet his. So serious. But warm. "You don't need a guy to give you self-worth. To make you feel special. You're worth all the people I've met this weekend plus some. Definitely more than that stick-up-her-ass Nicole chick."

He raised his other hand up to touch her cheek. It was almost electric, and she started. And suddenly she realized where they were. What they were. Their present state of undress. Her mouth went dry as she thought about lowering her head, pulling his toward her, and kissing those lips that had been tempting her since she first met him.

She pulled back, taking a step to increase the space between them before she did something stupid.

"I bet you say that to all the girls," she said, trying to pretend she was unaffected by his words, by his touch, by his proximity, but her voice was shaky. "But it's sweet of you to say it. And everything you've done for me this weekend. I really owe you."

He was silent as she crossed the room, but when she paused before entering the bedroom, he said softly, "'Night, Kate."

It almost sounded like a promise. Not a good night.

She was clearly delirious. After spilling her guts like that, the only emotion she could have engendered in anyone was pity. Not lust.

Damn, she'd almost made an idiot of herself. Although…

She couldn't help but wonder. What would have happened? If she'd kissed him? Would he have kissed her back?

Sleep. That's what she needed. And perspective.

Morning couldn't come soon enough.

$\cdots$

Kate sneaked a peek at Dominic seated comfortably in her grandma's easy chair, still amazed and touched that he was there. Most people heard the words "nursing home" and visibly flinched, as if warding off images of their own imminent end, and yet Dominic had not only agreed to come but actually looked like he was happy to be here.

He'd certainly surprised her. Not just today, but this entire weekend. Some men might have felt out of place at a lodge filled with stuffy lawyers, not the least of which was her ex, but he'd managed to seem completely at ease, holding his own with everyone. Especially Michael. He'd been like a white knight or something. And that wasn't even mentioning the crazy stirring of lust and attraction that had her nervous and excited like a fifteen-year-old girl again.

And the weekend hadn't even ended.

Dominic looked up and caught her eye. She saw a softness

in their depths and she tried to ignore the uncomfortable pressure building in her chest. Neither of them had mentioned what had almost passed the night before when he'd touched her and said the most beautiful things she'd ever heard. She almost wondered if she'd imagined it all. Maybe dreamed it. But there'd been no way she could have imagined the warmth of having him hold her hands, of comforting her. Making her want to throw off her robe and wrap her body around that delicious heat of his.

He was like the devil. Tempting her.

Fred Astaire's warm, rich voice pulled her attention back to the screen, where he was singing about dancing cheek to cheek with the starry-eyed Ginger Rogers. *Top Hat*, her grandma's favorite. Kate had lost how many times they'd watched this together, particularly this past year. There was something familiar and comforting to Grams about the movie that she couldn't get enough of.

Kate, though, was caught up with wondering how this gorgeous, sexy man could sit there like there was no other place he'd like to be.

Michael had come with her to visit her grandmother less than a handful of times in all their years together. Even before her grandmother's ill health had forced Kate to make the hard choice to settle her here.

"You know," her grams said, not taking her eyes off the screen, "for every move that Fred Astaire made, Ginger Rogers had to match it. Backward. And in heels."

Kate smiled and nodded, having heard this statement every single time they watched a flick that starred the duo.

"And makes it all look effortless," Dominic chimed in.

"She does, doesn't she? You know, it broke my heart

when Fred Astaire went on to dance in his movies without Ginger by his side. No one did it quite like her. Even that lovely Audrey girl was never a match to Ginger. Why men don't know a good thing when they have it is beyond me."

"You're absolutely right," Dominic said. "Sometimes men are idiots."

Grams smiled at him. "Oh, don't be too hard on your sex, young man. You men do have your moments. I'm sure this young lady can attest to that, right, dear?"

Kate swallowed a lump in her throat. She should be used to this by now, but she wasn't. For she was certain her grandmother had no idea who she was, even though she'd reminded her as they walked in an hour ago. As her grams usually did, she was polite and sweet to everyone, choosing not to use names since it was too hard to keep track. For all her grams knew, Kate was just a woman who came by for something to do.

Someone knocked at the door and Sara, the day nurse, popped her head in. "Hi, Kate. I just need to check Mary's pressure and give her her medication." She came in, closing the door behind her. "You doing okay, Mary?"

"Quite well, thank you. With such delightful company and Fred keeping me company, what more can I want?"

Dominic stood and walked around the room. He stopped at a photo of Kate and her grandmother, taken when Kate was probably around twelve. Gawky, with long braids and a toothy grin, she looked happy with her grandmother's arms wrapped around her.

He looked back at her and tilted his head, as if he was trying to picture her in those long braids again. She moved to join him, standing by his side as they looked at the picture.

In a soft voice, so as not to be overheard, he said, "I can see how much you love her, Kate. And even though she may not always know who you are, she can feel your love, too."

Damn. Why did he have to go and say something like that? Her eyes felt hot and she fought back the tears that threatened. "I like to think so. It's why I come here every week. She needs to be reminded that she has people who love her. I just wish I could get here more. It's tough, though, with work."

"I'm sure she understands. From what I can tell of this woman in this photo, she would be proud of you and all of your accomplishments."

"You have to stop being so sweet. You're ruining all your best boyfriend moments on an empty audience." She smiled but kept her attention on the photo, not trusting herself to look back at him, even though she knew he still watched her. Afraid that if she looked too deep into those eyes, she might start believing this thing between them was real.

That *they* were real.

"True. I guess I can use this as material later. Just try and pretend you're hearing it for the first time."

"Deal," she said and laughed.

She was standing so close to him that it seemed natural when he reached out to tuck her hair away from her face. Caressed her cheek again for a moment. As he had last night. She couldn't help but press her face into his hand, just for that moment. To feel his breath against her skin.

"All right, Mary," the nurse was saying. "You're set. I'll let you get back to your company."

They broke apart, and Kate glanced over to see the nurse give them both a full grin before she packed the items on the tray. Kate's cheeks grew hot and she tried to return the smile.

"You know, I'm feeling a little tired today, Sara. I might just take a nap. Would you be so kind to take me to my room?"

Kate knew it was unreasonable to feel the ache in her heart. Her grandma was tired, was all. She didn't mean to dismiss them. She didn't even really know who Kate was.

That did little to comfort her, though, as she watched the nurse help her grams to the next room. At least she looked happy. Content. Comfortable. It could be worse.

She walked to the television, about to turn it off when Dominic's voice stopped her.

"I don't know about you, but I'm dying to see if Fred gets the girl. Care if we watch it a little longer? We still have a couple more hours until we need to be at my parents', anyway."

She looked at him with some suspicion. He smiled, lazy and confident, but not teasing. She managed a return smile. "Since I wouldn't want you to wonder how the movie ends, I guess we can stick around. She'll be out for hours anyway."

"But you've got to promise me one thing. No breaking out in song."

She tried to look offended as she slid onto the couch next to him. "I haven't sung once—"

"You've been mouthing every word since the movie began. Don't try and hide it."

She bit back a smile. "Wait until we get to the car. I have the soundtrack."

"I'll just bet you do."

Chapter Ten

Dominic's sisters were busy chopping at the counter when Kate and Dominic walked into the bright, cheery kitchen. The aroma from the stove had Kate's mouth watering.

"You made it," Benny said and smiled.

His mom stopped stirring the big pot on the stove and wiped her hand off on her apron before stepping forward to crush Kate, and then Dominic, in a long embrace. "Welcome. I'm so happy you decided to come, Kate."

Kate looked over at Dominic. "Wouldn't miss it. Dominic tells me you're quite the cook. And it does smell wonderful."

His mother waved her hand dismissively, "Oh, this is nothing. Just a little stew."

"Don't let her fool you," Dominic whispered loudly. "Everything she makes, even a simple piece of toast, has to be prepared just right." He cleared his throat, and in a louder voice, asked, "So what exactly do we have on the menu tonight, ladies?"

"As if you couldn't tell," his mom said. "The pork has

been roasting in the green chilies all day. As soon as the tortillas are done we can eat. In the meantime, make yourself useful. Go see what the kids are up to. Last I saw them they were playing some video games downstairs."

Dominic was being dismissed. Meaning her anchor, her partner in crime, was leaving her alone with these women. But short of begging him to stay, there wasn't really any alternative.

He winked at her, and she knew he was trying to tell her everything would be fine.

She tried to relax. "Can I help you with anything?"

"Come over here. You can help Daisy roll the tortillas."

Nervous energy drove through Kate, not just at being left with the women, but at trying to do something she had no clue about. She went to the sink and scrubbed her hands with soap and grabbed a towel that Benny tossed her. "I should warn you, the most cooking I've done is frying an egg and making a mean pan of Hamburger Helper."

Daisy laughed. "This is easy. I'll walk you through it. You see these balls of dough?" She lifted a red towel from the counter, revealing a pile of little balls. "They're called *testales*. We're going to roll them into a round tortilla and cook them on the hot *comal*—or griddle. Easy. Take this."

Daisy handed her a long, rounded piece of wood and took an extra one for herself. "Now we want to lightly—very lightly or you'll have dry tortillas—flour the surface like this. Okay, now once your *testal* is in front of you, settle the pin over it like this... Now roll, stopping just before you get to the edge."

Kate stared at the ease at which Daisy had already flattened half the dough, and she pushed and made the same attempt. Only she pushed too hard on the left and it looked a little...

slanted.

Daisy smiled. "You're doing fine. Now, just turn the dough a bit like this, and do it again. And keep repeating until you have a nice flat disc."

Kate's mouth might have dropped open at Daisy's quick, easy movements that resulted in a perfectly flat, round disc. She watched as Daisy dropped it on the hot griddle, continuing to move it around just so, and flipping it, until at the end it was a poufy, round tortilla. It had only taken her about a minute to cook it and then she was placing it on a clean towel and covering it before moving to the next *testal*.

"How do you do that so quickly?" Kate asked in awe.

"Lots of years of practice. Now go on. You won't get any better unless you keep trying."

Kate turned and saw Elena and Benny watching her with hidden smiles. "Don't worry," Benny assured her. "You'll notice I'm resigned to chopping duty because even after all these years, mine look like a five-year-old made them."

"You just stick to bandaging arms and legs and saving lives and leave the tough stuff to me," Daisy said, tilting her head charmingly at her sister.

"I've told you, Daisy, you should really consider opening up a bakery or restaurant. You're an amazing cook." Elena cleared her throat and Benny shot her mother a grin. "Thanks to the tutoring, of course, of our dear mama."

Kate looked over and caught Elena's eye, who smiled jovially and winked. Just like Dominic.

But Daisy's own smile was more resigned now. "Maybe once upon a time, but now I have other things to think about. Bills to pay. My children to watch out for and feed."

Kate turned her dough and attempted to copy Daisy's

quick movements. This was a perfect opportunity to try and fulfill her part of the bargain. And help Daisy, too. "You know, Dominic may have mentioned to me a little bit about your problem. With your husband." She hazarded a look up and saw the other women had stopped their preparation for a minute and were watching her and Daisy carefully. "If you're interested, maybe I can meet with you some time. Talk about what you can do to protect your interests."

Daisy's attention remained on almost pulverizing the next *testal*. "Thanks, Kate. But I couldn't take your time like that without paying you, and right now, things are a little tight. I have an interview tomorrow. Maybe once I have more steady income, okay?"

"Actually, you would be helping *me* out. You see, at my firm, all associates are expected to put in a certain number of hours on pro bono work. That is, working for free for those clients who can't afford legal representation otherwise. Anyhow, I have been so busy this year I don't have nearly the number of hours I should." Which wasn't quite true, but it wasn't like Daisy could verify this. "So helping you out with your case would help me meet the minimum, while at the same time help you and your kids, too."

Daisy looked at her with skepticism in those dark brown eyes. "Pro bono? I don't know, Kate. Did Dominic put you up to this?"

Crap.

She hated lying, and especially to these wonderful women who were welcoming her so warmly. But she knew that if she told the truth, Daisy would outright refuse her and wouldn't get the help she needed. "No. I mean, he mentioned what was happening, but I'm volunteering here on my own accord. I want to help." That last part was 100 percent true and something in her tone must have assured the woman.

Daisy tossed the dough on the griddle and Kate watched as the little bubbles started to form across the surface. Kate tried one more time. "I'll leave you my card, okay? No pressure. Take some time to think about it and when you're ready, just give me a call and I'll set up an appointment."

Benny popped over and pulled one of the freshly made tortillas from the pile. "Sounds like a win-win to me. I don't see the harm in you at least meeting with Kate, finding out your options."

Daisy flipped the tortilla. "All right. Leave your card and I'll consider it."

Kate looked up and saw Benny and Elena smiling at her again. Embarrassed at their grateful looks, she returned a nervous smile.

They thought she was Dominic's girlfriend. Here to meet his family because she loved and cared about him.

Maybe even wanted to make a future with him.

Would they still be as warm and appreciative if they knew that she and Dominic were lying to them all?

. . .

Dominic found the kids playing an active game of Wii Sports. From what he could tell watching the screen, Paul was beating his older sister up (virtually speaking) and hurling her into the water below, sending both girls into fits of giggles. It didn't take them too long to convince him to give it a try, and fifteen minutes later, a remote in one hand and a nunchuk in the other, he was boxing his seven-year-old niece.

She was creaming him.

A sound from behind caught his attention. He turned to see Kate leaning against the wall at the bottom of the stairs, trying unsuccessfully to control her mirth.

"Hey, this is harder than it looks," he said, wiping his brow. "Care to give it a try?"

"And miss this entertainment? Not on your life."

But Kate soon discovered his nieces and nephew were as persistent as they were cute and, after some cajoling and pleading, she was standing next to him with the controls in her hands.

"I'll try to take it easy on you," he challenged. "I know how competitive you can be."

She smiled wickedly back at him. "Just try and keep up."

She held her hands up in front of her and jabbed forward, completely missing his avatar. But she didn't stop and after a few more jabs, she nailed him with a few solid hits that sent his avatar flying into the virtual water below.

The kids cheered, and Kate threw her head back and laughed. The sound was beautiful, as was her face when he glanced over to see her cheeks bright with the exercise, her eyes gleaming.

There was only so much a man could take.

Before he could question the good sense in his actions, he slid his hands around her waist and pulled her against him. Still winded from their play, her chest rose and fell heavily against his and it was hard not to appreciate the full swell of her breasts cushioned against him. But instead of showing anger or discomfort at the display, she seemed to melt further against him. And smiled.

"No fair, Uncle Dominic. You're cheating," one of his nieces called out. "Kate was so kicking your butt."

"You know how boys can get, Natalie," Kate said, still looking at him. "They don't like being beaten by a girl."

"Oh, is that right? I wouldn't really know, since my record in Scrabble, so far, is undefeated." He wriggled his fingers along her waist, earning a high-pitched cry as she tried to squirm away. Oh, she was ticklish all right. He did it again and she laughed and twisted her body to escape his fingers. "Oh, wait, you're not ticklish, are you? Paul, I think you need to come and help me out."

"Don't you dare, Paul. Remember, I thought we were buddies," Kate said, imploring Paul but unable to hide the next giggle.

In ten seconds, Paul was throwing his weight against her, trying to tickle her belly. "Help me out, girls." It was all the incentive his nieces needed before they pushed against them, too, and they all fell back against the couch, Dominic underneath Kate but holding her against him, trying to fight off the little fingers of the girls trying to get under his neck and arms.

"Hey, you loafers downstairs." It wasn't hard to distinguish Benny's voice from the others. "Dinner's ready, so get those butts up here now, or Cruz is going to eat all the tortillas."

The kids squealed as they piled off and ran for the stairs, trying not to be last.

Leaving the two of them alone. Kate still lying facedown on top of him, her chest rising and falling as she tried to catch her breath. She felt too good, her body fitting so perfectly against his, he didn't want to let her go.

His hand reached up and tucked a strand of hair behind her ear that was tickling his cheek. Her chin seemed to quiver as she sucked in her breath.

He would have to be a saint to resist taking advantage of the moment.

And he'd never claimed to be one.

With his palm, he cupped the back of her head and brought her mouth down to his. He'd been wondering what she tasted like more times than he could count, and as his lips teased hers, testing her to make sure she didn't object, he was reminded of honey. He didn't know what to expect when he deepened the kiss—resistance maybe, or disgust—but the heady feeling of her opening her mouth to him, allowing him to swirl her tongue with his own and fully taste her sweetness, nearly killed him. As when she climbed higher up in his lap and tilted her head to fully enjoy the kiss.

Trusting him.

"Hey, you two. If you're not up here in ten seconds, you'll be sitting at the kids' table," Benny yelled again. "I can't hold the rug rats off much longer."

With great reluctance, Dominic pulled back and watched as Kate's eyes opened, staring back at him, dreamy and languid. Her lips were swollen and begged him to steal one more taste, but the sound of running feet and scraping chairs reminded him he'd be testing fate. The sounds seemed to seep through Kate's consciousness, too, for she flushed and practically bolted upright and away from his lap.

"W-we'd better get up there." She pressed her hands down, smoothing her soft black sweater down over her curvy figure, then repeated the action with her hair.

He smiled despite himself, trying to decide if he should tell her that due to the dreamy look still in her eyes and the swollen lips, no amount of fussing was going to tell anyone less than the truth of what they'd been doing.

He stood and reached out to smooth a lock of hair that was poking up on top of her head. "Yeah. We better."

He should be reminding himself why that kiss was a bad idea. That it could go nowhere and might even risk things becoming awkward. But he didn't care.

It had been worth it.

• • •

Kate could not get enough of the savory, tender pork wrapped in warm tortillas. It wasn't as if she'd never had *chile verde* before. There were a number of very good Mexican restaurants within ten minutes of her house, but it wasn't the same as homemade. Store-bought tortillas would never taste the same again.

She'd eaten one full burrito made of the flavorful stew and was thinking about a second when she saw Dominic was watching her with that gleam in his eyes. And any further thought of food was dismissed.

Only the memory of that kiss.

And Dominic, so strong and firm underneath her, his shoulders as she had gripped him tighter, his chest that she'd pressed herself against. The softness of his hair that her fingers found their way to as she pulled him in to her as she gave into the heady heat of his kiss.

She'd been lost.

Even now his gaze dropped to her lips, and she almost opened them, as if he was there now. Her lower belly swirled with desire again.

Which was freaking crazy.

She and Dominic were not going to happen. They

couldn't happen. This proved it. Because now that he'd kissed her—really kissed her—she couldn't think of anything else.

Best to avoid looking directly at him for the rest of the evening if she wanted to retain any semblance of her sanity. Instead she sat back and listened to the chatter around her.

The kids were the loudest and she was glad to see their initial shyness had dropped as they talked animatedly with each other and Dominic and Cruz—who had shown up while she was downstairs. They were clearly trying to impress their uncles.

Dominic's father, who had been resting when they'd arrived earlier, had also joined them and taken a seat at the head of the table. A tall, broad-shouldered Viking with light blond hair and unsettling blue eyes, he was stoic and reserved while the rest of the family took part in more animated discussion. She couldn't imagine anyone being more opposite his petite, dark-haired wife, with her easy, warm deposition and proclivity for smiling.

But even though he didn't say much, she could see the love in the elder Sorensen's eyes as he glanced around the table at his family. He clearly was enjoying having his family surround them with their energy and love. And she was enjoying it herself. As the meal progressed and Benny and Cruz took to teasing Dominic again, she saw their father's eyes twinkle in amusement, a slight smile on his lips. When he caught her watching him, she was more than surprised when he gave her a quick wink. Kate blushed a little at his attention. She could definitely see where Dominic got his charm.

She closed her eyes for a brief moment, feeling the warmth and love that surrounded her. Heady, tempting. For a moment, she felt a dark, hollow feeling in her gut. This couldn't last, this glimpse she was getting into this family. Into Dominic's life. Eventually his work would be done, the terms of their proposal would be met, and Dominic would move on to the next woman who caught his eye. Especially once Kate earned that promotion to junior partner, and she was consumed with work. She doubted he'd understand or tolerate that.

And she'd be alone again.

Despite her promise not to look directly in his eyes, she sneaked another peek. He smiled at her, so sweet, and that twirling in her belly started up again. Delicious and tantalizing.

She just needed to keep a level head when it came to Dominic, that's all. But for the time being, she might as well enjoy the euphoria that being with him brought.

And the feeling of knowing that things were on track to getting everything she'd ever wanted.

Chapter Eleven

"This is me in shock," Payton said while dabbing at the iced tea spilled down the front of her shirt.

They'd been grabbing lunch at the deli by the park like they did every Monday when Kate dropped the news that Dominic had not only talked her into skiing, but that she'd actually enjoyed it. Evidently, that was so shocking it had made Payton miss her mouth. And Kate hadn't even told her about the kiss yet.

"I spend the past fifteen years trying to get you on skis, and after one game of Scrabble, he has you on the mountain." Payton almost didn't look like she believed her.

Kate laughed. "You know I never make a bet I can't win, and with my track record, I didn't think I could lose."

"I'm liking him better already." Payton stirred her tea with her straw and took a sip. "And have you heard any word about whether your little ruse was successful with the powers that be, or, more importantly, Michael?"

"According to my assistant, the break room was buzzing about who Dom is and how long I've been seeing him, which—come on—is either her overactive imagination or everyone seriously needs to get out more. But she did mention that Tim's assistant had a few questions, too, which makes me wonder if she's asking on her behalf or someone else's." Kate picked up her Reuben and took a bite, careful not to drip sauce on her blouse.

It was hard to miss the longing look that Payton gave the sandwich before stabbing a tomato with her fork. "Then your plan sounds like it's already a success. But you're being too vague. I need details here. About Michael's reaction, about Dominic's family, everything."

In the explicit detail that Payton had grown to appreciate, Kate gave her a blow-by-blow of the weekend, taking a moment to decide whether to give her the details of the kiss, but then she realized that her need for her friend's opinion outweighed any inevitable teasing.

Payton set her fork on the table and rested her hands on the top and leaned forward. "I can't believe you were just toying with my ass for the past twenty minutes. We've been friends for how long, and you wait until *now* to give me the good stuff?" Payton's eyes blazed, but more from avid curiosity and excitement than any real anger. "Tell me. Now."

Kate laughed again. "There's nothing more to give you. We kissed for a minute, maybe two, and then it was over."

"And you never interrogated him about his intentions, the ifs, ands, or whys the rest of the night? I don't know. That doesn't sound like you. You question everyone and every-thing."

"That's why I'm such a damn good attorney. But really… what was there to say? We just got carried away with the moment." Kate coyly brought her drink to her mouth. "Not that I'm saying it wasn't a freaking good kiss, because it was, but it's unlikely to ever repeat itself."

"But we can hope?" Payton said and grinned. "So, since the two of you have this pretend relationship going for a few more weeks, does this mean he's going to be your plus one at my engagement party? Because I'm dying to see Michael's green complexion myself."

"I'm not sure. I was so focused on this retreat I didn't even think that far ahead, but I can ask him. And don't give me that feigned outraged look, because I know for a fact you're trying to forget about the damn thing yourself."

Payton rolled her eyes. "Just don't let my mother hear you say that. This wedding and the party have taken over her life—and mine. Did I tell you she bought my engagement dress one size too small to force me to drop ten pounds?"

Kate laughed. "I wondered what was up with the whole salad for lunch, since you usually only eat one if they bring it as a side to your order. I just figured weren't very hungry."

"I'm practically starving to death." Which looked nothing farther than the truth with her smooth, glowing skin and healthy strawberry-blond hair that even now glistened in the sunlight that streamed in from their window. Then there were those darn adorable dimples. Kate would hate her if she wasn't her best friend.

Unaware of Kate's internal eye roll, Payton continued, "Normally I could care less about the dress my mother has selected for me and would tell her where she could take her advice—" She stopped when Kate raised a brow. "Okay, not so much told her where to take it as just ignore it, but the dress is a Jason Wu. His creations are just so beautiful."

Kate would have to take her word for it, since she never followed things like fashion as diligently as her friend. "Well, your mother is crazy. You're beautiful, and I'm not exactly seeing Brad complaining."

"That's hard to do when he's in Europe all the time." Payton reached across the table and grabbed Kate's dill pickle. "But I'm dying to meet Dominic. He has to come if only to appease my curiosity."

The prospect of having Dominic at her side, ready to slay dragons—or in this case, sharp-tongued socialites—on her behalf, filled Kate with tentative excitement. She did have one dress that she'd been waiting to show off, and to see Dominic's look of appreciation when he saw her—even if things were just pretend—might be something to look forward to after all.

She smiled back at her friend. "I'll try my best."

• • •

Kate pulled up her driveway the next evening, trying to settle the fluttering in her belly at the sight of Dominic's truck parked at the curb in front of her house. He hadn't been able to come by yesterday due to some unexpected problems at the site from the weekend, but he'd texted her at three today to confirm he was there and working demolition on her bathroom. He had wanted to warn her that it was going to look worse before it got better. But anything had to be better than the Pepto-Bismol–colored tile, and she was looking forward to seeing the changes.

And a certain someone.

The door was unlocked, and she dropped her keys on the table and climbed the stairs, following the sounds of destruction. She found him pulling drywall down with gloved hands, and he didn't appear to have noticed her arrival. She leaned against the doorway and appreciated the scene.

Broken pink tiles scattered around the floor along with more dust and debris than she'd have thought possible. But that wasn't what had her attention. It was the sight of his strong, bulging biceps as he smashed a section of the wall with the sledgehammer, often stopping to pull at the drywall with both hands, that had her pulse racing. And the beads of sweat sliding down his neck and through the black T-shirt he wore. Who knew sweat could actually be so sexy?

She must have been breathing too heavily, because suddenly he stilled and glanced back to see her.

"How long you going to stand there checking me out? I warned you it wasn't going to be pretty."

That was a matter of opinion.

• • •

"I can't believe you've never tried this," Dominic said and took another bite of his sloppy joe, enjoying the mix of sweet with salty and tangy.

Kate looked at his sandwich and visibly shuddered, and he tried not to laugh. "It's not so much the sandwich, but the piles of potato chips you've smashed on top. Are you trying to kill yourself?"

He ignored that last bit. "Come on. You can't knock it until you try it." He held his concoction in front of her. She eyed it with suspicion but finally took the tiniest bite, the crunch sounding through the kitchen. He stared a little too long at her mouth as she chewed, remembering how it had felt under his and wondering if he'd ever experience that again before this thing was over. He definitely was hoping so, even though he knew it was a bad idea.

She looked thoughtful. "Okay. So it's not horrible."

"That's what I thought." He wolfed down another bite, aware of Kate still watching him. Something she'd been doing a lot of since she got home, even though she would look away or pretend to be looking somewhere else when he tried to catch her. But it wasn't nearly as often as he'd been sneaking glances at her, only less obvious.

Like they were both in junior high. It was pathetic.

He blamed the damn ponytail, and the way her long red hair flipped around when she turned her head. The way her lips parted when she stared at him, as if she was remembering that amazing kiss from the other night. Or the way she flushed for no apparent reason, making him wonder what she might be thinking.

But he knew a small part of it was that he liked to look at her. To fill the ache he'd been experiencing since they'd parted Sunday night.

They had spent an amazing weekend together, though. It was perfectly normal for him to want to see her again. They'd become good friends. Right?

He swallowed some soda down. "So how were things in the office? Was everyone buzzing about who the dashingly sexy guy was at your side all weekend?"

"That's right, I was besieged by your fan club when I hit the break room for coffee. They've even posted a picture of you on the fridge in homage."

"Yeah, I should have warned you about the effect I have on people. They practically find me irresistible." He ignored her cute snort as she covered her mouth. "In another interesting development, my mom called me today. Told me that Daisy set up an appointment with you for later this week. She's already started gathering the documents you requested."

"I can't confirm or deny that. It's a matter of attorney-client privilege." But she smiled, confirming that it was true.

"Don't worry. I know if you're on the case, she'll be in good hands. Just make sure you hit that asshole where it hurts—his bank account."

"I'll give it my best. Which actually reminds me…I had lunch with Payton yesterday and she reminded me that I hadn't RSVP'd yet for her engagement party."

"Nice segue there. I can totally see how those two things would be related. Wait. You're her maid of honor. Aren't you already obligated to go to this thing?"

"Unfortunately, yes. But the real question she was asking was…who was going to be my plus one. I know I didn't specifically mention this when we made our arrangement, but Michael is bound to be there, and if I go solo, it might arouse some suspicions. So…I was kind of hoping that you might be willing to go with me?"

For a brief moment, Dominic wished that Kate had asked him to go because she wanted to be there with him. Not because she had some appearance to make—and especially not for Michael. But he shook it off. Despite their attraction for each other, this thing between them wasn't real. "They still do that sort of thing? Formal engagement parties?"

"The Vaughns do. Payton's mother was on the phone

with the country club the minute after Payton flashed them her ring. They're pulling out all the stops. Believe me, Payton's excitement level for this thing is barely higher than mine. But she knows a losing battle when she sees one."

He pretended to think about it for a minute. "Since we wouldn't want to disappoint Michael with my absence, I don't see how I have much choice. Please tell me I don't have to wear a monkey suit."

From the way Kate cringed and tried to smile, he got his answer.

"You owe me big."

"Yeah. Believe me, I'm not looking forward to this thing any more than you. In fact, you'll probably enjoy yourself more." She shuddered.

It was the same reaction she'd given at hearing the invite to Glenda's and later his parents' for dinner. He had to ask. "So what gives? I mean, no one likes to go to parties where they don't know anyone, but you seem to have an especially low tolerance for these things than I would say is normal."

"Let's just say my experience has taught me to be wary of social occasions. Most people are usually subtle enough not to come right out and ask about your family's background, your social connections, the amount of your investment portfolio and where you vacation every year. Usually weaving the questions in just when you're starting to feel comfortable. Not Michael's parents. They don't pull any punches."

"Sounds like a bunch of assholes. Where the hell do you find people like that?"

She shrugged. "Guess I've just been lucky. Take for instance the Vaughns, Payton's family. Well, her mother, anyway. Emily

Vaughn. Everything for her is about impressing people. The right people, that is. She can be pretty scary, not helped by the fact she totally loathes me."

"You?" He dumped some chips on his now empty plate. "If I were laying bets, especially considering I haven't met your friend yet, I would bet on you being the levelheaded one in that friendship, keeping Payton on the straight and narrow. Not the other way around."

"No. That sounds about right." She smiled softly and paused, as if remembering something before continuing. "Mrs. Vaughn's dislike stemmed more from the fact I was the charity case. Payton was supposed to be hanging out with other rich kids who had successful parents and good connections that Mrs. Vaughn could brag about. I was on" — she lowered her voice — "scholarship."

Anger twisted his gut at the possibility that anyone could make Kate feel like she wasn't good enough. Especially a younger, more impressionable Kate, whose life had been plenty tough. "Sounds like a bitch. Hope you didn't take her opinion to heart."

She shrugged. "It's easier now, but when I was twelve, not so much. You should have seen the look she gave me the first time Payton invited me to go skating with her." She laughed, but it was a short, dry laugh that he could tell cost her. "My grams was on Social Security and what with all the school fees, books, and uniforms that my scholarship didn't cover, we were just getting by. Spare cash wasn't a luxury we had. So instead of handing over the cash for my admission, Grams ran over to the window of Mrs. Vaughn's shiny black Lexus and handed her a buy-one-get-one-free coupon. You should have seen the horror on Emily Vaughn's face. A used

Kleenex would have been less abhorrent." Kate paused at the memory, a sad smile twisting her lips. "She's been giving me that same look ever since."

One thing was for sure, things were going to get really interesting when he met up with this heartless bitch. But for now, he pretended that Kate's words hadn't ripped at his heart. "But Payton didn't care," he prodded her as she paused to stare out the window a second too long.

She smiled. "No. Payton didn't mind. She's not like her mother. Used to love coming over for sleepovers, just to get away. We'd camp out in a tent in the backyard and stay up way too late eating Red Vines and reading each other contraband romance novels that I'd found in Grams's closet. I got lucky when I met her."

He imagined a younger, more gawky Kate, with long red braids like in her grams's picture. Mischievous. Funny. Undoubtedly sarcastic. But with a heart of gold.

Until people like the Vaughns and the Langfords came along and ripped away her self-worth. Made her doubt herself.

That wasn't going to happen at this party if he could help it. If he left Kate with one thing, it would be that she really was worth more than all of them. And that the little girl with the freckles and toothy grin was still inside. Ready to find happiness. A fearless happiness.

If she would only let herself.

But instead, he said only, "I'd say you both got lucky."

. . .

"Promise me you'll give this guy a call, Dominic. I've seen

his work and it's great. He promised to work something out for a reasonable price." She paused and her voice turned suspiciously soft. "It's time. Dad will understand."

Cruz entered the room and placed a coffee on Dominic's desk and went to his own.

"Yeah, yeah. Got it, Benny. Email me the details. Look, I've got to go. Cruz just got in and we have some numbers to go over."

He dropped the phone to the desk as he heard Cruz laugh softly. "Numbers, huh? And she actually bought that?"

Dominic ignored him and looked down, trying to remember what he'd been doing before his sister had called. She was really pushing him to get a website going for his business. Not that it was a bad idea, and it certainly was something he'd been thinking about for some time, but…

It was a big step.

He had to be sure Sorensen Construction — and his dad — would be okay before he jumped ship.

"What does Kate think about all this?"

Dominic looked up to find Cruz watching him. "About what?"

"Don't play dumb. About your future, whether you're staying here, opening your new business, going back to school… I'm assuming you are serious about her, considering it's been years since you brought anyone around to meet the family."

"Hasn't really come up."

Cruz's brown eyes beamed into him and Dominic shrugged.

"You're seeing some fancy attorney at some pricey downtown law firm and your career, your future, *hasn't really come up*?" Cruz sat back and folded his arms in front of him. "I knew something was suspicious about the timing of this whole thing, what with Daisy needing an attorney and your sudden infatuation. You're full of shit. Level with me. What's going on?"

Damn. He'd never been able to get anything past Cruz, and he guessed he should count himself lucky they'd made it this far. He shook his head. "Fine, you're right. I met Kate, like I said, because I was going to work on her house. But then we both discovered that we had some…issues in our life and that maybe we could help each other out." Dominic explained the details of the agreement to Cruz, who just shook his head and looked at him like he was an idiot.

"This isn't going to end well, you know. When Mom and everyone find out this was part of a scam, they're going to kill you."

"I don't see why they have to find out. People break up all the time. When the time's right, we'll amicably break up and move on."

"You're delusional." This time Cruz cracked a smile, his eyes more sympathetic.

"How's that?" Dominic sat back and waited.

"I saw the way you two looked at each other at dinner the other night and if you think this is just a business arrangement, then you're an idiot."

Dominic was silent. He couldn't convincingly deny that he was attracted to Kate and that she had recently taken a leading role in all of his fantasies. What that meant wasn't something he was ready to think about just yet.

"I'm a grown man, so I'll figure it all out."

"Fine. Dad's surgery is Friday morning. Have you and Kate worked out whether she's going to make an appearance at the hospital? You know, to show support as a dutiful and loving girlfriend?"

He hadn't thought about it. But Cruz made a good point. Man, this thing was trickier than he'd expected. But he'd figure it out. He glanced at this watch. Well, whatever lies he had to tell would be worth it since, as they were speaking, Daisy was meeting with Kate and getting the help she and those kids needed.

And if it meant he had to spend a little more time with the beautiful Kate, then so be it. It was a burden he was more than happy to bear.

Chapter Twelve

"I'll have my assistant file the divorce petition and motion for a temporary order with the court no later than tomorrow," Kate said early Wednesday afternoon. "The temporary hearing will be scheduled before one of the commissioners soon after, and my assistant will give you a call with the date, so be sure you call that number and schedule a time to attend the divorce orientation before then. There's no reason you and the kids should have to wait any longer for your husband to start making the child support payments you're entitled to."

"Thanks, Kate." Daisy nodded, her eyes still as sorrowful as they'd been when Kate first met her, but there seemed to be a new gleam in their brown depths. Hope, maybe. She was dressed in a pretty wraparound dress and heels, her black hair long and flowing. One thing was for certain—once Dominic's sister was ready to start dating, Kate couldn't imagine she'd have to wait long for some lucky guy to swoop in. She was beautiful.

"Like I said, you're doing me a favor, too, so I'm just glad we could both help each other. Although I think I'll enjoy making your husband squirm a little more than usual."

"Good. Because honestly? I'm through mourning for him. Waking up this morning, I think I had my first taste of anger." This time Kate saw a more steely, determined look in her eyes. "But really, I can't tell you how grateful I am for your help. It's almost fortuitous that you came into our lives right now. I know that I haven't seen Dominic look so happy, so relaxed in some time. You're good for him. I can tell."

Kate dropped her eyes, uneasy with the guilt casting a shadow over her. When she and Dominic talked about this plan, she hadn't thought any farther than getting everyone to believe they were a committed couple. She hadn't thought about how she'd feel having to look these loving, friendly people in the eye and continue to perpetrate a lie. How they'd feel if they discovered it was all a sham. And how attached she'd get to all of them. Wishing they were her family.

Daisy stood, unaware of Kate's conflicting emotions. "I better get going. I've got to pick Paul up from kindergarten and drop off a few more résumés. Will we see you at the hospital on Friday?"

Kate searched her memory for what Daisy was referring to. "I'm not sure yet about my schedule…" she said, hoping the answer was satisfactory.

"I hope you can, even for a minute. I'm sure Dominic played down the whole thing, but I bet he'd love it if you stopped by as a show of support. I know Mom probably would as well. She'll be such a wreck—you should have seen her in those days when it was touch and go with Dad. They're everything to each other."

Dominic's dad's surgery. She had heard some mention

about it, but she hadn't realized it was this Friday. She had never asked. Another wave of guilt hit her. Even if Dominic hadn't mentioned it, what kind of girlfriend—not to mention friend—would she be if she didn't try and make it? "I'm conducting a pretty big deposition that's scheduled to go Thursday and possibly into Friday as well. I'll try my hardest to break away."

"Well, I hope we'll see you."

Daisy waved and walked to the door. A male figure appeared in the doorway, and they sidestepped each other as she made her way out.

Michael. What did he want?

"Morning, Kate." Michael took a couple steps in, his hands in his pockets. "Meeting with a new client?"

"Something like that. It's a pro bono case. A custody and divorce matter."

"Are you sure a pro bono case—especially a messy custody and divorce one—is something you should be taking on right now?" Michael's brows furrowed in concern, and his tone became soft and protective. Something she remembered well. The feeling of someone watching out for her. Caring. Only now, his concern wasn't comforting. It was...annoying. "Even with Nicole's help, you have to be pretty stretched right now, preparing for tomorrow's first round of depositions and those in the coming weeks, not to mention your other clients. And this McKenna case is important to your career."

No, Michael was being downright condescending. Had he always been like this? "I'm not taking on anything I can't handle, but thanks for your concern. Was there something you needed?"

He stayed standing, shifting his weight to his other leg.

"No. I just know that you start taking depositions tomorrow and I remember how you get when you're in preparation mode. Since I was heading down to the coffee shop, I thought I'd see if I could get you your usual."

She crooked her head to the side. What was this about? He hadn't stopped by to get her a coffee since they were a couple. "Is everything okay with you, Michael?"

For a moment she wondered if there was some trouble in paradise with Nicole, but then dismissed that. She'd seen Nicole briefly this morning, preening and flashing that rock around like it was the Holy Grail or something. Smug in her confidence that she'd won the guy.

"No. I was just realizing we never have a chance to really talk anymore. You know, like we used to?" He jangled some loose change in his pockets. "How's the progress on your house? It's strange to think of you in this new place, a place I've never even seen. With a guy that's not me."

She sat back in her chair and savored the moment. Because she was nearly certain that what she was hearing was jealousy.

It was good to see the emotion on someone else for a change.

"Things are going better than I expected. How did your painting project go?" Nicole had seemed intent on getting rid of every last vestige of Kate and Michael's relationship.

"Oh. That. Well, I don't really have the time to take on that kind of project right now. So Dominic and you. Seems pretty serious. But what do you really know of this guy? I mean, I know it's really not my place to interfere, but even in the brief time I've met him, I just get this vibe from hi—"

"You're right. You don't have any right to interfere in my personal life. And because you only just met Dominic is precisely why you have no idea what you're talking about. But the issue is moot, Michael. I'm not discussing who I am or am not seeing with you."

She managed to say this calmly, even though as she spoke, the embers of her anger were being stoked. He had no right to say anything about her life. He'd left *her*, not the other way around. But she didn't want an argument today—she had neither the time nor the energy. "I've got a lot of work here. If that's everything…"

"Just don't let this guy distract you. I've heard the talk, and it seems like you've impressed all the right people so far, and if you play your cards right, you could be this firm's next junior partner."

Long after Michael left her office, Kate sat musing about what had gone wrong between them, and more importantly, what he meant to her now. In all these months since their breakup, she had secretly hoped that Michael would realize he had made a mistake by breaking things off—because what his parents thought shouldn't matter when it came to love—and he'd come back to her. Like in some movie.

It had taken seeing that ring on Nicole's finger to make her see reality.

But lately, he'd been showing an interest in her, an interest she'd feared was gone forever. And she honestly couldn't decide if she was pleased or annoyed.

She remembered Dominic's question, about whether she'd take Michael back if he asked. She really couldn't say. She'd thought they were going to be together forever, make a future together, and when he'd been too afraid to stand up to his parents and instead begged off, she'd been devastated. The wound had been deep, and she hadn't thought she'd ever get over him.

But now, it was as if some of that love and adoration had been replaced with righteous anger and, to be honest, disgust. Disgust that he hadn't been strong enough to stand up for her. It was like the veil had been ripped away and she could see Michael for what he was. Human, filled with faults, of course, but also weak, and frankly, selfish and arrogant.

She shook her head. This was wasted time. It wasn't like he was beating down her door, anyway. Not really.

Dominic, though. Her heart swelled uncomfortably for a moment as she thought about his smile. His charm. His natural ability to make her feel happy and good about herself.

Not to mention that freaking amazing body and the way his lips made her forget everything about their plan and think only about him. All of him.

Crazy.

That's what that line of thinking was. Dominic and she were so…incompatible. He needed someone without her baggage, someone sweet and loving and ready to devote herself to him entirely. Something she couldn't do. Not if she was going to be appointed to a judgeship before she was fifty. Forty-five if she was lucky.

And she needed someone as rational and practical as her. Someone who wouldn't make her want things like the big family, the all-consuming love and lust that being with him would demand.

• • •

"The first thing you want to do before you ever try this,"

Dominic said later that night while Kate sipped tea from her perch on a bar stool in the kitchen corner, looking sexy as hell even if her smile told him she was only humoring him, "is to make sure you have the main breaker off. You don't want to know what it's like to have a bolt of electricity surge through your body." He stood on the top step of the stool with wires woven between his fingers. The idea had been to show her how to install a new light fixture. Although he had to admit he might be showing off, just a little bit.

"You do realize I'm just humoring you here. Like I'd ever try to do something like this on my own."

"Well, continue to humor me for another minute, if you don't mind," he said and climbed down before walking over and turning the breaker back on and then returned. "You want to do the honor?"

She moseyed over to the switch and he couldn't keep his eyes off her rear end as her hips moved tantalizingly. She flipped the switch and the sparse kitchen was flooded with a soft glow from the new light.

"I love it," she said with wonderment as she stared around her and then back up to the light, and he felt that stupid skip in his chest as he watched her reaction. "I can't believe the progress you made on the bathroom today, getting the Sheetrock up already, and you still had time to do this. Benny's right. You really should get moving on getting that website up, starting your own business. You're so talented."

"You haven't seen anything yet. This is grunt work. Wait until you see the final creation."

"Okay, Dr. Frankenstein. So why haven't you? Gone out on your own yet?"

He gave her wary look. "Have you been talking to my

brother?" He shook his head. "I just wanted to wait until the time was right. Things with my dad can be...complicated."

"Yeah. Most everything related to family is complicated." She slid back on her bar stool and grabbed her tea. "Try me."

He went to the fridge and pulled out of the beers Kate had started stocking for him. "Want one?" he asked and held it up toward her.

She looked down at her now empty teacup. "Yeah, sure. Thanks." He pried the cap off and handed it to her, did the same with another one and took a pull, leaning against the fridge.

"When Cruz and I were growing up, my dad loved to bring us to the job sites, show us what was what. As we got older, he had us do some odd jobs until we were competent enough to work side by side with him and the crew. He never made it a secret that one day he wanted to change that sign from Sorensen Construction to Sorensen and Sons."

"What happened?" Her blue-gray eyes pierced him with their intensity, and he wondered if this was what it felt like to be the opposing counsel.

He wouldn't stand a chance.

He took another long pull, the cool liquid slipping down easily. "I like my work, but it was the beauty, the symmetry behind the construction—the drafting and design—that really intrigued me. I didn't want to just follow blueprints. I wanted to create them based on my own design. Dad was okay with me going to the community college, getting my drafting certificate. That could be useful in the business. But when I finally had the courage to tell him I didn't want to just work the construction end of things, that I wanted to go to school to be an architect, it kind of hurt him. Don't get me wrong, when I got into the program, he was all sorts of proud. But I could see that he was also sad at realizing his dream of having a business with his sons wasn't going to happen. Then he got sick, and you know the rest."

She tapped her fingertips on the counter. "But he won't be sick forever, and if things go well Friday—*when* they go well—you can start to get back to doing what you want to do. Your dad will understand."

"It's not that he won't understand." He paused and walked over to the kitchen island, standing across from her and meeting her gaze. "These past few years, having me back on board, he's been so damn happy. I'm not sure how he'll take hearing that I'm leaving again."

She leaned forward and placed her hand on his arm. A simple touch, one to offer comfort, but his arm was itching where she touched it. Liking it too much. "From what I saw of your parents, they both really love you guys. Your dad may be initially disappointed, but I'm sure he only wants your happiness. With time, I'm sure he'll be happy for you."

"Yeah. Well, all the same, I think I'll wait until after he's on the mend before I get the ball rolling. When I know he can handle it."

She nodded and took a measured sip of her beer. "I met with Daisy," she said, thankfully changing the topic of discussion.

He smiled. "I know. And she loved you. Mom said that she seems more rejuvenated. Ready to embrace the next stage of her life. And it's all thanks to you."

"Easy there. Like I told her, we don't know how her husband's going to react to her petition or what his angle will be in all this. It could get ugly and long, with a few setbacks along the way."

"Yes, but it's something. Anything is better than sitting in limbo. With your help, she's finally taking control of her life and not letting someone else make the choices for her. So…thank you."

She squirmed, avoiding his gaze and instead fidgeting with the label on her beer bottle.

"What's wrong?" he asked.

She looked up at him in surprise, and he could see she was about to object. Then she clamped her mouth and heaved a sighed. "It's just I hadn't expected to like Daisy and the rest of your family like I do. It makes me feel awful, the way we're lying to them. They think we're a couple and are opening their arms to me on that basis alone."

"You're not giving yourself enough credit. They like you. Not just because you're my girlfriend—" Damn. That had sounded pretty good. He stopped and regrouped. "Well, pretending to be—but because you're genuinely caring and nice and funny. Believe me, I've had a few girlfriends I've brought home in the past, and they didn't roll out the welcome mat like they have with you." Actually, with few exceptions, they'd loathed them. Melinda most of all. In hindsight, he could see they'd had good reason.

Not looking entirely convinced, she slid off the stool and took her empty cup to the sink. "I just hope that this whole thing doesn't cause more pain. But I am glad to be helping Daisy out, any way I can."

"Of course you are." He smiled and reached over and picked up the almost full beer she'd left on the counter and took a pull while she rinsed her cup.

She turned around, wiping her hands on a towel before

dropping it to the counter. "Anyhow, Daisy asked me if I might be stopping by the hospital. To lend you support. I had to think fast since I hadn't realized your dad's surgery was this Friday, but I don't think she noticed. Why didn't you tell me about it?"

"It wasn't intentional. I just didn't think it was something you needed to worry about." He also hadn't wanted to overburden her with his family problems. God knew that Melinda hated doing anything family related. It hadn't seemed fair to ask Kate, his pretend girlfriend, to stop in for what some might see as an unpleasant task.

She took a step forward and slugged him with surprising force. "Let me decide that, okay? I really like your dad and your whole family. And whether we realized it at the time, this charade has drawn me into your family and the drama that comes with it. I can't help but care."

He rubbed his arm but was unable to keep the smile from creasing his face. "Fair enough." He sounded offhanded, but hearing her talk about his family like that—like she really cared—was making him feel all sorts of crazy.

Maybe Cruz had been on to something. Maybe he was growing more attached to Kate than he'd originally envisioned. He pushed the thought to the back of his mind. Cruz was making him paranoid. That's what it was.

"I may have mentioned I have depositions I'm taking on the McKenna case tomorrow," she continued. "It's scheduled for two days, but I'm hoping to get most everything wrapped up tomorrow. Maybe freeing up some time on Friday, if I'm lucky. I can come by. The hospital, I mean. If you want me to."

"I think having you there might be kind of nice," he

said cautiously, not wanting her to know how much it would mean if she did. He didn't want to pressure her. "But I also know how important this case is to you, so if for any reason you can't be there, just know that I understand. But speaking of your big case…" He needed to change the subject. It was getting entirely too personal and he needed a breather. "Shouldn't you be cramming or something right now?"

She laughed and practically rubbed her hands together in front of her. "Nicole wasn't all that happy to see me bail before eight tonight, but I know the facts inside and out and sitting in my office reviewing them another couple of hours isn't going to make any difference at this point. Now it's all about the excitement, the wondering of how things will go tomorrow. I know what I'm hoping she'll say, but sometimes you never know. It makes it all so…terrifying but exciting at the same time."

He watched her describe some of the case details again, noticing the way her eyes lit up with excitement, turning them more turquoise than their usual blue gray. She licked her full lips and he was reminded of how sweet her lips had tasted, and how soft and pliant they'd been under his. If he kissed them now, would she taste like tea and honey? Or maybe like the beer she'd tentatively sipped?

Then the truth hit him hard in the chest, and he felt as if the air had been punched out of him.

Shit. Cruz was right.

He just might be falling for this smart, passionate woman whose heart was as beautiful as she was. And he just might be past the point of caring.

Chapter Thirteen

Ava Herrera, a woman in her early forties, was quite pretty, make no mistake about it. She was dressed for court in a conservative but stylish suit with a bright scarf tied around her neck that coordinated with the cherry-red stain on her lips, both of which further accentuated her pretty brown eyes.

Kate would have bet Ms. Herrera's dark brown hair, full and teased, would give even Miss Texas a run for her money. She was a woman who knew her attraction and, Kate had no doubt, played that to her advantage.

But was that so different from any other woman?

Kate tried to quiet the annoying voice that had been popping up all morning during the deposition, anytime Kate thought something snarky, something to help see this woman as the bad guy. It always made it easier when she had to ask the tough questions, particularly when this woman's dark, expressive eyes looked at her, damp with moisture and with a look that said Kate, as a woman, had somehow betrayed *her*.

"And what did you do after Mr. McKenna made this advance?"

"I was in shock. This was the first time he'd taken his flirtation past blatant sexual innuendo to something more… physical."

The woman continued to detail what happened that particular day and later, when they went on a business trip together and her boss actually attacked her. At times, she'd break down, and her attorney would hand her a tissue and they'd wait until the woman could gain her composure. But she remained consistent throughout, much to Kate's dismay. And credible.

"And did you tell anyone at the company what had happened up to this point? A coworker? The human resources department?"

She shook her head.

"I'm sorry, I need you to respond for the record."

"No."

This questioning went on another hour and a half, until it was time to break for lunch.

"Two months of alleged harassment and you finally made a formal complaint to Ms. Driscoll at human resources," Kate said, summarizing the morning's testimony. "Do you recall what she told you after you explained everything?"

"She said they'd start an investigation and would notify me of what they discovered."

"And do you know if they did, indeed, start an investigation?"

Ms. Herrera shrugged, a wry smile on her lips. "They started an investigation, all right. But I don't think they were looking to prove anything about my complaint. It was more a witch hunt—against me—for daring to bring such a claim against Mark. I knew Ms. Driscoll didn't believe me and wouldn't help me, despite what she'd said."

"And how could you know that?"

"Besides the fact she looked at me throughout the whole thing like I was some kind of lying schemer? A couple of days later, when I was dropping off some reports at Mark's office, I overheard her and Mark talking about me. I distinctly heard him telling her this is what happens when they hire trailer trash like me to fill some quota." Ms. Herrera's voice broke at this last part.

It was as if someone had slugged Kate in the stomach. *Trailer trash.*

She tightened her grip on her pen. She couldn't explain it, but the words hit something in her. She was more than relieved it was time for lunch and made a beeline to her office, trying to take deep, calming breaths. She could hear Nicole following behind her. Of course. They had to discuss the information they had so far and make sure they were on task. And discuss points they could tear apart, to get Ms. Herrera to backtrack.

It was dirty. And necessary, even if Kate felt nauseated at the prospect.

But this was what she did.

And the sooner she got her head in the game, the sooner she could wrap this up.

• • •

Dominic took a drink of the lukewarm coffee that Benny

had brought him and the rest of their small group seated in the waiting room. It had been a couple of hours and, from what the doctor had explained, it could still be another hour more.

Waiting sucked.

Benny sat next to him. "So Kate seems really nice. Smart but not overly full of herself."

He'd wondered how long it would take before Benny started talking about this.

"Are you guys serious?"

He could say one thing about his sister, she certainly was straightforward. "Kate and I...we're kind of complicated right now." Benny stared at him, waiting for him to continue, and he sighed. "I don't really want to talk about this right now, Ben. Can we save it for later?"

"Okay. But I wanted you to know. I like her. We all do. She's nothing like Melinda." Benny waited about twenty seconds and started again. "But what's so complicated?"

Dominic repressed a sigh and was just about to tell his sister she needed to learn the definition of "no" when he saw a familiar redhead in a knee-length navy skirt, matching blazer, and killer heels walking his way. And all other thoughts save one left his mind.

She came.

Even with her hair drawn into a tidy bun at the back of her head, she looked damned sexy. He wanted nothing more than to pull her into his arms.

She stopped in front of Daisy and his mom, and they both stood and welcomed her in a hug. If he weren't mistaken, Kate actually looked comfortable with the contact and seemed to return it—even if she hadn't initiated it.

He and Benny joined them, and he could feel everyone watching him and Kate. He spoke first. "You came. Did everything go okay with the deposition?"

She shrugged. "It went fine."

But he could see something in her eyes, and the dark shadows underneath told him there was more to the story. He'd have to pursue it later.

"Your mom told me your dad's still in surgery. How are you holding up?"

Dominic looked around at the curious faces and smiled. "I'm doing all right. I need to walk my legs a bit. Care to join me?"

He waited until he knew they were out of earshot to ask. "You look beat. You didn't have to come, you know."

She looked affronted. "Of course I did. We already went through this. I care about your family, just as I care about you." The words made his heart thud a little irregularly, even when she hastily added, "I mean, I think over the past couple of weeks we've become…friends."

"Okay, then since we can both agree that we've become friends, maybe you can tell me what has you so upset? Don't tell me you're fine. I can see you're struggling."

"Yeah, fine. This one seems to be taking a lot out of me. Making me wary of the whole process. I'm used to turning off my emotions when I question witnesses. Empathy doesn't have any room in a deposition or a courtroom. But something about this woman…" She paused and tried to force a smile. "I'll probably feel better a little later. After I've processed everything, had something to eat."

"You hungry? We can grab something in the cafeteria."

"No, but thanks. Not that hospital cafeteria food doesn't

sound appetizing, but I need to get back to the office. I'll just pick up something on the way. I have a meeting with Tim and Nicole to discuss the progress of the case and next week's round of depositions. How late are you going to be here?"

Dominic looked at his watch. Just past two. "If everything goes as planned, Dad should be out within an hour and in recovery. I want to see him before I go. Then I was planning on getting the tile laid in your bathroom."

"Dominic, you don't have to work tonight. Your dad just had major heart surgery."

"Which is exactly why I need to work. It'll distract me. I want to do this." And he wanted to see her. "Want to have dinner later?"

She tucked the slightest wisp of hair behind her ear. "Yeah, I'd like to, but I should warn you, I don't know how late this thing will go—or my meeting with Tim. I probably should head out now. Will you tell your family good-bye for me?"

"Of course." He couldn't resist the opportunity and reached his hand down to hers and held it for a moment, happy to see the way she jumped at his touch and then blushed. "Thanks again for coming, Kate. And don't let this case get you down. You'll do the right thing."

He watched as she walked away, turning back a brief moment to wave before disappearing down the corridor.

She appeared to have the weight on the world on her shoulders. Dinner together might be just what they both needed.

He was already looking forward to the prospect.

• • •

Heavy, wet snowflakes made her commute home from work Friday night treacherous and stressful. The sight of Dominic's truck in front of the curb at her house, after her long, bone-tiring day of finishing up Ms. Herrera's deposition, quickened her pulse—but in a more pleasurable way than the traffic.

She hadn't looked forward to a weekend away from work in a long time. Not just a weekend away from work, but a weekend with Dominic. It had taken every ounce of self-control not to race out the door after her meeting with Tim and Nicole and the long conference call with the client after.

Her feet seemed to fly up the porch to her door. Dropping her stuff inside the door, she stopped and listened for him. Hearing the noises coming from the kitchen, she headed in that direction.

He looked perfect.

And after the day she'd had, she felt an overwhelming urge to head directly into his arms, to have their strength around her, holding her. Smell his clean, musky scent. Feel the touch of his hands on her waist and hips as he pulled her closer and the stubble that darkened his jawline as she raised her mouth to his in a welcome.

He looked up then, and she had to catch her breath at the promise in his eyes when he saw her and his usual slow smile filled his face. Like a promise of fun and adventure and lots of laughter—and clothes-ripping, mind-blowing, make-her-beg-for-it sex. She let her breath out, trying to steady her rapidly beating heart.

It took her a second to realize that her old kitchen cabinets were no longer gracing her walls, and she was looking at blank, patched walls where they once had hung.

She blinked.

"Wow. You have been busy. And I guess this answers my question. We certainly will be ordering in pizza. So everything is going okay with your dad?"

"He's doing remarkably well. They think he'll probably be released by Sunday, so that made him feel a lot better."

"So fast? That seems crazy. You know what this means, right? Soon your dad will finally be on the road to good health and you can broach the topic of going out on your own."

"Yeah," he said, sounding somewhat distracted. "Soon, but I'll probably give him another week to recover. Thanksgiving is next week, so I might wait and broach it after." He rubbed the back of his neck and looked up her again, a nervous smile now on his mouth. "Which once again brings up another issue that I don't think either of us considered when we formulated this plan of ours. Thanksgiving dinner. My mom will be heartbroken if you don't come over and celebrate with us."

Thanksgiving? That was big.

Back when Grams was healthy, Kate used to go all out making the big feast—even though it was just the two of them. A turkey that gave them leftovers for the next week, pies, stuffing, homemade Parker House rolls, and her grams's special sweet potato casserole. It had been about…four years since they'd done that? She really missed it.

Really missed her.

"Dinner will be around four. I know how much your grandma means to you, and she's welcome to come, too. I can help you get her if you want."

He said it so easily, so ready to help make Thanksgiving complete for her. She smiled and shook her head, humbled by his consideration. "Thanks, and there would have been a time she would have loved the invitation. Now, though, she feels more comfortable and relaxed in her room, with the things that are most familiar around her."

But she could go, and Lord help her, she really wanted to. And that just might be the biggest shocker of all. Her choosing to go to a family event.

"You know…I usually hang out in the afternoon at the center and have dinner with her—they serve Thanksgiving dinner pretty early." Dominic was nodding in understanding, his face devoid of any emotion. "I suppose I could probably make it by four…"

It was hard to miss the smile that slid over Dominic's face, the strange light in his eyes as he processed that she was coming. Like he was actually glad she was coming, not just because his mom had invited her, but because maybe he wanted her there. And suddenly, the dread and depression that been like a shadow of her day seemed to dissipate. She was feeling alarmingly cheerful and optimistic. "But I'm going to have to bring something. I insist."

"You're going to cook?" His brow lifted and it was hard to miss the mischievous smile he now delivered. "I'll warn them ahead of time."

Chapter Fourteen

Kate wasn't sure what kind of work she'd envisioned getting done on Saturday with Dominic arriving bright and early, ready to get started on the next project. Even with the French doors closed while she worked at the dining table, her attention kept wavering every time she heard the steady sound of his work boots overhead or clomping down the stairs. And she'd look up from the table, anticipating the possibility of seeing him pass by the French doors, giving her that silly grin that turned her stomach inside out.

How much longer could she pretend to work before venturing out for his company?

Focus, Kate.

She stared at the words in front of her, but her mind was on the steady sound of footsteps arriving outside the dining room again.

Tap, tap.

She looked up to see Dominic waiting on the other side

of the glass doors. That man was damned temptation.

"Come in," she said. As if she could deny his company.

In a red flannel shirt, the sleeves rolled up above his fore-arms again —why even bother with long sleeves?—he had a down-to-earth appeal. "I'm heading out to the dump. Wanna take a break? We could stop and get something to eat."

"The dump, huh?" He had to be kidding, right? "Well, as tempting as that sounds, I think I'm going to take a pass. Besides"—she glanced outside her window at the dark sky that had consumed the bright sun of earlier—"you're not going to make it without being hit with a torrent of rain."

He grinned. "I like to live dangerously. Come on. You've got to eat. My treat. Besides, there was something I wanted to show you."

"Like what?"

"It's a surprise. You'll have to come with me."

Said the spider to the fly.

But, God help her, she really, really wanted to go.

She looked at the work scattered around her. She supposed she'd gotten more than enough done for now. There was always later. Who wouldn't want to spend their afternoon at the city dump? At least it would be an unlikely place for her to suddenly lose control of her hormones and maul him.

"Let me get my jacket."

The inside of the truck shook when Dominic slammed the tailgate closed. That had been faster than she'd expected since, between Dominic and a couple guys from the dump, they'd made quick work of unloading the haul. He climbed inside and buckled up before easing the truck from the dock.

Just in time, apparently, as the dark skies that had threatened rain for the past hour suddenly released their torrents. She loved a good rainstorm. Especially when she was still dry and cozy and warm inside.

"You know, that wasn't as bad as I thought it would be. I had envisioned acres of rotting garbage and the putrid smell of waste. And what do you know, my appetite is still intact."

"Good. Because I'm starving."

"Okay, so where are we going?"

He flicked the windshield wipers on and threw a smile at her. "All in good time. I thought we'd stop and pick up the food on the way. How does Chinese sound?"

"I'll eat just about anything."

"There's a menu in the glove box. Have a look."

She opened it to find a handful of different takeout menus. Mexican, pizza, Thai, Jimmy John's, and Chinese. He obviously came prepared. She wondered briefly what else she might find in the glove box but didn't think he'd take kindly to her snooping and shut it reluctantly.

Kate perused the menu while the bluesy twang of Emmylou Harris flooded the cab.

Thirty minutes later, a bag of Chinese food was nestled at her feet, and the aroma of sweet and sour filled the truck. With the steady beat of rain on the windows and top of the cab combined with the music and gentle swaying of the truck, Kate's eyes grew heavy.

This was nice. But drowsy as she was, she kept her attention on the scenery, especially when Dominic turned off the main road and they ascended a smaller road that wound higher and higher up the canyon. At least the road seemed to be recently paved.

It took her a moment to realize they'd reached their destination when Dominic put the car in park and looked over at her. "Ready?"

She looked at him like he was crazy. "For what?"

He grinned and grabbed the bag of Chinese food and a thick blanket from the seat and turned off the engine. Was he seriously taking her to a picnic in the middle of a downpour? "You'll see. Come on."

"It's pouring out there. Are you serious? We'll get soaked."

"Trust me."

Sheesh. She looked outside again as he pushed his door open and ran around to open hers for her. Reluctantly, she brought her coat over her head and followed him. The ground was muddy and they headed down a thinning path and into what felt like a veritable forest.

This was not how she'd envisioned this day going. A visit to the dump. Trudging through the woods for a picnic during a drenching cold rain shower.

The raging rush of lust and desire that was hitting epic highs every time she glanced down at Dominic's backside as they continued their hike.

They reached a slight clearing and she looked farther ahead. Was that a cabin? With no other choice but to follow him, she continued on, the coat held above her head already soaked through and dripping onto her. Without the protection of the woods, the wind hit them hard and she shivered.

They stopped in front of a set of steps, and she looked through the opening in the coat again.

Wow.

It was actually a house, not a cabin as she'd originally

thought. A massive house that spread over a good chunk of property. A wide porch wrapped around the front and side of the house disappeared around the back. The outside of the house was a mix of natural stone and wood, treated and stained a rich chocolate, which had probably been why she'd underestimated its size. It seemed to blend in with the surrounding environment.

Dominic climbed the three steps and stood on the porch, studying her.

"What is this?" she asked.

"My home."

She looked up at the low eaves that covered and protected the wide porch, almost hugging it and keeping it dry and protected. There was a wind chime hanging to his left.

This wasn't at all what she had expected.

"It's still a work in progress. But with the winter season ahead, I'll have the next few months to finish getting it into shape. So I'm taking my time. Making it mine."

She felt oddly humbled. Touched that he would bring her here to share something of himself like this. There were no words and fortunately, he wasn't waiting for any, already slipping a key in the heavy wooden door and pushing it open.

"After you." He stepped aside and she walked in, her footsteps echoing on the plywood under her feet. It was barely warmer inside than it was outside, and she breathed in the damp smell of rain and pine and…plaster?

The room was empty and bare and extended to the back of the house, where she could see full-length windows extend floor to ceil— She stepped forward and realized she had incorrectly assumed this was a one-story home. Ahead of her, she could see that the windows extended down to another floor below.

They reached a banister and stopped. Her mouth opened. The view was incredible. Both inside, where she could see a great room with a massive stone fireplace, and outside where she could see the lines of the trees, the tips of the canyon ridge, and the whole world, or so it seemed.

Dominic took the stairs to her right, and she followed. Several sliding glass doors opened up to a wide deck that would allow a person a view of everything. Nothing was out there now, probably because they were in the middle of November, but she could envision a patio set, a porch swing, a barbecue. Children playing in a tree house. Swings over on the north end of the lawn, maybe even a trampoline. The kind of stuff she'd dreamed about having as a kid.

"Told you there was a lot of work," Dominic said from behind her. He was standing at an island and pulling the boxes and containers of Chinese out of the bag. Bare cabinets were behind him and she spotted a basic sink and a small dorm fridge in the corner.

She cocked a brow. "I see you pulled out all the stops for the appliances."

"They'll be along when I'm closer. But this fridge holds drinks, leftovers, whatever I need when I'm up here working."

She looked behind her at the open expanse of windows and space. The stone fireplace. And even though the floor was still plywood, the walls only drywall, no appliances or light fixtures other than the glaring light from the work lamp in the corner, it was...breathtaking.

"It's beautiful, Dominic. I can't believe you're undertaking something like this on your own."

"Well, on my own and with the help from a few subcontractors we use at Sorensen Construction to get the walls up," he added wryly.

"How did you come up with the design? Did you hire an architect?" she continued, walking around, like she hadn't heard him. "This floor plan is amazing."

"I did it."

She swirled around and met his gaze. "You designed this? Imagined all of this and made it real? You really are a genius."

Dominic ducked his head, but not before she saw a look that could only be described as pride. He grabbed the blanket and came to stand next to her. "I wouldn't say a genius. Besides, I wouldn't have been able to go as big as this without the resources so easily at my disposal." He threw the blanket open. It curled up on the edges and she bent down to smooth them over.

"Now you're being modest. This place is incredible. You'll have to give me the grand tour when we're done eating." She sat back and turned to see Dominic at the fireplace. Within a moment, a blaze came to life.

"Gas fireplace," he said, as if he had to offer an explanation.

"Practical and environmentally correct."

"Precisely my focus when I was studying architecture up at the U," he said and returned to the island for their food.

Kate stood and helped him bring the cartons and a couple of paper plates over before taking a seat. "Pretty big space for a bachelor like yourself. Planning to open a bed-and-breakfast? Maybe an orphanage?" she teased.

"Nah. Just wistful thinking. Someday I plan on having a full house. A wife, kids. A dog or two. The works."

A lump filled her throat unexpectedly. Not that these

things were anywhere on her list of things to accomplish, but it sounded nice. He was going to make some lucky woman quite a husband.

"What are you going to do with the area upstairs?" she said, uneasy with the current topic and wanting to change courses. "It's kind of open for a bedroom. Unless you like that whole lack of privacy thing."

"A game room. Or an office. Not sure. Maybe both. There's also a master bedroom over that way with a master bath." He nodded to his left. It was next to the great room, which meant it probably had the same amazing view. "It's part of why I wanted to show you this place. I've started some work on the tub area, and I thought you might be interested in taking a look. Maybe you'll see some features you want to use at your place. Anyway, across from that master room is a smaller room. Downstairs is another open room and space for two or three more bedrooms."

"You are ambitious."

He delivered a devilish smile and raised his brows. "Or realistic."

Her stomach did a somersault, but she wouldn't let him see his effect on her. She rolled her eyes instead and took a bite of some kung pao chicken. Which was pretty fantastic. She took another bite. "Either this is the best Chinese I've had in a while, or I'm insanely hungry."

"Nope. It's pretty good. I'm friends with the owners, actually. They've been in business almost fifteen years."

"I'll have to go there more often."

She must have bit into a pepper because suddenly she was coughing, her eyes watering. Dominic sprang up and headed to the small fridge and grabbed a bottled water. She accepted it gratefully and took giant gulps. He went back to the kitchen and looked into the fridge as her coughing slowed.

"Want a beer?"

She nodded and Dominic grabbed two bottles and returned, settling back on the blanket. He twisted the top off one bottle and handed it to her before doing the same to his. "I hope you don't mind my asking, and if you do, tell me to mind my own business, but...what ever happened between you and Michael. Why'd you two end things?"

Why had *Michael* ended things might be the more appropriate question.

Kate tipped her beer and tasted the yeasty flavor as she mulled it over. She gave Dominic's question another minute of consideration and waited for the usual pain at thinking or discussing this subject.

Nothing. Except a little sadness at remembering the pain it had once caused her. Disappointment. The memory wasn't even as gut-wrenching as it used to be.

She realized he was still watching her and waiting. "It wasn't us, really. We were fine. It was more what Michael and I could never be. What I could never be."

There was a dark glimmer in his eyes, a tightening of his jawline. "What you could never be? What the hell kind of shit is that?"

She leaned back, crossing her legs in front of her to get comfortable. "My family lines don't trace back to the first settlers. I don't have a trust fund that would rival the per capita income of a small third-world country," she offered in explanation. "As I've mentioned before, to Michael's family, just like Payton's, that was important. The lineage most of all. They envisioned vacationing with their in-laws in Kennebunkport with little golden-blond grandchildren running around. Not redheaded rednecks."

"I would hardly call you a redneck," Dominic said, his tone light, but the tightening of his fist belied his real anger.

Unable to keep his gaze, she toyed with the beer bottle, tipping it side to side as she continued. "Michael was okay with it all. At first. But eventually it started to put pressure on our relationship. You probably remember Nicole mentioning the weekend brunch they were going to at his parents' house? That was something I was never privy to in the three years we dated. It reached a head when Michael's sister got engaged to a Huntsman. They fawned all over the happy couple. It wasn't long after that Michael came to realize we just weren't ideal for each other."

"Ideal for each other? What the hell does that mean?" This time he couldn't keep his anger from his voice. "You either love someone or you don't."

"He told me he still loved me. Was in love with me. But we wouldn't work out in the end. That was just over a year ago. Then Nicole started at the firm, and the rest is history."

"What a goddamn coward." Then reaching forward, catching her eye, he added, "I'm sorry, Kate. But what a shit. Not even man enough to break up honorably but instead leads you on to think he loves you except for *your* shortcomings?" His outrage was clear. "He couldn't even take the blame for ending things, pawning it off on his family and you—anywhere but on him, where it belonged." He waited for her to look at him before he continued. "You deserve someone better. Someone who will love and appreciate you for everything you are."

"Sounds nice. You should write Hallmark cards," she said and stood. "Why don't you show me the master bath? I probably should be getting back soon."

"All right," he said, not batting an eye at her obvious change in topic.

He took her through the kitchen first and showed her a laundry room tucked behind it—or what would one day be a laundry room. They hit the small room next with a window overlooking the side of the house and the sloping hill. Then they stepped across the hall to the master room.

She'd been right. It did have an amazing view. Even empty and unfinished, Kate could envision what it would look like someday. And for a moment, she let herself imagine what it would be like to lounge in bed in this room. Naked and with Dominic's warm, tanned skin pressed up against hers, enjoying a postcoital moment as they watched the sunset—or sunrise or rainfall or snowfall—just outside the windows.

The intimacy of it all unnerved her, and she quickly walked out and back to the main room. She stood in front of the fire, her hands raised to its heat. Dominic came to stand next to her, and she forced a smile as she glanced up at him. "Since you're all about prying into my pathetic love life, I think it's only fair that I turn the tables on you. Why is it that you're not already married with a dozen kids tearing this place down?"

"I almost did get married. Once."

She hadn't expected to hear that, and she couldn't keep the surprise from her tone. "You're freaking kidding me. You?"

And then the surprise turned to another emotion, one

that seemed to make her a little queasy.

Dominic had nearly married someone else.

Well, of course. That shouldn't be a big surprise. As she'd already discovered the past few weeks, he was quite the package, and it wasn't like he would have been living like a monk for all these years. So this insane moment of jealousy was absolutely ridiculous.

She hoped she sounded perfectly normal when she asked, "What happened?"

• • •

Dominic considered Kate's question, the same question he'd asked himself for three years. "Fate. When I had to drop out of the architectural program, let's just say Melinda was less than thrilled. We'd been dating about four years by then. And when I couldn't confirm with absolute certainty when and if I was ever going to go back to earn my architectural license, she decided to get out while she could. It was a tough experience, but I'm glad I found out when I did, before we got married, had kids. Now she's in California and married to some banker."

"Melinda was an idiot."

"She was only honest about what she wanted." He shrugged. "Marriage to a carpenter wasn't what she envisioned."

Kate scowled and continued to shake her head, not convinced. She whirled around and stepped into the center of the room and threw her hands out. "This place is amazing. A certificate on the wall wouldn't change your talent." She stopped, and her voice softened as she looked back at him. "But I am sorry, Dominic. That was a shitty thing for her to do."

"Well, like I said, it was a long time ago. I won't deny that it about broke me once, but with time, I've gotten over it and come to realize what a close call the whole thing was. She did me a favor."

"Even without a degree, you've accomplished so much." She stepped over to the window and looked out. With her face in profile, he studied the soft curve of her neck, the fullness of her lips as she considered her next words. "Do you think you'll ever go back to school and work on getting your license?"

His hackles raised, which was unfair, he knew. But going back to school had been such a point of contention with Melinda, he couldn't help but feel weary when he heard the inquiry. "Cruz thinks I should. To get on with my life. He thinks I've given up on it because of hurt feelings from Melinda. Throwing the baby out with the bathwater, so to speak. But it's not like that. I love the freelance jobs I've taken on, including yours. And with Benny on my back about this website—Sorensen Restoration, she wants to call it—well, I may not pull in as much as if I had an architectural license, but it might be enough for me. It makes me happy." And it did.

She sighed wistfully. "It would be nice to have that freedom. To do what makes you happy without concern for the financial risk or loss."

Relief flooded through him as he started to understand why she'd asked. Then he thought of what she'd said. Being happy. Having freedom. It was a curious statement from someone who seemed to have every reason to be happy. Her attention still outside, she watched a bird dive for cover from a branch.

Unable to resist, he took a few steps toward her until he was standing behind her, his breath so close to her neck that she had to feel it. Sense his proximity. Sure enough, he saw goose bumps rise on her skin, and she shivered. He wanted to reach out, wrap his arms around her. Tell her she deserved to be happy. Comfort her. But he kept his hands fisted at his sides.

His voice was thick with emotion when he finally spoke. "Whatever you do, Kate, make sure you never settle for anyone who doesn't show you in every breath, every word, every touch that he loves and adores you every day of his life."

She turned then, her eyes gray and dark like the skies outside. But there was a fierce yearning in their depths, and he knew that to take this next step might be dangerous to their friendship. But right at that moment, he didn't care.

He needed to feel those lips under his again. Feel her give way to the pressure of his own mouth as she had that evening at his parents'. When it was hard to miss the heat and attraction that burned like fire.

When her gaze dropped to his mouth, he was lost.

• • •

The moment Dominic stepped close enough she could feel his breath on the sensitive skin of her neck, it was as if every nerve ending in her body was sizzling with heat and wanting. Now, as he stood just inches from her, studying what felt like every breath she took, she felt like she was going to burn up with the heat that seemed to surround him.

She looked into those brilliant blue eyes that held a promise in them that she was almost afraid to ask for. Then she studied him with the same intensity, and she longed to reach up and touch the strong curve of his jaw, already peppered with bristly hair, just to see what it felt like. To feel the fine lines around his eyes and his mouth that she looked to next. Lines that told her Dominic smiled more times in his life than he'd frowned.

She waited for him to step away, to break the moment, but he didn't move. His gaze dropped to her mouth, and she caught her breath, suddenly terrified and also exhilarated at the prospect that he might kiss her again. Then he took an almost impossibly closer step toward her and she couldn't breathe at all anymore as her heart lurched in her chest. She tried to steady the pounding that hammered loudly in her ears.

His lips grazed against hers, soft. Almost like a whisper, and her belly twisted as a warm rush of wanting flooded through her. Wanting more. Of him, of his kisses…

She willed herself to keep her eyes open. Not wanting to miss the emotions that might play on his solemn face. She wondered if he could read the panic in her thoughts that he would do it again—or worse, that he wouldn't.

Then it seemed to hit her. The ball was in her court. She needed to decide what she wanted—he was giving her a choice here. Easier than any words, she let him know what she wanted as she raised her lips to his and breathed in his musky, intoxicating scent. The pressure was harder this time as their lips touched, and the stubble around his chin bristled against her skin. The slight sting was offset by the tingling pressure building south of her belly. Her hands gripped his shoulders, so firm and warm. His scent surrounded her, and she brought him farther into her mouth, feeling his tongue, his heat.

This was Dominic.

A man who would show a woman what forever meant. Who would love and cherish her, give her a family and a home and the most thrilling love that would claim her each and every day.

But...it was like a big flashing light was going off in her head.

A family? Kids? She had other goals, other things she had always wanted to accomplish. A partnership to earn and eventually a judgeship. The large house filled with kids and a dog and cat—they weren't anywhere on her horizon.

She had never wanted them. Those things had never seemed important before.

Not like they were to Dominic.

And to continue to kiss him, to encourage this thing between them, would be doing him a disservice. She'd be no better than Melinda.

Because as much as they might want each other right now, need each other, the hard truth was in front of her.

They didn't want the same things. They had different futures ahead of them.

She opened her eyes and stepped back, creating distance from this warm, strong man who only wanted to love her. She had to catch her breath.

"What was that?" she whispered. Her hands went to her mouth, still tingling.

He smiled. "Think that was what they call a kiss."

"I know it was a kiss, but... No. It can't happen. *This*

can't happen."

He didn't seem offended or alarmed by her reaction, more amused as he leaned back against the window. "It could happen. Let's be truthful. We both want it."

"But it would be a mistake. You and me?" She pressed her palms against the sides of her jeans, trying to collect her thoughts. Reason with him. Help him see that, rationally, this was a very bad idea. "We're just so...different. After everything we talked about, our past relationships, going forward with this would be continuing the mistakes of our past." Her voice had raised a couple octaves, sounding as panicked as she felt. "Getting mixed up with someone who doesn't share the same goals. Doesn't want the same things. It would be a mistake."

"I'm pretty sure you and I want the same thing," he said in a teasing voice, unfazed by her words.

"Yes. *Now*. But in a few months, when I'm working sixty-plus hours, day and night, even into the weekends, are you going to still feel the same way? When you're filling these beautiful rooms with furniture and wallpaper, you're also going to be envisioning the children that will live in these rooms and the love and laughter you'll share with your wife, waiting at home for you. Maybe even a dog or two. And that's just—it's just not me."

Hell, that wasn't true.

Her heart, her gut, told her she wanted it so much it scared the ever-living crap out of her.

But it was her head that reminded her of the foolishness of her thoughts. And tasked her with sticking to the promise she'd made for herself long ago. The plan she had for her life.

She was going to be someone. Someone important and

relevant, and no one was ever going to make her feel like she was nothing. That she was trailer trash.

But it was as if he wasn't listening, or didn't want to. He only smiled at her, almost indulgently. "I'm not asking you to marry me, Kate. But ever since you threw open your car door that day, looking so damned cute and ornery, I've wanted to pull that red hair of yours from the tight knot at the back of your head and spread it out around your shoulders. Feel its heat in my hands. And having known you and already tasted you, I can say with certainty I only want you more. I want to see and touch and love every part of you. What's so wrong with that?"

Kate couldn't deny the shiver of anticipation that ran through her at the thought of Dominic's soft lips, that hot mouth, on her. "I just—I'm just not the type who does the casual sex thing. I want to know I'm in a relationship with someone that can go somewhere because we're compatible. Want the same things."

His hand reached out to touch her jaw, his thumb sliding along the edge, and she couldn't deny the havoc the slight touch was causing her. "That you've got wrong, Kate. We do want the same things. We both want each other and that— for now—is good enough for me."

She stared into his blue eyes, so open and warm. It would be so easy to give in to the emotions he was stirring up.

And, Lord…that kiss.

He started to lean forward, as if reading her hesitancy for acceptance.

No.

No. She shook her head emphatically. She couldn't do that. She couldn't play with fire like that, not with her emotions.

Not with his. Not when she knew nothing could ever come of it. She had to be rational.

"I'm sorry, Dominic." This time she turned toward the kitchen area, needing to put distance between them. "It just wouldn't be a good idea."

He sighed heavily and gave her a wry smile, tinged with sadness. "You're the boss."

Needing to focus on something other than Dominic, she pressed the lids down over the food cartons. In a few minutes, the food was back in the bag and the empty beer bottles discarded in a recycle bin in the corner of the room. She looked around her and outside at the dark skies again. A darkness that seemed to match her spirits.

He followed her gaze outside. "Don't think it's going to let up. Might as well make a run for it."

By the time they reached the truck, they were both soaked through. Even the heat blaring from the truck as they wound their way back down the canyon couldn't warm the chill settling in her bones.

Over her heart.

An overwhelming sense of sadness crept over her.

When they pulled up in her driveway, she was trying to think of something to say to ease the discomforting silence that had surrounded them for the past half hour.

"I think I'll call it a day. I just have a few things I need to grab, and I'll be out of your hair," he said and pushed the truck door open.

Dominic already had the front door open and was starting up the stairs by the time she reached the threshold. Oscar darted in and nearly tripped her.

"You hungry, kitty?" She flipped on the lights and

sidestepped the persistent cat on her way into the kitchen. She could hear Dominic overhead.

This is what she wanted. This was smart. This was protecting both of their hearts.

But…it had felt nice being held, even briefly, in his arms. And then there was the hot, pulsating need his kiss had stirred that, even now, standing before the hideous blue wallpaper of her kitchen, hadn't diminished.

What would it be like, to be with him?

Wonderful. Mind-blowing.

God. Was she being foolish? Being with Dominic made her feel so…alive. Vibrant. Wanted.

The unmistakable sound of his boots trudging back down the stairs told her he was done. He was leaving. She had to go out there and see him again. Say good-bye. It would be weird if she didn't. Would he see the doubt in her eyes? The crumbling of her earlier resolution?

He stood there. Staring at her, his arms laden with his stuff. "I'll be back tomorrow to get started on priming the walls in the bathroom, not to mention the kitchen, since your cabinets could be arriving any day."

She nodded. He looked like he was already over it. They could have been discussing going to a movie, not making love, for all the effect her denial seemed to have on him. "Let yourself in if I'm not here, since I might go see my grams a little earlier than usual," she said and opened the door for him. The pungent, damp air rushed against her face. "Well, good night. And thanks for showing me your house. It's beautiful."

"'Night, Kate," he said and nodded, his face now cast in shadows as she stood on the porch.

Stay was what she really wanted to say.

Instead, before she could change her mind, she pushed the door closed behind him and leaned against it for support. The sound of the truck door creaking open and slamming shut caused a deep ache in her belly.

What she needed was a long, hot bath. That was safe.

The door pounded at her back, and hope and terror both burgeoned in her heart.

Steady.

But her hands trembled as she opened the door.

And there he was. Standing there, water dripping from his hair, his chin, his arms. Just staring at her for a long agonizing moment.

Then he was rushing toward her, and she was wrapping her arms around his broad shoulders, pulling him against her as tight as he was pulling her so she could feel his heart thumping through his damp shirt, beating almost as rapidly as her own. And his mouth, so hot still, was on hers. His hands pressing against her buttocks, pulling her even closer.

It felt so good, so right.

He kicked the door shut and pressed her against the wall. Kate's leg wrapped around his and he pressed closer, his need for contact as consuming as hers. She couldn't hold him close enough. His fingers tugged at the hem of her shirt, and he pulled it over her head in a smooth movement, and together they did the same with his.

Hot desperation surged through her. She wanted to feel every inch of him on her. To hold him.

Strong arms anchored her to him, grasping her hips tightly, and her legs wrapped higher around him. Dominic carried her to the center of the room, where he sank to his knees and laid her on the couch.

For a brief second she tried to remember whether she'd shut the drapes. Then his mouth was on her and she stopped caring.

He looked up then, meeting her gaze, and she sucked in her breath.

There was a promise in those kind blue eyes. Then her head lolled back in pleasure.

Just for this moment, this night, she was going to let him be her forever. She was going to pretend they had a whole future together. In that beautiful house filled with bright-eyed, mischievous kids with Dominic's smile and spirit.

Just for tonight.

Then he was stretching out on top of her, kissing her and loving her until she forgot everything else. Except to feel.

Chapter Fifteen

Kate stirred in Dominic's arms, pulling him from the sleep that had finally taken them both sometime during the night. Faint morning light streamed into her front room, and he guessed it to be close to seven. They were lying naked on top of the couch, the back cushions tossed to the floor to give them space.

Damn. The fantasies he'd had about this couch…they'd probably run through about half of them. He smiled. There were still a few more. He looked at the woman asleep in the crook of his arm.

Peaceful. Beautiful. He supposed he could let her sleep a little longer.

His thoughts turned to last night. What the hell had they done? What the hell had *he* done? She'd made it clear that she didn't want anything more from him except his friendship. That she had other priorities in her life. That he wasn't part of her plan.

And of course there was the fact that he wasn't Michael. Couldn't offer her the same things as his royal highness.

But none of that had mattered when she'd looked at him like she had, and he'd inhaled her scent, watched her lips open, wanting him to kiss them. He had only wanted to be with her.

And now they were going to be back to square one. Except...

He wasn't convinced that there wasn't something there between them. Kate had wanted him as much as he'd wanted her. He still wanted her.

She stirred and nuzzled deeper into his arm. He sensed the moment when she realized where she was, as she seemed to hold her breath a real long time. Her eyes opened slowly. Awareness hitting her.

"You're awake."

She glanced down at how she was pressed against his side and then looked furtively around the room, probably for something to cover herself. Her eyes widened when she looked outside, surprised at either the promise of sun this cool autumn day after yesterday's rainfall—or the fact they'd done what they had with the drapes wide-open.

He grinned. He'd bet on the latter.

Jumping up, she grabbed her T-shirt from the floor and threw it on, then slid into her black cotton panties. He sat back and watched, enjoying the show. Half dressed, she raced to the curtains and pulled them shut. Her shoulders dropped with some relief. Then she raised her head again. And stood there awkwardly.

"Come here."

She walked more shyly back to him and sat primly on

the edge of the couch. Cute.

In one quick motion, he pulled her back so she was lying on top of him. "Morning."

And before she could speak the objection already forming on her mouth, he pressed his mouth to hers. For a few seconds, Kate's lips were soft under his. But then just as quick, she tensed and her eyes fluttered open. And she pulled away from his kiss.

Her eyes were gray and held uncertainty as they gazed into his. "Dominic—"

Before she could finish, he headed her off. "I'm going to grab that Chinese food from the truck. I'm famished."

She blinked and sat up as he stood and pulled his jeans on. She looked momentarily confused. "It sat in your truck all night. It can't still be good."

"Since it dropped down to thirty overnight, I think we're safe."

"Your funeral. I'll go start the coffee."

Kate was pressing the start button on the coffeemaker when he set the bag of leftover Chinese food on the counter. Her hair was a sexy mess as it fell around her shoulders, and he remembered its texture and softness. His fingers itched to touch it again.

Kate turned around, chewing at her bottom lip, and her eyes stared, beseeching, at him. "You didn't see Glenda outside, did you? I don't know what she's going to think of me if she knew I spent the night with her nephew."

"Nah. Didn't see her." He didn't think it would be a good time to mention Glenda was an early riser, probably up two hours ago, her morning paper—which he'd noticed was absent her doorstep—likely spread on the kitchen table as she sipped from her mug of tea.

She nodded. "Good. For all she knows, you arrived early to get started on the bathroom."

"Probably." *But unlikely.*

With the coffee brewed and poured into mugs, they stretched out on the couch again, their feast spread around them. Kate took a bite of lo mein. "I think we need to talk about what happened last night."

"I am sure you do." He grabbed the carton of sweet-and-sour pork and grabbed a fork. "But is there any chance we might agree, just this once, not to talk about it? To just let things happen as they might. No second-guessing our choices. I had a good time last night, and I'm pretty certain that you had just as much fun." He looked over and got some satisfaction at seeing her blush. Again.

She set the food down and met his gaze again, still flushed but determined. "I meant what I said. Nothing has changed. And I think that it's best if what happened last night — "

"And early this morning," he added, not able to stop himself.

She paused and this time her cheeks looked like they were scorching her, because if he wasn't mistaken, the second time they'd made love just before dawn, *she'd* been the one to initiate it.

She tried again. "What happened between us should just be chalked up to poor judgment. Something we shouldn't let happen again. Because I really like having you in my life right now and I'd hate to do anything that would make it impossible for us to continue to be friends. Okay?"

He wasn't going to argue. It would be pointless. Instead he was going to show her in the coming days and weeks that he wasn't going anywhere. That her future could be whatever she wanted it to be, whether with him or someone else.

That it wasn't decided for her.

So he sighed heavily, making it look like he was giving in. He could pretend if that made her happy. "Okay."

"Good." She nodded again in agreement and picked up her food again, probably feeling back in control again. "I should probably hurry and get showered. I want to get up to my grams's house and back in time to get that work done I missed yesterday." She paused and looked over toward the dining room, where her stuff was still lying out. "I can't wait for this one to be over."

He hated how she almost sounded defeated as she said that. He put the now empty carton on the table and grabbed the rest of the lo mein that Kate had left. "I probably will need to clear out of here by five if I'm going to make it on time to my parents' for dinner. Should I assume you won't be able to make it tonight?"

"Shoot. That's right. Your dad's getting released today." Her brow furrowed and he could see the stress surround her eyes. "I wish I could go with you, but Daisy's temporary hearing for support and custody is tomorrow afternoon, and Mark's deposition begins Tuesday, so I'm going to be swamped. But let them know I can't wait for Thanksgiving."

"I'll tell them you'll be there with bells on."

She stood, modesty taking over again as she pulled the T-shirt down over her hips. "Guess I better go jump in the shower and get going."

Images flooded through his mind of what she looked like under that formfitting T-shirt, the sounds she'd made as he nuzzled her, the line of moles on her belly that he'd traced down with his fingers and then tongue before she pulled at this hair in frustration and pleasure...

"Yeah," he rasped, grabbing his coffee from the table. "You'd better."

• • •

Kate had a hard time dragging herself out of bed Monday morning. She spent half of Sunday night and early this morning remembering Dominic's touch and how for those moments she'd never felt so happy and alive. She'd spent the other half second-guessing her decision not to fall into bed with him again.

Which was why today she had less than two hours of sleep to go on and a week from hell to look forward to. Most particularly having to look into Ms. Herrera's eyes as she sat through Mark McKenna's depositions on Tuesday, seeing her anger and hurt and need for justice even though Kate knew that things weren't looking so good for her at this point.

Seeing Mark's smug face because he knew the same thing.

Not to mention the mind-numbing hours reviewing the testimony with Nicole to make sure everything they'd heard from Ms. Herrera's deposition lined up with the facts they wanted to glean from Mark.

There were four voice messages waiting for her when she arrived in the office. Including a message from Ava Herrera's attorney saying that he had recently attained some discoverable evidence that he'd have dropped off later that day.

How convenient. Was it an accident that they'd waited

until after her deposition and just before Mark was scheduled for his testimony? But the rules of civil procedure were pretty generous in this respect, and it wasn't worth trying to object to the late admittance. If there was anything they wanted to address with Ms. Herrera, they'd schedule a follow-up later.

Kate picked up her extension and dialed her assistant. "Trish? Ms. Herrera's attorney is sending some documents over today. Keep an eye out for them and let me know the moment they come in. I have to run out soon for the hearing on Daisy's divorce case but should be back around two."

"Sure, Kate. I also stuck several invoices that have come in on the McKenna matter for your approval."

"I'll start looking through them now. Thanks."

Kate hung up and found the stack of invoices in her basket and scanned them.

Wait. This couldn't be right.

Kate glanced down through the invoices again. The Radisson had sent them a bill for $24.95, the cost for copying and mailing a video dated…two weeks ago. On the McKenna matter.

After a few more minutes of looking up a number for the Radisson, Kate reached the billing person listed on the receipt.

"Right." The woman said as she shuffled through some papers. "It was for that security footage you requested a couple months ago. Our tech guys were able to retrieve the information you were looking for."

Where the heck was it, then? "Great, but for whatever reason, it didn't seem to reach my desk. Would it be possible to resend that again? Of course, we'll reimburse you for both copies."

"Certainly, Ms. Matthews. I'll FedEx it to you today."

Kate hung up the phone and stared at the bill. She picked up the phone again. "Hey, Trish. Do you remember seeing a video—I'm guessing maybe a thumb drive or DVD—arrive from the Radisson recently? It was for the McKenna case."

"No. I haven't. But if it was for McKenna, all documents have been flagged to first go through Tim's office."

Since when? How come she hadn't realized this? "Hmm, okay. Maybe I'll check with his assistant and see if she remembers anything. Thanks, Trish. I'm running out now, but keep me updated the moment those other documents arrive."

· · ·

Kate followed Daisy out of the courtroom and found a bench in the hallway to discuss what had just happened.

"You can breathe, Daisy," she said and smiled to try and comfort the woman, whose face was still pale and tense. "The commissioner has pretty much signed off on everything we asked for. Leo has to start sending money for you and the kids. This is good."

Daisy nodded and breathed out slowly. "It was just seeing him again. So smug and cocky. And to tell the truth, it was an eye-opening experience. For the first time, I could see him for the man he's become—not anywhere near the man I first met and fell in love with. He's different. And so am I."

Kate nodded, agreeing with Daisy's assessment of her future ex-husband. Attractive but with an unmistakable oily quality about him, Leo had certainly been smug. She placed her hand on Daisy's shoulder. "And soon you can move on. He'll still have visitation rights with the kids."

Daisy smiled sadly. "I would love it if he would exercise his visitation rights. The kids—mostly Paul—really miss him. Even though the past months he's been so absent, this not seeing him at all or knowing if they would has taken a toll. I'm just glad their uncles have been making efforts to include them. It's helped them."

Yeah. Dominic was a really good guy like that. He loved those kids, no doubt about it. And he would never skip out on his kids like Leo had. He was a good man. *Too* good for Kate.

"I'll start drawing up the order now for the commissioner's signature. In the meantime, you call me with any questions you have, okay?"

Kate waved good-bye to Daisy and was scanning her phone for any messages when she heard her name called. She looked up to find an old friend heading her way. An attractive woman in her forties with short, sandy-blond hair and shrewd brown eyes, Jessica walked with purpose down the hall.

"Hey, stranger," Jessica said and slid onto the bench next to Kate. "It's been a while since I've seen you in this part of the building."

"I'm handling a family law case pro bono. Custody, spousal support, the whole complicated mess."

"Since when does Strauss farm you out for free?" Jessica smiled. Kate had had run up against Jessica on a dozen cases over the past few years since starting at Strauss and had grown to respect the no-nonsense woman. Jessica was not only a partner at a small employment law firm that focused on plaintiffs' rights, but also a well-respected member of the legal community.

"It's for a friend. But I could ask the same from you. What're you doing over here?"

Jessica grinned. "We all love to take the meaty employment cases and take all your clients to task, but they don't pay the bills—at least not on a regular basis. Family law and wills and estate matters are the bread and butter at a small to midsize firm. Only we get to pick and choose which cases we take. So, how are you doing these days, Kate? I haven't seen you for a while. Still working with Tim?"

"I do," Kate said and laughed when Jessica smiled at her with sympathy. Jessica had worked with Tim at Strauss and Fletcher years before Kate arrived. In fact, both Jessica and Tim had been in the running for the same position. Tim had ended up with the honor and a year later, Jessica Lund had left Strauss to join Price Bennett, now renamed Price Bennett & Lund. Jessica and Tim did not get on, Kate had gleaned over the years. "Don't look like that. Tim can be a stickler for details and is maybe a bit of a micromanager, but I've learned a lot. In fact, he recently recommended me for a junior partner."

Jessica's smile turned speculative. "I'm not surprised. You deserve it. If I didn't think so, I wouldn't have been trying so hard to get you to jump ship for the past couple of years. It's about time they appreciated what they had in you."

"Thanks, Jessica. That really means a lot coming from you."

"Let me know if you ever decide to change your mind. Come and be a David against those big Goliath clients of yours."

Kate laughed again and rolled her eyes. "You'll be the first to know if I ever do."

. . .

Just after four o'clock, Ms. Herrera's documents arrived. With her breath held, Kate hastily skimmed the pages.

Most of the documents weren't terribly harmful to their case. Except for two recently dated affidavits, which stated, in short, that despite her client's insistence there were no previous complaints similar in nature filed against Mark, two former employees would say otherwise.

Kate's earlier unease began to grow to a near panic, and she reluctantly picked up the phone to call Nicole and Tim.

"We'll object to their admission and any testimony Mark gives about it," Nicole said dismissively half an hour later and dropped her copies on to the desk before glancing over for Tim's reaction. "And the other women's claims are barred by the statute of limitations, so they can't be added as parties to the lawsuit."

The crackle from the speaker, where Mark and the CFO of McKenna were conferenced in, drew their attention. Mark cleared his voice. "Look. I have nothing to hide. Those two women were some of the worst employees we've ever hired. They never could do their jobs right and if I so much as corrected them, they cried foul. I never laid a finger on them. They conspired to make those stories up to try and hurt me. This is nothing more than a witch hunt."

"So these two women did file complaints against you?" Kate asked, unable to keep her frustration and anger from her voice. Tim, who had remained silent so far, looked at her sharply.

"Give us a minute, please." Kate recognized the voice as

Jonathon's, the CFO of McKenna.

There was a long pause and then silence as the client muted the speaker to confer. Another minute passed and Mark came back on. "As best as I can recall, I think one of the women had been upset with a performance evaluation and felt she had earned a higher score. So she complained to Kathy about it. When nothing came of it, she claimed sexual harassment."

"Okay. I think I understand," Tim said in his usual firm voice. "Why don't you see if you guys can find any more documents about this complaint and get those to us ASAP. Unless you guys feel differently, I'm confident in going forward as scheduled. The sooner this is done, the sooner we can make a motion for summary judgment and get it dismissed."

Tim paused as the two men on the other line agreed. It was hard to miss the way Tim's gaze had rested on Kate at that last part. *The sooner this is wrapped up, the better.* No more delays and last-minute surprise documents.

"Sounds good, Tim," Mark said. "I'm really relieved to hear you're going to be around tomorrow. Thanks for your insight, Nicole. Kate," he finished a little more stiffly.

"I don't think he's telling us everything," Kate said when the call was disconnected. "I have a bad feeling about proceeding with this when we don't know what's going to come out."

"Just because they find a couple of bitter and disgruntled former employees doesn't mean we throw in the towel," Nicole said.

"I think this is more than that, and I don't think Mark's leveling with us here, and if he can't level with us, then—"

"Nicole," Tim finally said. "Can you give me a minute

alone to talk with Kate, please?"

Nicole cut her gaze to Kate. "Sure, Tim. I'll wait in my office."

After Nicole closed the door behind her, Kate spoke. "Tim, I know Mark's a friend and all, but I'm not so sure if—"

Tim raised his hand, stopping her. "Kate. I usually respect your professionalism. Your ability to see through the crap to the legal argument you usually hit so eloquently. But today, how you spoke to your client—our client—was disappointing. It was disrespectful."

Kate felt like he'd slapped her. "Tim, for months I've asked Mark and his staff to provide me any information, any names or details of complaints they'd received over the years against Mark. I was told repeatedly I had everything. The fact that Mark isn't really even surprised by these allegations and *now* remembers one of these other complaints tells me they haven't been up front with me. How can I put on the best defense when they're holding back?"

"Come on, Kate. You know most of the time our clients walk the line on what's the truth, what to come forward with, hoping against hope that if they forget something, everyone else will, too. That's why we don't really prod their memory too carefully. From what I've seen of this case, Mark and the company haven't done anything that can't be salvaged. If you have your head on straight and can stay focused on what really matters, that is."

She bristled at his tone. "I'm thinking quite clearly, Tim. I don't think Mark is the best guy to be laying our bets on."

"You say you're focused on what really matters?" Tim tented his fingers in front of his mouth and paused, almost melodramatically. "How about this pro bono case you spent the afternoon at? The afternoon when you should have been prepping with Nicole on this deposition. Can you really tell me your priorities are where they should be, Kate? You know, once you're a partner—if you're made partner—you're going to need to figure out where your time and resources are best spent for the good of the firm. And hours of lost billable time on a messy custody battle is not one of them."

"I've always thought that this firm found that public service to the community was invaluable, too. Are you saying you don't want me to help this woman anymore?" It took effort, but she managed to keep her voice even and respectful.

"I'm not telling you anything, Kate. Just be aware that everything you do—and don't do—will be considered at the quarterly meeting. And the most important thing you can do is make sure you get this McKenna matter nailed. No mistakes. No loose ends."

For a moment, Kate remembered the missing video and an alarming thought occurred to her. Had Tim known about it and intentionally hidden evidence? He wanted to win this case, whatever the cost. She considered broaching it but realized that would be stupid. Until she actually knew what was on that video—possibly nothing—then she couldn't make such an accusation.

But the thought remained.

Tim came to his feet and moved toward the door. "Tomorrow you have an opportunity to turn this around." He paused and turned around and met her gaze. "Show me that I wasn't wrong to bet on you, Kate. To trust you're capable of handling this job and the other responsibilities that would be yours if you should make partner."

She swallowed and nodded. "Of course, Tim. You can count on me."

Chapter Sixteen

Dominic was in the kitchen painting when he heard the front door shut late Monday night. A moment later he sensed Kate standing in the doorway, but she didn't say anything, possibly taking in today's progress. He was working on the last coat of the soft buttery-yellow paint she'd chosen, a choice that reflected the brightness and warmth of the room—and the client.

"How long you going to stand there checking out my ass?" he asked finally.

But instead of shooting him the usual quick comeback, she stayed quiet another minute. "Just appreciating everything you've done. It looks great."

"Since your cabinets could come in soon, I thought it would be a good idea to get this finished before I started reworking the floors upstairs." He turned to look at her, noticing the tension in her forehead and shoulders, the tightness around her lips. "Hey. Everything okay?"

"It's gone better." She paused, as if considering whether or not to confide in him.

He smiled at her. "I'll sign a waiver of confidentiality if you like. But either way, you know you can tell me anything in confidence."

He climbed down from the stool and grabbed them both a beer and brought her to the other room and sat her down on the couch. After some more coercing, she finally spilled, telling him her concerns over the case and the recent discovery of missing evidence and conference call with the client. Finally she mentioned the possibility that her boss might be hiding evidence on the case that would show the truth on a major issue of contention.

"And the thing is," Kate said, "I get the feeling there's even more I don't know. And I don't like it."

Dominic didn't have much patience for companies that thought they were above the law. There were a lot of things he wanted to say, but he exercised restraint instead. "If your clients aren't going to be forthcoming with you, then they're the ones sabotaging their case. Not you. You may lose this one, but I'm sure there will be others."

"There may be others, but *this* is the one that will decide my promotion to partner now. Something I've been working for since day one at Strauss," she added and raised her chin almost stubbornly.

"I'm sorry, Kate. For what it's worth, I think your cautiousness is appropriate under the circumstances, and if they can't appreciate your concerns, then they're the ones making the mistake. But you also have to ask yourself what's going to happen if you find out Tim is holding onto this evidence. Can you work at a place that would try and bury the truth?"

A more appropriate question might be...would she want to? A question he wasn't sure he wanted the answer to.

She bristled and straightened. "You don't seem to understand everything that's at stake here, Dominic. I've been working years to be at the place I am now, poised for this partnership, and in another five years, I'll be ready to step into a senior partner position and, if I've played my cards right, a position as a state or maybe even a federal judge. Everything I ever wanted." She brought her hands to her temples and rubbed them. "You make it sound like the answer is so easy, but as I see it, the answer is to keep the status quo and reach my dream or lose everything."

He paused, not wanting to push her away, but needing to give her another perspective. "Is there no other path for you? Is this judgeship the only thing that you want? I've let this go before, but what's so wrong with having other goals? Like a job that makes you actually happy? That doesn't demand all your time and attention but lets you enjoy other interests, too. Interests like, maybe..." He paused, realizing he was putting out more than a mere suggestion with his next comment. "A husband you can share your life with? Who'll be at your side to hold your hand as you make your way through life? Experience it alongside you."

Her shoulders sank. "You just don't understand. You've never had people tell you to your face every day since you were a kid that you weren't good enough. That you don't matter. All I've wanted is to show them all that I do matter. That my opinions are worth something. That *I'm* worth something."

"But you already are." Unable to stop himself, he sank

to his knees next to her, taking her hands in his. "You matter to me and all the people who really care for you. You're so passionate and loyal to the people and causes you care about. You're not only smart and funny but beautiful and witty. Who the hell cares what the Michaels and the Ms. Vaughns of this world think? You have a lot to offer this world and you should do it, but on your terms."

She smiled wryly and met his gaze, steady. "It's easy for you to give advice, but how about taking a little of what you're dishing out? How long are you going to hide out at your family construction company? How long are you going to settle for getting by instead of taking the steps you need to be happy? To fulfill your dreams? That's what I'm doing and I have been doing for the past ten years, maybe longer. I'm not going to settle for less."

Her words hit him like a bat to the back of the head. He wasn't hiding, was he? Then the last part of what she said sank in.

She wouldn't settle for less.

Was family, a husband to support and love you, a different career path short of a judgeship…was that settling for less? It ripped at his heart to think she felt like that. He looked again into her eyes to see the truth, but she would no longer meet his gaze, instead staring at the wall behind him.

She pulled her hands from his. "I'm sorry, Dominic. I'm kind of tired tonight. If you don't mind, I think I'm going to take a bath and get some sleep. I have a long day ahead of me."

He stood, knowing when he was dismissed. "Sure, Kate. I understand. But I'm here if you ever need someone to talk to."

Dominic returned to the kitchen to finish and clean up. He had tried to sound unaffected, upbeat, even. But what he felt was frustration and disappointment. That Kate couldn't see what she had in front of her, all the opportunities. Opportunities that might also include…him.

But what could he offer her? In some ways, he and Kate were more alike than she realized. Neither of them had an illustrious name, hefty bank accounts and trust funds, or the social connections that Michael had or that Melinda had wanted. They both knew what it felt like to not be enough.

The difference between them, though, was he didn't care about those things. But it was beginning to hit him that to Kate, it meant a lot.

And maybe that was the biggest truth of all. He could never be Michael. He couldn't give her the things that Michael could. The things that she seemed to want.

. . .

Dominic got off the phone Wednesday evening, exhilaration puffing his chest. Hell, he should have created a webpage months ago. Having taken Benny's—and Kate's—words to heart, he'd stayed up Monday night and well into Tuesday morning working on his own webpage. It hadn't been nearly as difficult as he'd imagined. And twenty hours after taking his webpage live, he'd just had his first inquiry from a potential client.

Normally he would have been at Kate's right now, doing little odds and ends as they talked or worked in companionable silence together. But since the bathrooms were finished and the kitchen painted, there wasn't anything more to do until the cabinets arrived.

And it wasn't like she wanted to see him right now anyhow.

She'd make that clear when she texted him yesterday to say she was working late the next couple nights and if she didn't see him before then, she'd see him on Thanksgiving.

Well, she could hide all she wanted, for now. But he'd see her tomorrow, Thanksgiving Day, and he'd remind her how good they could be. How happy she was when she was with him. How happy he was with her.

But she'd been right. He had needed to take some of the advice he was giving out so freely and make some tough choices of his own. He'd planned on waiting until after Thanksgiving to break the news to his dad, but he'd only been putting off the inevitable discussion, and he wasn't going to do that anymore. It was time to embrace life. Take those risks.

And he was going to start right now. He grabbed the keys to his truck, already lighter at the prospect of talking to his dad.

It was time.

It was a bit of a shock to see his dad sitting at the kitchen table with Cruz when he arrived at his parents' house just after seven. He'd grown so used to seeing him lying in bed when Dominic's mom wasn't railing on him to join everyone for dinner that he'd forgotten how reassuring it could be to see him in good health. His bathrobe was hopefully permanently retired.

He looked up now and smiled when he saw his son.

"Dominic. Nice to see you."

Dominic shared an incredulous look with his brother, who gave a slight nod of assurance. "Dad. You look great." And he did. The usual gray pallor that had shadowed his face these past few years was gone, as was the fear in his eyes when he looked at his family. Like he was going to lose them any moment. "How you feeling?"

Petter Sorensen nodded, his blue eyes free from fear now. "Like a new man. And happy to see both of my sons making unexpected visits."

Dominic looked down at the papers in front of the men and the Cruz's laptop open in front of their dad. "Yeah. What's going on here?"

"Wanted to fill Dad in on the recent progress with the company. And show him some ideas I've been working on."

Dominic nodded. Cruz had been tied up in as many knots as Dominic these past few months, anxious to talk to Dad about plans for the future. The difference being that Cruz's plans included further involvement with the company and further growth—while Dominic's were to hopefully make his escape. From the slight creases in Cruz's eyes and slight turnup of the lips, things had gone well. He was almost smiling. "And what do you think?" he asked, taking a seat at the table.

"I think Cruz has his work cut out for him. And he's ready to take the lead. Which, surprisingly, is something of a relief. You boys have done a great job of holding things down these past three years. It's really set my mind at ease."

His dad looked so happy. Proud. And Dominic's stomach tightened at the thought of disappointing him. "It was the least we could do for you, Dad. Which is kind of something

I wanted to talk to you about today."

Cruz sat back, clearly knowing what was coming as he gave his brother another reassuring nod. His dad just waited, mildly curious.

"You know how much I love working with you and the company," Dominic started. "Stepping back in a few years ago was something I was more than happy to do. You needed me. And don't get me wrong, I've loved my time there, working with Cruz and all the men I've known practically my entire life, but…well. I just think it might be a good time for me to get back to what I was doing before. Renovating houses, designing things. Maybe start my own business. And as you can see, Cruz has things well in hand."

His father had crossed his arms during this litany and now studied him quietly. The clock above the stove ticked loudly in the quiet of the room. Then his face broke out in a grin, and his blue eyes twinkled. "What took you so long?"

Dominic blinked a few times. Wait. His dad not only didn't sound surprised, but he sounded like he'd just been waiting for Dominic to make the announcement. "You're okay with it then? You're not upset?"

His dad actually chuckled. "Hardly. I can't tell you how much it meant to me when you dropped everything and jumped in when you did. All of you. I count my blessings each day. And I can't wait to see what you can do now that you're ready to get out on your own. Maybe with a certain someone next to you for support?"

Kate. Right. His pretend girlfriend whom he no longer wanted to pretend with. Having her at this side, supporting him through this new endeavor, would make him feel invincible. But that possibility was looking more and more bleak of late.

"Maybe" was all he said, though. Not yet ready to confess the whole thing was a farce.

He still had hope.

. . .

Kate looked at her watch as she reached the front steps of Dominic's parents' house and breathed a sigh of relief. Ten minutes to spare.

She had seriously underestimated the time it would take to visit her grams, dig out the old recipe for the sweet potato casserole, and put it together. Not helped by the last-minute return trip to the grocery store when she'd realized she should have drained the can of yams *before* she mixed everything up. Her dish now actually looked and smelled pretty good, kind of surprising even her. She just hoped it *tasted* as good as it smelled.

Kate reached the front door and took some deep, even breaths to calm her nerves. Not just at seeing Dominic's family, but at seeing him. She'd been avoiding him for the past few days, and they both knew it. But she told herself it was easier this way—as they drew nearer to reaching the end of their plan, she'd have to get used to being on her own again. Save for her work.

The past couple days at the office had been tough, though, and it was only by going on autopilot that she'd reached the end. Mark's deposition had gone brilliantly, fortunately, with her cutting off the opposing counsel's questions and objections when necessary.

Even if it left her with a sick feeling in the pit of her stomach.

Why did Ms. Herrera's attorney have to be so freaking incompetent? He hadn't even put up much of a fight. If it had been Jessica who sat across from her at that table, Kate might have felt a little better knowing Ava Herrera was getting the best representation she was entitled to.

Kate managed to pin a smile to her face when the front door swept open and three eager faces cried out her name and pushed her inside. She managed to hold onto the dish as they bounced around her, and she couldn't help but laugh at their exuberance. She was met with an interesting array of aromas, including roasted turkey, buttery rolls, and also something… spicy.

"There you are, Kate." Dominic's mom tapped the spoon she'd using to stir and rested it on the large roasting pan. Wiping her hands on a towel, she came and took the casserole from Kate and set it down, then pulled her in for a long, full hug.

"So glad you could make it," she said softly and stood back, a beaming smile on her face as she looked Kate over and nodded. Patting Kate's shoulder, Elena returned to the stove.

"Hey, Kate," Benny said and continued to drop rolls into a basket. Daisy looked up and waved before returning her attention to the steaming pot in front of her. She was holding tongs and pulling out steaming corn husks.

Kate raised her brows. "Homemade tamales?"

"Of course, is there any other kind?" Daisy asked and smiled.

"Just wait until you bite into one of Daisy's pumpkin empanadas," Benny added. "Heavenly."

"I can't wait." Kate turned and looked into the main

room, where Dominic's dad sat on the couch, Cruz on the other end, both fixated on the television in front of them. They managed to look up and called hello when they saw her before returning their gaze to the screen.

Kate spotted Glenda seated in the corner of the room at a card table and went over to greet her. Just like everyone else, she stood and wrapped her arms around Kate. "Hi, neighbor, glad to see you here."

Jenna, the oldest of Dominic's nieces, grabbed her hand. "We're playing Candyland. But we can start over if you want to play. I was winning, anyhow."

"I don't want to play that anymore. How about Apples to Apples," Natalie asked. "Kate can be on my team."

"Let's give Kate a minute to catch her breath."

She stilled, recognizing the voice behind her. Before she could turn to meet his gaze, Dominic reached his hand out and wrapped it around her waist. She caught her breath at the familiar touch and tried to slow the yammering of her heart as he pulled her up against his side.

His body was like fifty degrees warmer than hers, as she remembered, and his musky scent with a hint of spice surrounded her. His breath was warm on her neck as he leaned down and pressed a kiss that nearly brought her legs out from under her.

"We were getting worried something happened," he said, loud enough for everyone to hear. "You should have let me pick you up." Then, softer, he whispered for her hearing only, "Or were you afraid to be alone with me?"

She looked up and met his gaze. Eyes brilliant and blue stared back into hers. Had it only been three days since she'd seen him? His hair was ruffled and sexy with that familiar piece teasing down over his left brow and that lazy smile that crooked his lips just so. She remembered the touch of those lips on hers—and on a few other more intimate parts that immediately brought warmth to her face.

Now she remembered why she had avoided being alone with him for the past few days. Even now, her resistance to him was melting away.

"Hey," she finally managed to return, but her voice seemed clogged with emotion. She noticed the glass of red wine he held out for her, and she took it, careful to avoid his fingertips.

"Dinner will be on the table in about ten more minutes," his mother called. "Kate, if you're hungry, there are snacks on the table. Please help yourself."

She became aware of Dominic's hand resting lower on her hip, and it took all of her concentration to reply as if she were unaffected by his touch. "Thanks. Everything smells wonderful."

"We'll be back in a few minutes, actually," Dominic said. "There were a few things I wanted to talk to Kate about before we ate. About her…kitchen cabinets."

"Yeah, right. Nice try, bud," Benny said. "There'll be plenty of time for you to discuss her 'cabinets' later," she said, in a voice that told them she had other ideas of what Dominic meant, "but this turkey is ready to be carved and there's no way I'm letting Cruz do it again after the fiasco last year. Kate can keep me company while I set the table."

Cruz came out of his television coma long enough to call out, "Hey, my turkey carving kicked ass last year. We can't all be surgeons like you."

"Really? It looked like rabid dogs chewed on it first. Just

to be safe, I hid the electric knife." She smiled and held out a long, gleaming carving knife and fork to Dominic, who looked uneasily at them and sighed.

"You could save us all the pain of your critique, Ben, if you'd just carve it every year."

"And miss the fun of showing you two up next year? Not on your life. Besides, you're always bragging about how good you are with your hands, let's see what you can do."

Dominic stared at his sister. "You realize you just made a pass at me."

The room was quiet for a moment. Then Daisy giggled, followed by Elena, and everyone joined in. And for once in the short time since she'd met her, Kate had the privilege of seeing Benny shut her eyes in mortification, completely speechless.

"No fair! That's traveling," Dominic yelled while Daisy cut him off. Their bellies full from dinner, Benny had wrangled everyone outside for a little activity to work off some calories. And to everyone's surprise and relief, Daisy had not only agreed to participate, but she also had the familiar gleam of competitiveness back in her eyes.

The siblings held nothing back as they scrimmaged around the cement padding in the Sorensens' backyard. Since Kate had no talent for basketball and a limited understanding of the rules, she'd begged to sit out to watch them and was joined by Dominic's nieces, Jenna and Natalie.

From what she could tell, Dominic, Benny, and Paul were kicking Cruz and Daisy's butts. But despite their loss, Daisy was laughing and throwing back the barbs they slung. Kate had never seen Daisy so lighthearted and happy in the short time she'd known her and had a sneaking suspicion it was due in large part to the check that had arrived Wednesday evening, as well as the fact it had actually cleared the bank.

According to Daisy, who'd stolen Kate away after dinner to share the news, Leo had dropped it off personally and even took the kids to McDonald's for ice cream. It was something. And despite the crap that Tim had given her about taking the case, the smile on Daisy's face made it all worth it. Kate would never wish otherwise.

She watched Dominic and Cruz face each other, Cruz almost taunting as he pulled the ball back every time Dominic tried to steal it. But Dominic psyched him out on the next one and stole the ball and passed it to Benny, who threw it high. And scored.

"Point and tied," Benny shouted and pumped her arm.

For a moment, Dominic looked back at Kate, and she received a rush as he smiled. She was completely under his spell.

"On that high note," Daisy announced, "I think we should call it a game."

Paul immediately objected but stopped when Daisy mentioned the fact the empanadas were ready, then raced his sisters for the door.

Dominic was out of breath when he reached Kate and extended his hand to give her a boost up. Unable to resist, she put her hand in his warm callused one, expecting him to lift her, but instead he ran his thumb across her skin, sending a shiver of pleasure shuddering through her. Then he pulled her up so she fell against his chest.

He was really playing up all the little public displays of affection tonight. Not that she was complaining as he stared down into her eyes, his own twinkling with mischief. Before she could blink, he pressed his mouth to hers and another bolt ran through her. Instinctively, her hand shot out to his chest, whether to push him away or bring him closer she couldn't say, since as soon as the kiss started it was over and he was grabbing her hand and pulling her inside.

An hour later, the kids were in another heated game of Candyland while the adults sprawled out on chairs and couches. Dominic grabbed a blanket from the closet and after tucking a bottle of wine under his arm and grabbing two glasses, motioned her to follow.

The cold air that greeted them was even chillier than during the game and she shivered as she sat on the cold cement step until Dominic wrapped the blanket around them. His body was like a heat lamp, and she leaned toward him despite herself.

The biting air helped to cool the sudden flush of her cheeks at this new intimacy and she floundered for something to say. "They say it's supposed to snow tomorrow." Lame, but it filled the silence as he poured the wine. "At least I won't have to worry about a heavy commute, since everyone will either be chilling at home or heading to the malls."

"You're working tomorrow?" He actually sounded disappointed.

She nodded. "I want to get a jump start on drafting the summary judgment motion on the McKenna case."

Almost tentatively, he asked, "How'd it go, then? Did you get what you needed?"

"Enough to make a pretty good argument why this case

should be dismissed."

"Then we should celebrate." He handed her a glass and held his up to hers. "Here's to getting everything you want, Kate."

Whether he was talking about her case, her promotion, or something more, she didn't care. She raised her glass. Who wouldn't want all the luck they could get? "Cheers."

They each took a drink and stared up at the sky. The moon was hidden behind clouds and the night was impossibly dark, making it difficult to see Dominic's face.

"So it's next week?" he asked. "When they decide about your partnership?"

"Friday. I'll be a bundle of nerves until then."

"Then we'll have something else to toast to at Payton's engagement party that Saturday night, besides the completion of your kitchen."

"My kitchen?"

"Yep. Got the call. Your cabinets should arrive Wednesday and with a couple of guys I use for my freelancing, we should have them up within a day."

Which should make her excited and thrilled. Only…all she could think about was that Dominic's work would be done and there'd be no more reason to see him.

She swallowed the lump in her throat and tried to smile. "And what about you? Now that the surgery is done and your dad looks to be on the road to good health, are you ready to make a decision?"

He took a drink and set his glass down. "I already did." He pulled his cell phone from his back pocket and held it in front of him. "You all were right, of course. About him just wanting what was best for me. And it helped that Cruz was already talking to my dad when I arrived, showing him a new business plan he'd drawn up for what he envisions for Sorensen Construction. My own plan for going out on my own seemed to be something Dad already had accepted. In fact, he actually asked me why I took so long."

He laughed, and he sounded so happy, as if the weight of the world was off his shoulders, she joined him.

"Here." He held his cell phone out to her. "I want you to see something."

She took the phone in her hands and stared down. On the screen was a gray backdrop and a black-and-white photo with the facade on an old house. The words "Sorensen Restoration" in bold letters crossed the top.

"You did it? You actually created a webpage?" It was beautiful, too, as she touched the screen and was brought to a portfolio of some older homes and the work he'd already done.

"Not only created it, but registered the LLC yesterday. And here's the kicker. I've already had someone give me a call and received two more email inquiries."

Her smile was wide and genuine as she looked at him, beyond impressed. "Wow. I can't believe how much you've done in such a short time." *Without me*, she wanted to add. But that would be silly. She'd shut him out, not the other way around. "I'm not surprised, though. I'm so happy for you, Dominic. You're going to do it. You're ready to start working on making your dream come true."

He looked at her, and she felt as if he was going to say something, and her heart thumped loudly, almost deafening in her ears.

But he only smiled a little wryly and winked again. "I'm trying."

Chapter Seventeen

Kate made it to the office in record time, considering traffic was sparse and the parking garage was practically empty. The office was quiet, too, without the usual bustle from the staff. Even the phones were strangely quiet. One of the reasons she usually loved coming in on holidays. Although now... she was starting to understand the allure of being at home.

If there was a certain someone to spend time with.

By eleven, she was busy typing her draft and barely noticed when one of the legal assistants dropped the mail off at Trish's desk. After another half hour, she finally stood to stretch her legs and took a look at the mail that arrived. It was hard to miss the padded white FedEx envelope on top of the pile. Taking it to her desk, she dumped it out, already confident in what it contained before she even saw it.

The video surveillance from the Radisson.

She slid the disc into her computer and waited the long minute it took for the computer to recognize the software.

Then it was starting. A long narrow hall, the picture a little grainy. A date was time-stamped in the corner. Same date as the day Ms. Herrera claimed Mark McKenna assaulted her in his room.

It took a good fifteen minutes of her forwarding through scenes of an empty hall before she finally spotted Mark arriving at his room. Alone. She exhaled a small sigh. She skipped forward again until she saw a woman with dark hair approach the door and go in. It was Ms. Herrera.

It was another six minutes on the video before the door was suddenly wrenched open and Ms. Herrera rushed out. Even in the short time she was in the frame, it was hard to miss the way her shirt hung open, the look of terror on her face before she raced down the hall.

A wave of nausea swept through Kate. She'd had her suspicions and doubts before, but now there was no denying what she knew was true. He'd done it, the bastard. And if his assault hadn't been bad enough, he'd made sure to take not only the woman's dignity but her income and then her job. She stopped the video.

Now she had to face another realization. Because now that she had seen what was on the video, there was no doubt in her mind that the first copy hadn't mysteriously gone missing. Someone had deliberately hidden it.

It would be easy to lay the blame on Nicole, a woman who Kate had little doubt would stoop low enough to hide evidence if it meant getting ahead. But there were two things wrong with that theory. Nicole had nothing to gain by hiding it, as it was Kate's neck — or promotion, rather — on the line and, in fact, hiding this might actually benefit Kate. The other problem was that Nicole didn't have access to her mail.

She knew only one person, other than Trish, who was screening any mail coming in on the McKenna matter.

Tim.

It wasn't difficult to see why he would try and suppress it. One look at the footage and their defense would be blown out of the water. Mark had lied about what happened, and it wouldn't be a stretch for anyone to believe everything else that Ava Herrera claimed had happened also.

She pressed her fingers to her head again as the pounding pain increased. If she brought this footage to light, she'd not only sink this case, but she'd sink her chances at partnership.

But what choice did she really have? Could she sit on the evidence, as Tim seemed content to do? Wrestle with her conscience and code of ethics later?

"Hey, Kate. Thought you might be in today."

Oh, crap. Not now. *What is he doing here?*

She didn't even lift her head. "Hey, Michael. Now's not really a good time…"

But he didn't leave, and instead took a few steps inside until he reached the other side of her desk and perched on the corner next to her. She hazarded a peek from behind her fingers to find him half smiling at her.

"Come on, Kate. This is me. What's going on?"

She rubbed her forehead again to try and relieve the aching pressure. "Honestly? I don't really know anymore. But for starters, there's this damn McKenna case."

He nodded. "Nicole mentioned that you seemed to be… struggling with things of late. But I heard you nailed the deposition."

"I did." Yep. Couldn't fault her there. She'd done an

impeccable job of making Mark McKenna come off as a veritable saint. She should win some award or something.

"So what's the problem?"

"The problem is my client is a liar and a predator and I'm pretty certain he sexually assaulted at least three women from his company. Then, when they tried to complain, he had them dismissed. And here"—she hit the keys and brought the footage back a few seconds to show Ms. Herrera leaving his hotel room again, ripped shirt and tears impossible to miss—"is what happened after he assaulted Ms. Herrera at the Radisson. Interestingly enough, this is the second copy of this footage the firm has received. The first went mysteriously missing."

"Are you saying you don't think it was an accident?"

"What I think is that Tim wanted to make sure this footage didn't get into the hands of the other side, and he buried it."

"Well, of course not. It's our job to protect our client. You can't take these things personally, Kate."

Looked like Michael also wasn't above hiding evidence that they were bound by the rules of evidence to provide.

"Sure, I guess it would be easier if I could flip a switch and turn off this inner moral compass that tells me this is wrong," she added flippantly. "That my life is on the wrong track and I'm working for the wrong side."

He sighed. "Kate. You can be so adorably naive some- times." He leaned over, closing the space between them. "You have a good heart, which is one of the things I love about you."

Love about her? Present tense?

"But you'll get through this. You're a great trial attorney and you'll do what you need to do and probably join the ranks of junior partner. I know how much that means to you, and you're almost there." In a softer tone, he added, "You just have to hold on, and you can have everything you've ever wanted."

That made him the second person in two days to mention getting everything she'd ever wanted. What the heck did she want?

Michael reached out and tucked a strand of hair back from her face, but instead of breaking the contact, his fingers trailed lightly down in a caress to her jaw, her neck, then stopped at the collar of her shirt.

She sat frozen, trying to figure out what was happening as Michael continued. "Once upon a time you wanted me as much as I wanted you, and for a crazy moment, I thought I could let you go. But—hell. I've missed you, Kate. And no matter how hard I've tried to move on, I can't get you out of my head or my heart."

She swallowed, trying to process. "What are you saying, Michael? Are you saying that your engagement to Nicole is over? And if so…why now?"

His brown eyes crinkled and he smiled. "Let's just say seeing you with the wrong guy was a good kick in the pants to realize who was the right one. That guy—" He shook his head. "Dominic? He doesn't know what you need, not like I do. He can't give you what I can, Kate. You know that."

It was as if she was in a dream, finally feeling his fingers softly caress her. Hearing the words she had wanted to hear for so long.

Only now that he was saying it, it sounded flat. Her heart wasn't skipping or racing anywhere near like it had when she was with Dominic. How was that even possible?

She had loved this man. Wanted to marry him, spend forever with him.

Kate pulled back, away from his hand. "It's kind of convenient, Michael. How on earth could I ever trust you again? Trust that you're not going to change your mind?"

"Sorry to interrupt." A low voice cut through the silence of the room, and her gaze flew to the door where Dominic was standing. Like someone had splashed a bucket of cold water on her, she jumped back in her chair.

How long had he been standing there? Dark, anguishing guilt hit her, but when she forced herself to look into his eyes, they didn't reveal anything.

"I stopped by because I thought Kate might want to grab lunch." His gaze dropped to settle on the area of her neck where Michael had just caressed her.

Still perched on the edge of the desk, Michael swiveled around to face Dominic, smiling a little too widely. "Dominic. How you doing, bud?"

"Doing fine, Michael." Dominic didn't give any indication of his feelings, but he didn't return Michael's smile. His gaze returned to Kate. "I realize we didn't make any arrangements, but I thought you might want to catch some lunch. My mistake. I didn't realize you would be so…busy. Next time I'll call." He turned as if to go.

"Dominic, wait. Michael, would you mind?"

Michael came to his feet, looking too satisfied with this latest turn of events. "Sure, Kate. But if you want to talk about this"—he lowered his voice, as if he was sharing an intimate conversation with Kate, but not low enough that Dominic couldn't hear it—"another time, I'm here for you. Always."

He strode to the door. "Well, see ya, Dominic."

Dominic watched him leave and turned back to Kate.

Finally coming to her senses, Kate crossed the room and shut the door. "Dominic. I don't know what you saw, but it's not—"

She stopped. Actually, she had no idea what it had looked like, let alone what it was. Was Michael saying he wanted her back?

"It looked like Michael was trying to tell you he wanted you back."

She closed her eyes. That was the same conclusion she had reached, too, so how could she deny it?

"Looks like you're finally getting everything you wanted," he said, his tone distant. Aloof.

Everything she wanted. Did that still include Michael?

For the past year she'd been convinced it did. And then Dominic had showed up and helped her see what life could be like without him. What it could be like with someone else. And it had seemed...pretty darn good.

But what she and Dominic had together—as they'd agreed—was only temporary.

He wasn't exactly standing there telling her to pick him.

She looked up at his face, so achingly calm. Completely unaffected by the possibility that Michael wanted her back. And that she'd accept him.

Dominic's gaze fell to the open FedEx envelope. "So what were you two talking about—I mean, before the big profession."

Crap. That's right. Michael was just the tip of the iceberg. The bigger crisis was her career...wasn't it? "The video surveillance arrived, and it showed exactly what I feared, that not only is my client guilty, but it's likely my boss and mentor is burying evidence."

"You work for one hell of a boss." He tightened his jaw, as if he wanted to say something but decided against it. "Guess you have a lot of life-changing decisions to make, then."

She smiled wryly. "You think?"

With a sigh, she looked around the office. Seeing the diplomas, the certificate showing she'd been on law review, little trinkets she'd once prized. Proof she had worked so hard to get where she was.

And yet the one thing she really cared about right now was the opinion of the man in front of her.

A man who looked cool and detached, nothing at all like the man she'd come to know these past few weeks. And it was like small shards of glass were piercing her heart.

"Well, I can see you have a lot on your mind, so I'll let you go." He started to turn away, pausing as if he remembered something. "Just to give you a heads-up, I'm going to be in over my head for the next few days, getting things worked out at Sorensen while also getting my own business off the ground. I probably won't be around until next Wednesday, when the cabinets arrive. Like I said, with some extra hands, I'll make short work of it and can be finished and out of your hair by the end of the week."

"Oh, well, of course. I can't wait to see those cabinets up, finally." She faltered. What had just happened? "I'll see you at Payton's party next Saturday, right?" Her voice sounded desperate even to her.

He ran his hand through his hair, and she could see regret flash through his eyes. She sensed his withdrawal from her but was helpless to stop it.

"Yeah, well, it seems kind of pointless, don't you think? I was posing as your boyfriend to help you land this partnership, but as of Friday, you'll know the decision on that. And keeping the pretense up for Michael seems kind of...counterintuitive. He wants you back. And having me hang around would be—well, like a third wheel. And I'm not really one for wearing those monkey suits, so, if it's all the same to you, I'll pass."

Why was she having such a hard time catching her breath? She was breathing in but it seemed like she wasn't getting any air in her lungs. She felt light-headed and reached out to steady herself on the desk.

Just like that, he was disappearing right out of her life.

"You're right, of course. There really isn't any reason, I suppose, for you to come."

Except to be with me.

But she couldn't say that. It was clear that he was already getting that itch to leave. They'd had their fun, but now that Daisy had things going in the right direction and Kate had her partnership nearly in the bag, they didn't need each other.

And technically, he was right. She didn't need him to come on Saturday to keep up the pretense. It would all be over by then, whichever way the dice fell.

But she wanted him to come.

"I should get going," Dominic said finally, and her heart squeezed painfully. "I know you have a lot on your plate. And try and remember what I said. Don't sell yourself short. To anyone. You have so much to offer."

He studied her a few more seconds, and then that top lip

curved up into that crooked grin she loved before he turned and walked out of her office and out of her life.

Like so many others had before.

. . .

Dominic's smile slid off his face as he staggered out Kate's office feeling like a man who had gone ten rounds with a heavyweight boxer. In the space of five minutes, his emotions had shot from excitement as he had anticipated surprising Kate to white-hot rage at seeing Michael touch Kate so intimately and promise the words he knew she'd been wanting to hear. Then jealousy took root when she hadn't immediately rebuffed him, changing to sick disappointment and finally...acceptance.

Michael was right. He'd always been what Kate wanted. What she needed to put the final piece in the puzzle of the life she'd made for herself.

Who was he to stand in her way, to throw a wrench in her machinations? She'd made it clear that whatever they'd shared had been a mistake.

He'd fought for a woman once before, laid his heart out to her, only to have her walk away from him and everything he could offer her because of what he wasn't. He couldn't make that same mistake. He wouldn't.

So he'd done what he had to do.

And he was walking away from the one woman he'd had fallen the hardest for. Even if it felt like it might kill him. Nearly as much as when he'd seen her waver under Michael's attention. But he knew he could never make her happy, and he didn't want to risk the same pain when she realized it and walked away.

Just like Melinda.

So he'd done what he had to and walked away first.

He reached the elevator and pounded the button to the lobby.

"I'm sorry if I ruined your plans."

Dominic turned to find Michael standing next to him, but "sorry" wasn't exactly how he would paint the guy's face. He looked smug and satisfied. And Dominic wanted nothing more than to ball his fist and smash the asshole's face with it.

"Let's be honest here for a minute, Michael. You're not sorry. And the only reason you're not unconscious and on the floor right now is because I don't want to do that to Kate. But let's be clear. Kate is the best goddamn woman either one of us could ever even hope to be with. And for some reason, she seems to still be hung up on you. But if at any time she gives me reason to believe she could be happy with me, I will be in your face so fast you won't know what hit you."

The smug smile only widened. "That's not going to happen. The only reason Kate was even in your life was because of my shortsightedness. Maybe she wanted to see what it was like to slum it for a while." Michael shrugged. "In the end, she'll come back to the one and only person who can make her happy. But good luck to you, Dominic. I'm sure I can talk her into giving you a referral for the work you've done so far. But that's all you'll get from her."

He'd tried, he really had. But sometimes people just didn't know when to shut their mouths. And with that, Dominic strode the two steps to close the space and socked Michael in the eye.

The satisfaction at seeing his head fall back and him stumble to the ground was short-lived as Dominic stepped into the elevator and descended to the lobby.

Because Michael had still won the girl, in the end.

. . .

Kate walked into her house Friday night, her body feeling as heavy as her heart. It was dark and empty and quiet. Oscar had slipped out the minute she'd opened the door, so it was only her. And she didn't know if she'd ever felt so alone in her entire life.

She dropped her keys on the table but didn't make a move to turn on the lights. Not just yet. The sounds of her shoes on the hardwood echoed through the house. She stood in the doorway of the kitchen a long moment, knowing that soon the cabinets would be on the walls and Dominic would be permanently gone from her life.

A few weeks ago, this wouldn't have fazed her at all. She hadn't even known him. But now, in the short space since she'd met him, she couldn't imagine her life without him.

Which was completely ironic. Because here she was on the cusp of getting the promotion she'd been working on for five years—a step toward that judgeship she'd coveted so dearly for so long—and maybe even the love and commitment of the man she'd always wanted. Or thought she'd always wanted. And she didn't care.

She thought of a future with Michael. The parties, the social events, the acceptance into the holy circle that she'd always wanted. The love of a man who she'd never thought could ever want her. And it sounded…empty. Just like this house. Empty and without any real meaning.

So contrary to the warmth and laughter and love she'd experienced in the time she'd known Dominic and his entire family. A family that had made her feel so at home. A part of something. Something real, just like her grams had had. She thought about the love she saw between Elena and Petter Sorensen. It was forever, and they had shared so much already and still had so much more to look forward to.

Something like she could have had with Dominic. But she'd lost her chance, if she'd ever had it in the first place. And she'd had to watch him walk away.

A sob from deep in her chest nearly choked her. What was she doing with her life? What did she want? You'd think a grown woman almost thirty would have a handle on that right now.

The only thing she was sure of, though, was that somehow everything had changed. What she wanted had changed.

And it might be too late for her to do anything about it.

Chapter Eighteen

Dinner Sunday evening was unbearable as Dominic rebuffed his family's efforts at drawing him into the conversation. It was hard to miss the glances his sisters and mother kept sharing, the worried looks on their faces. But what could he tell them? The truth?

He looked at Daisy, who was already back to her bossy ways, ordering her kids to have at least two more bites before they were excused and even chastising their dad for not eating enough to keep up his strength. How would she take the news that he'd offered to pretend to be dating Kate so that he could bum free legal services on her behalf?

"Before you go, Dominic, remind me to give you Kate's casserole dish. She left it here on Thanksgiving."

He nodded. He could drop it off next time he was over.

Bites dutifully taken, the kids ran from the table and downstairs to watch television.

"How is Kate?" Benny asked, despite the warning glances

their mom was giving. "I was hoping she might be here tonight. I wanted to talk to her about Christmas. If we're drawing names for gifts again this year, I thought maybe we could have her name added, too."

Oh, hell. He couldn't have them placing her name in the hat to draw Christmas presents. He might as well grow a pair and own up to the truth. All of it.

When he was done, the room was eerily quiet. Then Daisy dropped her napkin on the table and pushed her chair out before fleeing the room and all hell broke loose, with everyone shouting at him at once. Even Cruz, who'd known about the ruse since almost the beginning, was sharing a piece of his mind at the insensitive way he'd finally spilled the beans. As if there'd been any way to make this better.

And he sat there and accepted their anger. Because it was nowhere near the anger he felt at himself.

Not for the charade itself, though.

No. But for the chickenshit way he'd taken off Friday. He'd been a coward. Too afraid to tell her how he really felt. Hadn't even tried to throw his hat into the ring, but pulled it out entirely. Practically congratulated her on winning Michael back and gave her his blessing.

He should have been up front. Told her to forget about Michael.

Told her that he loved her.

And that she should choose him.

So the anger his family was throwing around helped in a way. He didn't deserve to have anyone feel sorry for him. He deserved their anger and disgust. It echoed his own.

• • •

If Kate had thought last Monday was tough, waking up this morning and looking forward to a week without Dominic, a week knowing that a woman's life and career might be in her hands, and a week with a career-changing decision to be made at the end of it made her want to bury herself under the covers for another month.

Reaching the sanctity of her office, she slid behind her desk and stared down at the stupid DVD that had helped bring her walls falling around her. She didn't know how long she sat there before Trish popped her head in to remind her she had an appointment in four minutes with Tim and Nicole to discuss their strategy on the case.

Kate was expected to deliver the outline of her argument for the summary judgment motion, but first she had something else that she had to get out of the way. Grabbing the DVD and stuffing it back into the envelope, she made her way to the small conference room already reserved for the powwow.

She wasn't surprised to find Nicole seated and sipping coffee, a folder open in front of her. Tim hadn't yet arrived.

"Morning," Kate mustered as politely as she could manage. After everything that had happened with Michael on Friday, she hadn't even thought about Nicole. Had he told her anything? Cautiously, she took a seat a few chairs away.

Nicole barely looked up. "Morning," she muttered and kept reviewing the documents.

Were those actual dark circles under Nicole's eyes? Impossible. It must be the lighting.

To kill time, Kate pulled out her cell phone, hesitating a moment before she activated it as she had every five minutes this past weekend. Checking to see if she'd missed a call, maybe a text or even an email from Dominic. But like it had been the last few days, the phone was absent any such notification.

Kate was more than a little startled to look up and find Tim seated at the head of the table and staring at her oddly. She hadn't even noticed him arrive.

"You all right?"

"Yes. Certainly." She slid the phone back into her pocket and straightened. No time for daydreaming.

"I think we can all agree that last week's depositions were a resounding success. You were phenomenal, Kate. And Nicole, thank you as well for all the behind-the-scenes support you gave Kate. I don't think there's even really much to discuss this morning, since I know you'll all agree that a motion for summary judgment is the next logical step." Tim looked positively gleeful as he looked around the table. "Nicole, would you mind preparing a summary of the case that we can present to our client, explaining our strategy? I think Kate's going to be a little busy for the next week or so getting the motion drafted, isn't that right?"

Kate looked at the envelope still in her hand. She would wait until she had a moment in private to confront Tim about it. She owed him at least that. In the meantime, she nodded. "I started the draft last Friday."

"Yes, I have no doubt you did. Nicole? I think you have enough to get started on that memo. I'm hoping to deliver it to the client by tomorrow."

"No problem."

"Good. I'll look forward to reading it. But I have some other news I wanted to discuss with Kate. You wouldn't mind excusing us, would you, Nicole?"

Nicole kept her face averted, and Kate had no idea what

might be running through her head as she left. Truth be told, the woman seemed almost as distracted as Kate. And probably for good reason. Kate felt a twinge of pity for the woman she'd loathed and hated for the past few months. Sure, she was stuck-up and unfriendly—and everything Kate always wanted to be. But she knew what it was like to feel someone slipping away and feel helpless to stop it. It really sucked.

"I meant what I said, Kate," Tim said when the door closed behind Nicole. "You really came through, despite the little surprise that came in last week. You affirmed for me and all the partners what a strong asset you are for this firm. Which is why I wanted to share this news with you now."

He was really making it hard for her to get a word in, and she stared down at the package in front of her as Tim warmed to his topic.

"This morning during the usual weekly meeting, we had a rather unorthodox conversation. Unorthodox in that we usually don't discuss these matters until the quarterly meeting, but I couldn't help but share with them all how you came through for our client. What I'm saying, in a surprisingly long-winded fashion, is that we had a little impromptu and informal vote, and I can say with authority that you have more than your performance to celebrate. You have your promotion to junior partnership, a fact that will be announced formally on Friday after the official vote. Congratulations, Kate, Strauss and Fletcher's newest junior partner." Tim even cracked a bit of a smile as he added this last bit.

It had been the last thing she'd expected to hear today, and she blinked a few times, trying to process this surprising news.

She was going to be a partner. It was as good as hers.

And instead of the overwhelming giddiness and excitement she thought she'd be feeling, Kate still felt, oddly enough…nothing. Okay, maybe not nothing. Maybe more like a thick rope was being tied around her neck and slowly beginning to tighten.

Now was her moment. The moment she should ask him about the DVD. What he knew about it, and now that they had it, what they were going to do with it.

But for some reason, she couldn't quite do it. It would be suicide to her job and her career, and she knew it. Instead, she reached out her hand out and accepted his proffered hand. "Thank you, Tim," she managed to say. "For your encouragement over the years and your belief in me."

And a few minutes later she was back in her office, not even remembering how she'd gotten there. She looked around her office again, at the diplomas on her walls. The small expensive treasures she'd picked up at each milestone along the way to where she was. And instead of feeling victorious, she still had that hollow feeling. As if she was still missing something.

And if she buried this evidence, just as she knew Tim would want and expect her to, she'd risk losing something else. Herself. Her values. Her moral integrity.

Now, more than anything, Kate wished she had someone she could talk about this with, someone who might understand her dilemma and what she was going through. Someone who could share in her worry, her excitement, her uncertainty.

Okay. Not just someone.

She wanted Dominic.

• • •

Dominic stood in front of Kate's refrigerator for a couple minutes first thing Friday morning. Trying to ignore the feeling that his heart had been smashed by a sledgehammer.

It was there. A check for the rest of the work he'd done. Sure, he was owed it, he knew that. But for some reason, seeing the payment clipped to the fridge like she would the water bill or the electric bill made everything they'd been to each other over the past months feel…worthless. Like it was all just another job. Like he was just a contractor and nothing more.

What had he expected? After what he'd seen last week, he'd bet that Kate and Michael had already made up and were going to paint the town red after she heard the word about her promotion. Because they'd be idiots if they didn't give it to her.

Only it made him sick to his stomach to think of Michael walking through this house that had come to almost feel like home. To place his hands on the woman Dominic had also come to think of as home.

Hell. She was better off. He'd been saying since the beginning that Michael was the exact type he envisioned for Kate. And he'd been stupid to think for a minute that she might have felt him something more than a friend, a cohort in this plan they'd come up with. But nothing more.

He took the check, holding in his fingers for a long minute, and ripped it in half. Then he took the two halves stuck them back on the fridge with the magnet.

• • •

It was nearly eleven thirty. Half an hour before the formal announcement went out that she and one other associate had been promoted to junior partner. But instead of celebrating, Kate sat at her desk, her chair turned to look out over the Salt Lake Valley. Thinking about her lunch meeting yesterday with Jessica Lund.

There was a lot to consider.

In confidence, she'd shared with Jessica the impending announcement of her junior partner position. But Jessica must have seen some of the doubt on Kate's face as they sat across from each other, because instead of congratulations, Jessica had renewed her offer to find a place for Kate at her firm.

And this time, Kate actually listened as Jessica laid out everything that the small, employee-focused firm could provide Kate.

Fewer, less intrusive billable hours.

A decent health care plan.

The perk of only taking on the cases *she* wanted to take on. Cases like Daisy's.

Never before had the offer been so tantalizing. Having the discretion of declining a case if the facts—and the client— weren't scintillating or bearable sounded like heaven. God knew she'd have dropped the McKenna case long ago had she had the ability to say no—and the promotion riding on its success.

Flexibility was what it offered. Freedom.

Her work hours at Strauss had never really bothered Kate before. She'd kept her nose to the grindstone, not really looking around to see where she was and how she'd gotten there, determined to reach that long-awaited goal of partner.

And now that it was hers…now what? Continue at her frenzied pace until in ten or twenty more years she might have that judgeship and the respect that might or might not come with it?

But what else would she have? Someone to share with and rejoice in her accomplishments? To rejoice in all the milestones? Or would she likely be alone?

Kind of how this past week had gone. Without Dominic.

She was only grateful that Michael had been in California the past week closing some real estate deal, so she'd been able to put off having to deal with that mess. But this partnership couldn't wait. It was time to make a decision. Set the course for the rest of her life.

A course she could live with.

Enough. She needed to speak with Tim, and before she could change her mind, she grabbed the DVD one more time and marched out to find him.

He sat in his office sipping a seltzer water, reading some journal. She took a breath and knocked on the door.

"Kate? Can I help you with something? We didn't have an appointment, did we?" He glanced at his watch.

"No. We didn't. But there is something we need to discuss, and I can't put it off any longer."

He waved her in. "All right. Have a seat."

She was surprised at the calm sureness that came over her as she walked across the rug and took a seat. Folding her hands over the package, she started. "I don't know if you remember my mentioning that I had contacted the Radisson about getting a copy of the surveillance video from the time Mark McKenna and Ava Herrera went on that business trip."

Tim nodded, his face devoid of any telling emotion.

She continued. "Funny thing is, we received a bill last week for some security footage they recovered and sent on to us. But I never received it. Did you happen to get it by mistake?"

For the briefest moment, Tim hesitated and his eyes flew from her to the door. When he returned his gaze to her, steady again, she knew the truth.

"I never saw it," he lied. "But it could be floating around the office, I suppose. Might be sitting in someone's mailbox by mistake. I wouldn't worry about it. Just put the invoice on the firm's bill."

"Of course. I'll make sure to do that. Only…when I got the bill, I called the Radisson and asked if they could send me another copy. Which I've since received."

He looked coldly at her, his brow raised. "Oh?"

"And I took a look. It's not good. It pretty much confirms Ava Herrera's account of what happened that night, down to the torn blouse."

"I see." But he waited, both brows raised. "And?"

"And I think we have a dilemma. Under the rules of discovery, any relevant evidence must be provided to the other side. I'm trying hard not to reach the conclusion that we should notify Ms. Herrera of the DVD's existence."

"Ms. Matthews, I'm perfectly aware of the rules of evidence. But I don't see why this is even an issue. If Ms. Herrera was diligently protecting her interests, she'd have already attained a copy of the surveillance. If they had any interest in the video, they could contact the hotel, as you did, and request a copy. It's not like it's very hard. And it's certainly not up to us to hand deliver them any evidence that they were too lazy to discover themselves." It was practically the same argument she had made to herself. "Am I making myself clear here?"

Kate chewed her bottom lip. Perfectly. She nodded.

"Good. Because I'd hate it if I helped you get this far only to have you shoot yourself in the foot at this stage in the game."

He'd helped her, all right. But only for what it could gain him, not out of any personal affection, as she once had believed. Had the McKenna depositions gone any other way, she'd have been hung out to dry without a qualm. And if she went through and produced this DVD for the other side, she'd not be only saying good-bye to her partnership, she'd be out the door in a blink of an eye.

She stared at him clearly for the first time since she had known him. The halo she usually saw encircling his head wasn't just tarnished but had evaporated entirely.

It made this next decision all the easier.

She stood. "I completely understand what's at stake. Here, this is a copy of the DVD from the Radisson," she said and placed it on his desk. It was hard to miss the satisfied grin that crossed his face. She paused, relishing the moment and what she was about to say. "Because it's only fair you retain that copy so you know what's on it after I send the copy I've made to Ms. Herrera's attorney. It's going out certified mail today."

"Kate." This time his voice raised several octaves and Tim half stood in his seat. "Wait. You need to understand what you're about to do. This is a decision you can't come back from."

"I know, Tim. And I wouldn't have it any other way. My resignation will be on your desk by the end of the day."

Seeing the look on his face as she sailed out of the office was priceless. She just wished she'd be around to see Mark McKenna's when the stories he'd fabricated came crashing down.

Her heart lighter, she reached her office and shut the door. She had a call to make and a letter of resignation to write.

She stared at the phone for a long minute, though. Because the call she wanted to make wasn't to Jessica to take that offer, not just then. It was to one person only. The one person who would understand the sacrifice she'd made, and who would make her feel like her choice, no matter what, had been the right one.

Because he had that much faith in her.

Swiping an errant tear, she picked up her phone and made her call.

"Jessica Lund, please."

• • •

"You gonna stand there all day and watch me work?" Cruz asked Saturday afternoon as they worked on framing the basement at Dominic's house.

"I would if I thought you had any idea what you were doing," Dominic quipped. He had to get his head in the game, though, and he couldn't keep letting thoughts of Kate and the last time they'd been here together flood his mind. It was pointless.

When Cruz had called him this morning to see if he needed some help, Dominic had considered refusing. Knowing that this last-minute offer probably had something to do with his announcement at dinner last Sunday.

It had taken a few days, but it seemed as if his family had come to terms with what he'd done—if the growing number of voicemails on his phone were any indication. Even Daisy had called and after three voicemails where she yelled at him for butting into her life and lying, she'd calmed down enough by the fourth to tell him she loved and appreciated what he'd done for her but if he ever tricked her again, the time she'd shaved his head in high school the night before class pictures would be child's play. She'd even mentioned finding a job as a baker at an up-and-coming neighborhood café that gave her flexibility she needed with the kids and the pleasure of getting paid for doing something she loved.

Unfortunately, none of the calls were from the one person he really wanted to hear from.

But he had to join the land of the living eventually, and today seemed as good a time as any. Dominic needed someone to talk to. It was time.

Especially when he thought about the evening that he'd once imagined for them tonight. Celebrating her promotion and dancing with the most beautiful woman in the room at that engagement party.

Now he had images of her and Michael together.

"Don't tell me. You're thinking about a certain redhead. If you're still so obsessed with her, why don't you pick up the phone and tell her whatever you need to so she can forgive whatever stupid thing you did and you guys can make up and move on?"

"It's a lot more complicated than that. Kate's probably back with her ex by now."

Cruz stopped what he was doing and glanced over at him. "Sorry. I was hoping things would work out. She seemed really nice. And you guys were great together."

"Come on. You know the reason we were doing all that. For Daisy, and so Kate could get her promotion."

"Yeah, but you guys played your roles as girlfriend and boyfriend *too* well. I saw how you two looked at each other, and that wasn't pretend. That was real."

Dominic laughed, but it was mirthless. "Then you should have seen the sparks that were flying between her and her ex when I saw them together last week."

Needing perspective, Dominic opened the cooler near his foot and grabbed two beers, handing one to Cruz. They went to the backyard, despite the frigid, icy cold, and sat on the stoop and he told Cruz about Michael and Kate.

Cruz took a long draw from his beer and mulled it all over when he was through. "One thing you haven't told me in this long story of yours is how you feel about Kate."

"I told you, she and her ex are as good as together by now."

"Yeah, but that still doesn't answer my question. How do you feel about Kate? Do you love her?"

Dominic didn't have to think very long, because he damn well knew the answer. "Without a doubt. She's the only one for me."

"And in all this time you've been spending time with her, have you ever told her how you feel?"

Dominic didn't answer, only took a pull from his beer and stared out over the tree line ahead.

"I'm going to take that silence as your admission to not telling her how you felt. Any reason you didn't?"

"You know, you're as chatty and inquisitive as Benny. If

I wanted to discuss my feelings, I wouldn't have called you. Cut me a break here."

"Hell if I will. You and I both know why you didn't tell her. And that was totally unfair to Kate. She's not Melinda. You've been afraid to tell Kate how you really feel because you didn't want to risk her rejection. Or being hurt. Your ex really played a number on you, but that doesn't mean Kate will."

"Not intentionally. But eventually, she will come to her senses. Realize that I can't give her the big fancy house and the fancy friends that she needs and wants."

"Have you looked at this place? Don't sell yourself short, bud. More importantly, don't sell Kate short. Tell her how you really feel about her, no holds barred, and give her that chance to make a choice. You think Michael is the man she always wanted and maybe, before she met you, that was true. Just like before you met Kate you thought Melinda was who you wanted. But things change. And from the glow I saw in her eyes whenever she looked at you or touched you, I'd lay bets she loves you, too. You just need to make her see it."

It hit him hard, hearing Cruz laying it out like that. Because he was right. He'd bowed out because he thought he was giving Kate what she wanted.

He needed to be honest with Kate. Tell her before it was too late.

Because until he heard the words from her mouth, heard her say she chose Michael or just outright denied him, he was never going to move on.

He owed her that chance.

He owed them both that chance. Because he loved that

woman and could make her happier than a million Michaels, and he was not just going to tell her that, but prove it every single day.

Dominic started back inside the house and for the stairs.

"Are we done?" Cruz asked his back, his laughter echoing after Dominic.

Chapter Nineteen

The band Mrs. Vaughn had secured for Payton's engagement party wasn't too bad. They were attempting to play one of the Beatles' love songs while the happy couple danced under the adoring attention of their family and friends. Kate held her glass of champagne, swirling the fluid under the lights.

Trying to pretend she was happy.

She was still sitting there, staring despondently into her glass, when Michael's voice made her jump. "Hi, Kate."

"Hi," she said and barely looked up. But the shiner around his left eye immediately caught her attention. "What happened to your face?"

"Your boyfriend is what happened. Dominic?" he added at Kate's confused look. "That day outside your office. I'm guessing he didn't tell you."

"No. We haven't exactly been talking lately." She looked around, not seeing Nicole, but it didn't mean she wasn't lurking.

"You know, you've already become an urban legend at the office. Turning down junior partnership like that after all the work you did. No one really believes it." He slid into the seat next to her, in the space where the place card still read Dominic's name. "So that's it, then? All that work, all that time, and…you're gone?"

She smiled wryly. "I wouldn't put it quite like that. I'll be around another couple of weeks, closing out some cases, sending out notices to my clients that I'm moving to another firm and that their cases will be reassigned. General housekeeping."

"Can you tell me where you're moving? Which big firm snatched you up? MacKenzie? Jacob Snell?"

"Actually, I've decided to downsize. I'm going to work at Jessica Lund's firm. Specializing in employee rights."

His brows furrowed. "That's quite the downgrade. I don't think they have more than ten attorneys on staff. What suddenly made you decide to change your course?"

"Just wanted something different for myself."

"Kate…" He took a breath and leaned toward her. "I meant what I said in your office that day. And I've given you some time and space to get to the same conclusion as I have. We're meant to be. And I don't care what anyone says anymore, I can't bear to be without you."

"And Nicole?" Kate looked around. "How does she feel about this development?"

"I don't think we're cut out for each other after all. I'm here alone, aren't I? Same as you." He smiled and leaned forward.

"I'm sorry to hear about you and Nicole. Really. I thought you were pretty perfect for each other."

He shrugged. "Her priorities were all skewed. And she

was always railing on you and my parents' interference. I got tired of it."

Michael was running away from another relationship. Why didn't that surprise her? But instead of any kind of satisfaction, she only felt sadness.

"Look, Michael. I want to be straight with you. I've come to realize a lot these past few days, and one of those things is that…I'm not in love with you anymore."

"Kate, stop. I know that you're hurt and upset because of how I—"

She held her hand up. "I was hurt and upset, but I'm speaking from a place of absolute honesty. And all I want for you right now is…happiness. Whether with Nicole or someone else. But you should know, a relationship, any relationship, is going to be tough. It's not always going to be roses, and you can't keep running away when things get tough. Before you blow this thing with Nicole, you should be sure you're not making a huge mistake. Whether her priorities are skewed or whatever, what matters is how you feel about each other. Whether, when you come home at the end of the day, it's her face you want to see waiting for you on the other side of the door. Her smile, her touch that will be the last thing you experience when you fall asleep. That's what matters."

Kind of how she felt about Dominic.

Michael sat back, blinking. "Wow. That's…interesting."

And she knew with absolute certainty at that point she meant everything she'd said. She no longer felt any tie to Michael. She only wanted to be with one person and make his future her future. Now.

Kate saw Michael's parents on the dance floor, their

attention focused on the two of them sitting there. They looked worried and Kate couldn't help but burst out laughing. She waved at them.

"Michael. There's something I have to do. Will you excuse me?" And she rose and grabbed her purse before he could respond.

There was a person she needed to see. Someone to whom she had a new proposal to make. Her fingers flew across the keys of her cell phone as she headed toward the club's fancy powder room, where she might have some privacy.

Please pick up.

Half an hour later, her calls were still going to voicemail and her texts were showing unread.

Why wasn't he taking her calls?

On the eighth call, she decided to leave a quick message.

"Dominic? It's me. I really need to talk to you, so please call me when you get this message. I—I need you to know something." She thought about how much to share and finally thought, *To hell with it.* "I love you. So when you get this message, please call me. No matter your answer."

Okay. She'd done it.

Oh. God.

What had she done?

She should have at least waited to tell him face-to-face. What if he didn't feel the same way? What if he'd never even come close to feeling that way? After all, they'd made love and then he'd taken her request to stay professional without any argument. Maybe she'd just been another notch in his tool belt before moving onto the next attractive client.

He might be on a date right now.

It *was* Saturday night.

She didn't know how long she sat like that before she realized she wasn't alone. Payton's hand was on her arm. "You okay, Kate?"

Kate looked into her friend's caring eyes, full of love and sympathy. "He's not answering. I think I waited too long to tell him how I felt."

Payton patted her back, not even needing to ask whom she was referencing, aware of what had transpired over the past few weeks. "It's only been a week. He couldn't possibly have already moved on. You're hard to forget. I should know, I've been your best friend since we were twelve."

Kate tried to will the tears away but they slipped down her cheek. "He's not taking my calls. And I just left him a message telling him I love him"—she glanced at her cell phone—"ten minutes ago. And he hadn't responded."

Payton pulled her in and hugged her tight. "You've got to have faith. It's all going to work you, just watch. You're too sensible a person to fall in love with someone who wasn't smart enough to love you back."

Kate drew back and accepted the tissue her friend handed her. She hiccuped. "Yeah? What about Michael, then?"

"Oh, come on, we both know you didn't really love Michael. Not when love has been making you all moony eyed these past few weeks. In truth, I've been a little envious of you."

Kate paused as she held the tissue to her eyes. She'd never asked outright if Payton was in love with her fiancé, but she had always had some doubts. But Payton, for all her open friendliness and exuberance, wasn't one to share everything when it came to matters of the heart. More softly, Kate asked, "Aren't you in love with Brad?"

For a moment, Kate thought she saw something wistful

in her friend's eyes, but then it was gone and Payton laughed. "Of course. He's the perfect guy for me—just ask my mother. You don't mind me. I'm trying to be sympathetic and doing a terrible job. Come on. Let's go have too much champagne and dance to my mother's horrified distress."

Kate smiled and took Payton's extended hand. She was lucky to have her. And as for Dominic…she'd at least put it out there. He—and she—finally knew how she felt about him.

No regrets.

Two glasses of champagne later, Kate was almost able to forget the fact that Dominic still hadn't returned her call. She looked out on the dance floor, where Payton and Brad were whirling around. They did make a beautiful couple. Like Barbie and Ken—although if Payton heard her say that she'd murder her on sight.

Mrs. Vaughn looked deliriously happy as she and Payton's future parents-in-law sat back and watched the two as if she'd orchestrated every dance step herself. Hell, maybe she had.

Kate had one thing going for her. She didn't have the overbearing weight of a mother like Emily Vaughn on her shoulder. And from here on out, she'd let the usual arrows and barbs the old crow threw at her slide off.

She didn't care what the woman thought about her anymore, because she knew the only person who could make her bad was herself. And making the wrong choices all these years had indeed made her feel bad.

But not anymore.

She only wished she'd realized all of this sooner. Before she'd lost Dominic.

"Is this seat taken?"

Her fingers tightened on the champagne flute. She must be hallucinating, because there was no way...

She glanced to her right and saw the disarming crooked smile on the achingly familiar face of the man standing next to her. Her stomach rose to her throat like she was about to go over a big drop on a roller coaster. And her hands were up in the air. Not holding on.

He slipped into the seat, not waiting for a response, which, frankly, she was having a hard time forming.

His fingers went to the collar of his white shirt and a sleek bowtie, pulling it away from his throat.

He was wearing the dreaded monkey suit. For her.

And looking mighty damn fine in it, too.

He leaned forward, his breath tickling at her ear. "You look beautiful."

Somehow she found her voice. "What are you doing here? And why haven't you been taking my calls?"

"Your calls?" It was hard to miss the sound of relief and excitement in his voice. "Have you been trying to reach me?" He patted his pockets for a moment. "I must have left my cell at home. I took off in such a hurry to find someplace that might be open to rent me this thing. I won't bore you with the details of the number of threats I had to make, just shy of needing you to come and post bail for me."

So he hadn't been ignoring her calls.

And he hadn't heard her proclamation of love.

"But to answer your question," he continued, "I'm here because I promised to escort you. And because if I didn't tell you that going back to Michael would be the biggest mistake of your life then it would weigh on me the rest of *my* life."

Her heart was about to pound out of her chest. "Oh, really? And why is that?"

"Because he could never love you as much and as devotedly as I do." He leaned forward, a soft smile on his lips, his eyes holding a definite promise. He slid his fingers through a strand of her hair, almost caressing it, and she shivered. "I love touching you, and ever since that incredible night we shared, I've dreamed of many more nights like that. Of being able to memorize every mole and freckle on that amazing body of yours with my lips, my tongue, my fingers, and my eyes. Of learning every special touch that will leave you quivering with pleasure. But most of all, of being able to hold you in my arms, sated and happy. Knowing that I could repeat it all the next hour, the next morning, the next night…forever."

It was almost too good to be true, as if she were in a dream, a fantasy, really. Because no man could be this good. This perfect. The tears she'd finally stopped earlier were now threatening again, and she didn't care. She only wanted this moment to continue. This feeling, this euphoria, to last always.

But he wasn't done, and his fingers now touched her bare shoulder, featherlight, and the goose bumps revealed his effect on her. "And I don't care what you do for a living or what you aspire to be. As long as you include me in all that planning, I'll be happy to be along for the ride. Because I know that no one will ever be a better fit for me than you."

She closed her eyes, the tears slipping out. When she opened them, he was still there, smiling at her. How had she ever come to deserve someone like him? And why had it taken her so long to see he was the only man she could ever love?

He cleared his throat. "I'm hoping those are happy tears, because I don't ever want to cause you to cry unless they're tears of laughter. Or because I've made you the happiest woman alive."

This time she did smile. "They are tears of happiness." Her voice sounded mangled and not the clear, confident sound she wanted to convey. "I just can't believe you're here. And that this is real."

"Because you're completely in love with me and not because you're mentally taking notes to file a restraining order against me, right?" he teased.

This time she did laugh and tilted her head against his shoulder. "Right. And yes. I'm completely, totally in love with you. If you knew the crazy thoughts I was thinking right now you might just file a restraining order against me."

"Don't bet on it." His fingers touched her chin and tilted her head up toward him. A second later, he brushed his lips across hers, and she didn't care if she was surrounded by a hundred different people who might all be looking scandalously at them, shaking their heads in disapproval.

The only person whose opinion she really cared about was holding her right now, his breath on her lips, his tongue even now teasing her mouth open. And giving her a full, languorous kiss that made her want to wrap herself around him and never let go. Naked, preferably.

But he apparently had the good sense to pull back and exhaled a loud sigh of relief. "I thought this was going to be harder," he said and chuckled.

"Fortunately for you, I'd already reached the same conclusion. That you and I—we're inevitable."

For the first time this evening, he looked nervous. "Michael decided to stay with Nicole?"

"I couldn't tell you. When I told him I didn't love him earlier tonight, I didn't bother to ask him what his plans were."

His face relaxed, and his grinned again. "Really? I'm sorry I missed it."

"Me, too. Dominic, I owe you an explanation and an apology." She took in a breath. "I've been doing a lot of thinking recently. About my priorities. And how freaking screwed up they were. What the flying fig do I care about the opinions of people who don't respect me for reasons beyond my control?" She turned and glanced around the room. "I can't control their opinion of me, and frankly, I don't care anymore. Because I realize what's more important is the people I surround myself with. The people who accept me for who I am, who are warm and loving. People like you."

This time she reached her hand and held that strong chin in her palm, let her finger rub the smooth surface where he must have recently shaved.

"Growing up, I was so alone. I missed so many things, not having the love and support of a family—at least, not until my grams came into the picture. She loved me unconditionally. Kind of like your family does, I imagine, no matter what brainless thing you might do." She smiled and felt more tears light her eyes. "And that's what I want. This past week at work, I finally achieved everything I worked for—the job, the promotion, the house, and all the other materialistic things. Everything I *thought* I wanted. Before."

His brows raised at this little correction. "Before?"

"Yep." She nodded, feeling so deliriously happy at finally being free from her previous fears. "Before I met you. Because even when I finally achieved all those things, I still wasn't happy. I felt hollow. Like something was missing. And I realized what it was. You. The someone who I had fallen in love with and who accepted me for myself. Who never make me feel like less of a person for what I didn't have. If anything, you made me feel more loved and accepted than anyone. Oh, and I quit. I quit my job and told Tim just where he could take that promotion."

This time he threw back his head and rocked out a hearty laugh. "You don't do anything in half measures, do you?" He sobered then. "But what are you going to do now? What about your plan?"

"I'm making a new plan. Starting with you, and then I'll work everything else around you. Around us. But no worries, I'm not exactly jumping without a parachute. I'm taking a position at my friend Jess's firm. Less pay but more flexibility. I'm ready to find myself again. Find what makes me happy."

The band started to play the familiar opening to Van Morrison's "Crazy Love."

"Stuff like that begs me to take you back to your place right now and show you just how much I love you. But then I'd miss this opportunity." He stood and with panache, he swept his hand out. "Care to dance?"

She looked over to the floor where, up to now, only Payton and Brad had been dancing. The thought of getting out there, making the public declaration of her love, sounded devilishly exciting.

She saw Payton watching them now, and by the huge smile on her face, Kate would bet she'd figured everything had worked out, as she had promised. Payton lifted her hand and waved them toward the floor in invitation.

How could she resist?

She placed her hand in his and stood. Without waiting a beat, Dominic put his hand around her waist, and he swept her out to the dance floor. "Let's go show them how it's done."

She nodded and smiled, not trusting herself not to tear up.

The lyrics of the song filled her head. Crazy love was right.

Lord, how she loved him. And she couldn't wait for her life to begin.

Epilogue

"I warned you," Dominic said and laughed when Kate shot him a look that told him his warning was not appreciated before she resumed her search for her bra.

It was Christmas morning. After a late night at his parents' house for Christmas Eve dinner, a later night where they attended midnight Mass, and an even later night of debauchery, Kate had intended on sleeping in until noon, waking up only to show the man in her life how much she loved and adored him before they headed to brunch at Glenda's at one.

But from the sound of voices in the foyer below, her plans were going to be altered.

She spied the strap of her black lacy bra under the bed and reached down to grab it. But Dominic's hand stopped her.

"There is a lock on the door, you know. I installed it myself," he breathed in her ear. "Should I…"

"Don't even think about it, buddy," she said even

though for the tiniest moment she considered the possibility. "Besides, from the sounds of it, your whole family is downstairs, and they're expecting us."

"Believe me, if you know my mother, she'd be up here giving us pointers if she thought it could gain her a new grandbaby in the coming year." He moved her hair from her neck and placed a kiss, sending goose bumps along her arms. Dominic was making it nearly impossible for her to remember why she needed clothes.

The sound of silverware clattering downstairs told her they had made it to her kitchen, at least, and were unlikely to be sneaking up the stairs. He bent his head then and sucked on the vulnerable spot below her right ear he knew all too well.

This was sick. This was depraved. Heavens, what would they think about her if they knew what they were up here contemplating this very minute? As if he knew her resolve was weakening, he placed another kiss at the base of her neck.

She had a decision to make. She could push him away and go down and greet his family in record time so they wouldn't think they'd been up here doing…this. Or she could turn around and wrap her arms around him and let him wish her a proper good morning.

Lord, she was a weak woman.

Twenty minutes later, she and Dominic headed down the stairs, hastily dressed in jeans and T-shirts and with a soft glow around them. She knew her face was flushed and bright from their little…escapade, but felt it flush a few shades deeper when she saw Dominic's dad and brother, Cruz, sitting on her couch. Both men gave her a look that told her they knew exactly what they'd been doing. The elder Sorensen winked at her.

Paul and his sisters were playing cards on her dining room table that someone had carried in and set up under the morning light of the front windows. The little Christmas tree she and Dominic had bought two days ago was already lit and, if she wasn't mistaken, had a few more packages poking from underneath than she remembered seeing last night.

Dominic's mom came in from the kitchen with a tray Kate didn't recognize and holding a pitcher of what looked like Bloody Marys. It was hard not smile in the face of all this love and acceptance.

"*Feliz Navidad!* Merry Christmas! You'll have to forgive me," the beaming woman said as Benny and Daisy followed on her heels with more trays filled with plates and silverware and a casserole dish that smelled like butter and cinnamon and brown sugar. Heavenly. "But we thought it would be a wonderful new tradition if we held the family breakfast here, with you both."

"I tried to convince her we should call first," Benny said, grinning, "but she wouldn't hear of it. It had to be surprise. Surprise!" she finished, and by the look she gave them, Kate had no doubt that, other than the kids and Dominic's mother, everyone else was on to them.

"No problem," Kate said. She looked around the large room, bright and cheery and filled with everyone she'd grown to care so much about.

Dominic's arms wrapped around her as he pulled her close. "No regrets?"

Kate touched her fingers to the ring that Dominic had placed on her hand last night and smiled up at him. "No regrets. They are family, after all."

Acknowledgments

I can't begin to express my gratitude and appreciation to my editor, Alycia Tornetta, for believing in this story and offering her amazing insight to making this the best it could be—and then some. Saying you're awesome just isn't enough.

Also a big thanks to all the people behind the scenes at Entangled, from book publicity to cover design, who've been there to provide support at every step in the process.

And finally, to my family for all the dinners of cereal and frozen waffles you've consumed during Mom's crunch time. And to many, many more. Love you guys.

About the Author

Ashlee was thirteen when she sneaked her first Kathleen E. Woodiwiss book hidden away in her mom's closet. After two days of staying home "sick" from school to finish it, she was hooked. Her rabid love for romance has continued ever since, and after a misadventure in the world of law, she is finally settling into her dream job of writing about people finding their happily ever afters—the only stories worth reading, after all.

Ashlee lives in the greater Salt Lake Valley in Utah with her sweetie, two fabulous kids, and a dog and cat that vie equally for her attention. Sometimes by sitting on her computer when she's trying to work. And although surrounded by picturesque mountains and beautiful landscapes, she's practically allergic to direct sunlight, the outdoors, and anything that involves communing with nature. Give her a book, an abundance of coffee, and a shady (enclosed) spot with a view and she's happy.

Whether writing contemporary romances or romances

with mystery and suspense, Ashlee aims to create down-to-earth heroines and heroes that will make you laugh and fall in love all over again.

You can find her on the web at www.AshleeMallory.com or lurking on Twitter (@ashleemallory) and Facebook. Drop her a line! She'd love to hear from you.

Don't miss the next book in the Sorensen series

HER ACCIDENTAL HUSBAND

Payton Vaughn's trip to Puerto Vallarta for her friend's wedding was her big escape from her ridiculously overbearing mother – oh, and that little matter with her cheating fiancé. Now, her flight's been cancelled, and she's crammed into a tiny car with the gorgeous-but-irritating best man. He has no business getting to know her better—not even for all the tequila in Mexico... until they wake with grande-sized hangovers as man and wife. Now Payton and Cruz must decide if they've reached the end of their journey...or the beginning of a new adventure.

Also by Ashlee Mallory

YOU AGAIN

LOVE YOU MADLY